THE BODY IN THE ICE HOUSE

KATE HARDY

Ebook ISBN: 978-1-80508-089-3
Paperback ISBN: 978-1-80508-090-9

Cover design by: Lisa Brewster
Cover images by: Shutterstock, Alamy

Published by Storm Publishing.
For further information, visit:
www.stormpublishing.co

ALSO BY KATE HARDY

A Georgina Drake Mystery

The Body at Rookery Barn
The Body in the Ice House

*For Gerard, Chris and Chloë Brooks – the best research crew ever
:)*

ONE

'It's so good of you to let me tag along with you to Hartington, Georgie,' Lady Wyatt said as she climbed into Georgina's car. 'Especially as I know this is a work meeting.'

'It's a work meeting I wouldn't be having in the first place, if it wasn't for you,' Georgina said. Sybbie had talked her into photographing Hartington Hall for her goddaughters, Henriette and Rosalind Berry. The gardens were already open to the public several days a week, but the girls were planning to open the family's ancestral home to the public and needed some publicity shots for their website and their planned guidebook. The gardens were closed today, so it would be a good opportunity to take photographs without getting in the way of visitors.

'Hmm,' Sybbie said. 'I still feel a bit guilty about – well, *wheedling* you into helping Hattie and Posy. I know you specialise in portraits, not landscapes.'

Georgina smiled. 'I've been saying for weeks that I'm going to get back to work, and without you giving me a nudge I'd probably still be pottering around in my darkroom, doing nothing in particular. Besides, the last thing you, Cesca and Jodie wheedled me into is working out just fine – isn't it, Bert?'

There was a soft wuff of agreement from the liver-and-white spaniel in the back of the car.

'You're quite sure they don't mind me bringing Bert?' Georgina asked.

'Dear girl, they have spaniels themselves,' Sybbie said. 'The dogs can all romp around together and have a lovely time. I almost suggested bringing Max and Jet as well, only I think a six-pack of dogs might be a little too much.'

Georgina hid a smile at the 'girl'. At fifty-two, she was only a dozen or so years younger than Sybbie: hardly a girl. But she appreciated her friend's foibles and her ready laugh.

'We've got a good day for it, anyway. Wall-to-wall sunshine,' Sybbie said gleefully.

'Road trip,' said Doris, equally gleefully, from the seat in the back next to Bert.

If Georgina had been stuck in one place for fifty years, she would've loved the chance to travel as much as Doris now did; they'd discovered by accident that Doris could leave the confines of Rookery Farm if she was with Georgina. But the only ones who knew that Doris was sitting in the back of the car were herself and Bert. Even the car's sensors, which normally made a fuss if Georgina left so much as a small handbag on the seat, couldn't register the presence of a ghost. The only technology that did seem to register Doris was that of Georgina's hearing aids, which picked up Doris's voice. Nobody else could hear her.

'Hopefully Karen won't be there today,' Sybbie said. 'I know Henry was lonely after losing Millie' – Camilla, Sybbie's best friend, who'd died from breast cancer four and a half years previously – 'but I wish his new wife was a bit more... Well, not Millie the Second, exactly, but someone who would at least *try* to be civil to her old friends.' She shrugged. 'Still. It is what it is.'

Sybbie chatted about gardens for the rest of the trip, and Georgina thought how lovely Norfolk was in the middle of summer, with the gold stalks of ripened barley rippling in the fields ready to be harvested, ancient oak trees casting dappled shade, hedgerows full of frothy Queen Anne's lace, and the wide azure sky with the odd white, fluffy cloud drifting across.

They passed through a pretty village full of flint-and-brick cottages, their front gardens bursting with roses and summer blooms; then the narrow road took them through fields again. Woodland began on their left, and Georgina could see a wall, the bricks a deep shade of red.

'Here we are. Next turn on the left,' Sybbie said.

Georgina took the turn and drove down a very long driveway flanked with beech trees. To one side, there was a lake. At the end of the drive, the vista opened up to the house: a rectangular Tudor pile built of deep red brick, with dormer windows on the top floor, barley-sugar chimney pots rising above the tiled roof, and large stone mullioned windows. There was a formal garden in front of the house, with herbaceous borders, a rose arbour and a fountain; between the lake and the house there was an enormous oak tree.

Sybbie directed Georgina to park at the back of the house. 'In days gone by, this would've been the turning circle for carriages,' Sybbie said, gesturing to the shingle. 'The girls normally run a pop-up tea tent and plant shop here on days when the garden's open but, now that they're also going to open the house three days a week, they want to turn the old stable block into formal tea rooms and a gift shop, with an exhibition space above it. The old workers' cottages, behind the stables, are going to be used as holiday accommodation.'

'That sounds like quite a lot of work,' Georgina said.

'It is, but the girls are like their mother – they work out what needs to be done, make a plan and then just get on with it,' Sybbie said.

Georgina clipped Bert's lead onto his collar, then unclipped his harness from the seat belt. She'd just closed the car door when three black-and-white springer spaniels rushed over to greet them, their tails a blur.

'Byron, Keats, Shelley – sit!' a voice called, and the dogs obediently sat. Bert sat, too, though it was clear he was itching to greet the other spaniels and bounce about with them.

The owner of the voice – a woman in her late twenties with a shock of red curls, piercing blue eyes and a ready smile – came striding over. 'Aunt Syb! It's been *ages*. So good to see you.' Sybbie was crushed in a bear hug. 'And you must be Mrs Drake,' she said, turning to Georgina and shaking her hand. 'Lovely to meet you. Thank you so much for coming to help us. I'm Rosalind, though everyone calls me Posy.'

'She called herself Rosy-Posy as soon as she could talk,' Sybbie said with a grin. 'And it suits her – doesn't it, cherub?' She ruffled Posy's hair.

'Lovely to meet you, too, Posy. And please call me Georgie,' Georgina said.

'Welcome to Hartington, Georgie.' Posy smiled. 'Hattie's putting the kettle on and rummaging in the cupboards for biscuits.'

'I can do better than that. I come bearing cake from Cesca,' Sybbie said, handing her a brown paper bag. 'It's her *nonna's* apple cake, fresh from this morning's batch for the farm shop, and it's still warm.'

'How wonderful. I love Cesca's cakes. If I thought I could get away with it, I'd try and poach her for our new tea rooms,' Posy said with a teasing grin.

'You can *try*,' Sybbie said, matching the grin with her own.

'Georgie, we're quite safe from traffic here, so if you're happy to let your dog off the lead to charge about with ours and wear himself out, it's fine by us,' Posy said. 'What's his name?'

'Bert.'

'Hello, Bert. You're a lovely boy, aren't you?' Posy made a fuss of him.

'He is. He belonged to Valerie Waring, my friend's neighbour, but she's not well enough to take care of him, anymore,' Georgina said. 'Your godmother bullied me into taking him on, three months ago.'

'Don't give me that. I merely *suggested* it. You love him to bits,' Sybbie said, laughing.

'I do. And he gets to see Val once a week, which is lovely for both of them.' Georgina crouched down and let Bert off his lead again. 'Go on, then,' she said. 'Make friends.'

'Go and play, boys,' Posy said, and the dogs rushed around, chasing each other in wide circles, their tails wagging happily. 'We'll head for the kitchen. No doubt in a few minutes the boys will pile in, grab a drink of water and trail half of it across the kitchen floor.' She rolled her eyes. 'Spaniels never swallow that last mouthful, do they?'

Georgina laughed. 'Bert certainly doesn't!'

'Hang on,' Sybbie said as Posy led them towards the cottages behind the stables. 'Where are we going?'

Posy winced. 'Hattie and I moved into one of the cottages, three months ago.'

'I see,' Sybbie said crisply.

'It saves all the rows with the Faultfinder General,' Posy said, rolling her eyes.

'Faultfinder General?' Georgina asked.

'Sorry. I'm being a bitch.' Posy sighed. 'But Karen's so negative, all the time. It's really wearing. She looks for faults that aren't there, much like the Witchfinder General deciding women were witches, when they weren't anything of the sort.' She shook her head. 'I don't mean to be so unkind, but she drives me mad with all the sneering and sly comments. Anyway, it's better for Hattie and me, having our own space. It stops any awkwardness if you stay out for the night, or if someone stays over. Plus now we can honestly say from personal experience that the holiday cottages are comfortable.'

'Hmm,' Sybbie said, clearly aware that her goddaughter was trying to look on the bright side. 'Giles moved to the farmhouse next door to us, but that was only after he married Cesca – and of course newlyweds should have their own space.'

'It sounds to me as if Posy and Hattie really don't get on with their stepmother,' Doris said quietly.

Georgina gave a nod of agreement; if anyone noticed, she hoped they'd assume she was agreeing with Sybbie.

'It's fine, Aunt Syb, really. We're quite happy here,' Posy said. She opened the door to one of the cottages, which led into an entrance hall, and ushered them through into a bright breakfast kitchen with a red-tiled floor and primrose yellow walls. There was a pine table and four chairs with a small matching dresser in one half of the room; the other half held a fridge, freezer, washing machine and cooker slotted between pine cupboards. Pine shelves sat above the worktops, filled with jars of pasta and lentils and home-made preserves; an array of ancient, polished copper pans hung from hooks underneath the shelves.

'Borrowed from the Hall?' Sybbie asked, gesturing to the pans.

'Rescued,' the woman Georgina assumed was Posy's older sister corrected, pouring boiling water into a teapot. Her hair was the same colour as Posy's, but rather than being a mop of unrestrained curls it was straightened into a bob and held back from her face by a black velvet Alice band. 'Aunt Syb. Lovely to see you,' she said, giving Sybbie a hug. 'Mrs Drake, welcome to Hartington. I'm Henriette.'

'Named after Papa, of course,' Posy chimed in.

'But everyone calls me Hattie.' Hattie smiled. 'Good to meet you. Would you prefer tea or coffee?'

'Please call me Georgie,' Georgina said, 'and coffee would be wonderful, thank you. Forgive me for asking, but why did the pans need rescuing?'

TWO

Hattie took a cafetière from a cupboard, shook in some grounds and added boiling water. 'The pans have been in the Old Kitchen since for ever – even though they probably hadn't been used for well over a century and I don't think the old range cooker would even light, now. Mummy loved them. She kept them polished and on display.' Her face tightened slightly. 'We overheard Karen talking about putting them in an auction room, a few months ago, so Posy and I liberated them before she could do that. We'll put them back once the house is open to the public and they can be on show. And then there'll be no way she can sneakily flog them off to the highest bidder.'

Georgina winced. There was obviously little love lost between these two and their stepmother, and Sybbie had made it clear on the way here that she didn't like Karen, either. Though, at the same time, Georgina felt a twinge of sympathy for the second Lady Ellingham. It must be hard to join a close-knit family, particularly after the loss of someone as much loved as Millie seemed to have been.

'She isn't here today, thank God,' Posy said. 'She had a row with Papa yesterday and flounced off to London. She'll probably come back in a day or so, when she's cooled off.'

'With the usual armfuls of designer carrier bags,' Hattie added, rolling her eyes. 'Let's just say Karen's big on retail therapy.'

'Still. You haven't come to listen to us moan about her. We really appreciate you giving up your time to help us with the photographs,' Posy said.

Hattie placed the cafetière on the dining table, adding a jug of milk, a bowl of sugar lumps with silver sugar tongs, four bone china mugs and plates, and silver forks, while Posy made a pot of tea and put the apple cake on a plate with a silver cake slice.

'Very civilised,' Sybbie said as Hattie ushered her and Georgina to a seat. 'I presume Henry isn't joining us? Or is he off skulking with his cars?'

'He's gone out,' Posy said. 'He doesn't mean to be rude, Aunt Syb, but... you know how he is.' She winced.

'Seeing me reminds him of Millie, so he can't face me,' Sybbie said bluntly. 'I understand.' She rolled her eyes. 'Though seeing you two reminds me of her, and that always makes me happy.'

'Papa finds things... difficult,' Hattie said.

'You mean,' Sybbie said, 'your father dithers over decisions and he couldn't organise his way out of a paper bag. Ask him a question and he'll go all tetchy and His Lordship on you, then disappear to tinker with his cars. Meanwhile, everyone else rushes round sorting things out, until all he has to do is append his signature and pretend it was all his idea.'

Hattie winced. 'Aunt *Syb*.'

'We might as well be honest. It's why the two of you are doing his job for him and dragging the estate into the twenty-first century,' Sybbie said, looking cross. 'And you ought to get the credit for it – just as Bernard always gives Giles credit for what he does at Little Wenborough. Your father is a *nightmare*.'

Hattie gave her a rueful smile. 'I know, but he's not going to change, so it's pointless trying to make him be any different. I'm so sorry, Georgie. You've been kind enough to come and help us, and it's not fair of us to bang on about family tensions.'

'No need to apologise,' Georgina said. But maybe talking about why she was here would make everything less awkward for the Berrys. 'How much of the house are you opening up?'

'The kind of rooms people want to see,' Posy said. 'Hattie and I want to style the experience as a look round Hartington through the ages.'

'It's not in consecutive order and we're doing it as self-guided tours,' Hattie explained.

'We'll start below stairs in the Old Kitchen, which was remodelled in Victorian times; as Hattie said, we'll put the copper pans back where they belong on the day the first tour arrives,' Posy said. 'The dining room and withdrawing room are seventeenth century, and the music room's Regency. Upstairs, we'll show a couple of the bedrooms – including the one that Elizabeth the First allegedly slept in – the Regency sitting room, and the Victorian library, which used to be the Tudor long gallery.' She smiled. 'Best of all, I'm getting a local carpenter to make us a display cabinet with museum-standard glass, so we can showcase the Red Book.'

'What's the Red Book?' Georgina asked.

'An invention of Humphry Repton,' Sybbie said, looking wistful.

'I'm still none the wiser,' Georgina said.

'Repton took over from Capability Brown as the leading landscape gardener of his day. He produced watercolour designs for his clients, which were usually made into a book and bound in red Morocco leather afterwards – hence "Red Book",' Sybbie explained. 'You'd see the view from your house as it was currently, and then you'd lift a flap to see the view as it would be if you made Repton's suggested improvements. Moving or hiding a fence, adding a lake or a bridge, that sort of thing. Very clever and years ahead of his time.' She smiled. 'I'm fairly sure our lake and bridge at Little Wenborough were designed by him, but I don't have the paperwork to prove it. If we had our own Red Book at Little Wenborough, it's long gone. I always envied Millie hers. She used to tease me that they'd have to pat me down before I left to make sure I hadn't stolen it – not that you'd be able to hide a quarto-sized book very easily.'

'Mummy loved that book, seeing how the garden developed from his ideas. She loved the historic side of it as well as the practical side, too,' Posy said. 'It's one of the things she had in common with Granny Rosa. She always had secateurs in her pocket, to give a little snip here and there whenever she was in the garden – whether it was her own or someone's she was visiting.' She gave her godmother a fond smile. 'A bit like someone else we know.'

Sybbie grinned, completely unrepentant. 'I agree with your mother – and your grandmother, for that matter. I liked Rosa very much indeed. And one needs to be helpful, dear girl. You're from the same stock as your mother and Rosa. I guarantee by the time you're my age, you'll keep secateurs in your pocket and do a bit of sneaky snipping.'

'Perhaps I could include a shot of the Red Book for your website and the guidebook,' Georgina suggested.

'Absolutely. It's very important,' Sybbie said. 'And it's worth a fortune because of the historic aspect, not just its value to gardeners. The last one I heard of for sale fetched almost six figures at auction.'

'When Mummy and Granny Rosa were sorting out the taxes after Grandpa died, Papa suggested selling Hartington's Red Book,' Posy said. 'They said he'd sell it over their dead bodies and suggested he sold his vintage E-type Jag instead, because that'd make the same amount of money. He harrumphed a bit and backed off.' Her face looked slightly pinched. 'Given what Karen was going to do with the pans, I worry that, now Mummy and Granny Rosa are gone, he'll sell the Red Book, with Karen egging him on – and it belongs *here*, with the house, not locked up in some collector's library.'

'I'm sure he won't agree to sell it, Posy,' Hattie said, giving her sister a hug. 'Or maybe we could liberate it like we did the copper pans and put it in a safe deposit box at the bank. Aunt Syb could always "borrow" it after we've taken the pictures today – though we might have to fight her to make her give it back.'

Posy smiled at the teasing, but Georgina could see genuine worry in her eyes; clearly she was really upset about Hartington's Red Book going missing.

'Of course I'll give it back,' Sybbie said. 'Or you could always entrust me to look after it at Little Wenborough. I'd like to see Karen try to get past Max and Jet into our library.'

'She loathes dogs, too. It's another reason we moved out,' Hattie said. 'She kept on at Papa to make the boys sleep outside. At least here they can sleep in the kitchen, in the warm. I mean, what's the point of having dogs if you're not going to let them be part of the family?'

Georgina privately agreed. Bert slept in her kitchen, but he had a favourite spot on the sofa. Apart from when she was in the darkroom, he went wherever she did in the house. He was definitely part of her family.

'Anyway, we were telling you about the house. We're thinking of doing special occasional tours as well as the standard house tour,' Posy said. 'Maybe the attics and the cellars, and on summer evenings we could have a bat walk around the woods and the ice house. Ellen said she'd get a bat licence so she can lead that.'

'Ellen's one of your garden team?' Georgina asked.

'No. She's Karen's daughter,' Posy said. 'And, thank God,

she's nothing like her mother. She's a bit quiet, but sweet, and she mucks in with the rest of us.'

'She's in the second year of her degree in ecology. She's particularly interested in bats,' Hattie said. 'Apparently the old ice house in the woods by the lake is a bat hibernation place in the winter, and she thinks there's a maternity colony in one of the hollow trees in the woods. We've got a government grant to restore the ice house, but we'll have to fit the work in around the times when the bats use it, once the surveyor gives us the go-ahead. Ellen thinks we can replace some of the bricks in the ice house with special bat bricks they can sleep in.'

'Sleep *in* the bricks?' Sybbie asked.

'Yes. They're like normal bricks, but with slits cut into them so the bats can squeeze in and be comfortable while they hibernate,' Posy explained. 'She says we have Daubenton bats and Natterer's bats, and she's doing a special project on them.'

'That sounds as if it'd be good publicity,' Georgina said. 'Perhaps I can have a chat with Ellen about the bats and take photographs of the ice house, if it won't disturb the bats? Plus she might have photos of the bats already that we can use.'

'I don't think she's around today,' Posy said. 'At least, her car isn't here. But I can show you the ice house and I'll ask her to get in touch with you when she's back, if you like.'

'That would be good,' Georgina said.

Once they'd eaten the cake and agreed that Cesca's cooking was to die for, Posy offered Georgie a tour round the house.

'Leave your Bert with our mob,' Hattie said. 'I'm going over to the estate office in a bit and I need to talk to the accountant, so I might as well do that while you're photographing the house. The dogs can stay with me so they don't trip you up.' She opened the kitchen door, rattled a tin, and a few seconds later four spaniels skidded through the door.

'I'm expecting you to sit nicely for this, boys,' Hattie said with a grin, and they all sat perfectly still, waiting in turn for a biscuit.

'Let me go and grab my camera from the car,' Georgina said.

'I hope you can get your photos done before this Karen woman comes back,' Doris said, when Georgina was on her own outside. 'She doesn't sound like someone you or I would get on with. My parents were farmers, and our dogs always lived indoors with us. Why would you make them sleep outside?'

'Don't ask me. Different people have different ideas,' Georgina said. 'It'll probably be a bit awkward if she turns up, given that she doesn't seem to get on with Posy and Hattie, but I'll just have to smooth it over as best I can. It's part of my job, dealing with difficult people.'

'Rather you than me,' Doris said. 'Though I'm looking forward to the tour of the house. I do love a good nosey-round.'

THREE

Posy took Georgina and Sybbie over to the house, where Georgina photographed the Victorian kitchen with its black-leaded range, large butler's sink and shelves stacked with patterned china dishes; the seventeenth-century dining room, with its huge oak table set for twenty, an enormous fireplace and dark panelled walls studded with tiny portraits in gilt frames; and the music room, a light and airy room with walls lined in apricot silk, delicate pale furnishings and plenty of gilt-framed mirrors to reflect the light and dazzling chandeliers, as well as a beautiful ornate grand piano.

Next was the withdrawing room with its rich blue damask curtains, comfortable sofas and small tables. Then Posy took them up the sweeping staircase to the first floor. The first corridor contained Elizabeth the First's alleged bedroom, a dark-panelled room with a carved oak tester bed and deep red velvet bed-hangings, an oak chest with linenfold panelling, a matching set of bed steps with a silver candlestick sitting on the top step and two carved chairs and an enormous tapestry.

'Did Elizabeth the First really sleep there?' Georgina asked, fascinated.

'We know that she visited Norfolk in August 1578 on her summer progress,' Posy said. 'The records suggest she didn't go any further north than Norwich, but who knows? Blickling is only a little bit north of Norwich – where the queen's mother was born, before the Boleyns moved to Hever Castle – and we're not very far from Blickling. Maybe Elizabeth wanted to see her mother's childhood home, and she might've visited Hartington afterwards. After all, not everything was recorded.'

'In other words, it's a lovely story, but there probably isn't a scrap of truth in it,' Sybbie said.

Posy laughed. 'Remind me never to let you be our tour guide, Aunt Syb!'

'I'd rather guide people round the garden, anyway,' Sybbie said with a grin.

The next bedroom was very different in style: Victorian, with a brass bedstead, cast-iron fireplace, a chest of drawers boasting a large mirror and silver-backed hairbrush, comb and mirror set, a bedside cabinet with a pretty glass lampshade, and wallpaper and curtains whose design Georgina recognised instantly.

'This is the Sunflower Room,' Posy said.

'Named after the fabric design?' Georgina asked.

'Absolutely,' Posy said, looking pleased.

'I love William Morris,' Georgina said, taking more photographs.

'Me too,' Doris said. 'Those curtains would look good in our living room. And matching cushions. And a rug.'

A little further along the corridor was a pretty sitting room, light and bright with a plaster ceiling, apricot silk wall-hangings, comfortable sofas in a slightly deeper shade, a couple of occasional tables with framed photographs on them, a harpsichord and a desk.

Georgina sniffed. 'That's lovely. Beeswax and lavender,' she said. 'The perfect scent for a country house.'

'You can smell lavender?' Posy asked, her face paling slightly.

'Yes.' Georgina frowned. 'Is that a problem?'

'No-o. Just... oh, never mind,' Posy said. 'Just me being silly.'

It sounded as if Posy was hiding something, but Georgina didn't get the chance to draw her out because then Posy said quickly, 'Let me show you the library.'

It was a long narrow room that ran the length of the house.

'Imagine curling up in a chair here, with all those books to read,' Doris whispered. 'That's my idea of heaven.'

Georgina agreed. 'This is stunning, Posy,' she said, taking photographs from several angles. 'I think, if I lived here, you'd always find me in this room. And I'd never get any work done.' She walked over to the window. 'Oh, my. You can really see the garden design from here. It's a perfect knot garden.' She took more snaps. 'That must be the lavender I smelled earlier.'

Again, Posy looked awkward for a moment, then changed the subject. 'They used this room in Tudor times for exercise,' she said, 'mainly promenades and practising swordsmanship. It was known as the Long Gallery for a time because there were lots of paintings here, but my four-times-great-grandmother turned it into the library in the nineteenth century. The house was requisitioned as a maternity hospital in the Second World War, and the library was used as the main ward; apparently, when they were doing some work on the floorboards, they found these little balls stuffed with moss, so it's possible that tennis was played in this room in Tudor times.'

'I hope you've still got the tennis balls,' Georgina said. 'It's the sort of thing your visitors would want to see. And I'd love to photograph them.'

'I think they got packed away somewhere,' Posy said. 'Maybe they're in the attic. They're on my list of things I'd like to find, because I want to do an exhibition about the war years. As soon as I find them, I'll let you know.'

Georgina took a couple of shots of the ceiling, with its geometric patterns, pendants and bosses. 'The ceiling's stunning,' she said.

'Classic Tudor showing-off,' Posy said. 'Did you notice that the pattern up there is exactly the same as the knot garden?'

Georgina looked up, then went over to the window again and took a shot of the garden. 'So it is. That's wonderful. You need to put the two photos together in the guidebook, to make the point.'

'But you're making us wait for the *really* exciting bit,' Sybbie said. 'Dragging your feet, young lady. Tsk.' She tapped one foot against the wooden floor.

Posy laughed. 'All right, all right. I know you're dying to see the Red Book again, Aunt Syb.' She went to a map cabinet in the corner of the library and opened one of the drawers.

Then she frowned. 'Oh. Maybe Papa's moved it.'

She checked all the other drawers in the cabinet, and her frown deepened. 'That's odd. The Red Book's not here.'

'Maybe, as you said, your father moved it,' Georgina suggested.

Posy's mouth thinned. 'Or maybe Karen took it. Maybe that's why she's in London. Seeing a dealer.' Her eyes narrowed in anger. 'I'll kill her if she's sold it! The Red Book doesn't belong to her. She has no right to sell it. It should stay here, in Hartington.'

'Sweetie, even if she *has* taken it to London, she won't get very far,' Sybbie said, trying to calm her goddaughter down. 'If she's taken it to a dealer or an auction house, they'll contact your father to make sure of its provenance before they agree to list it. At the very least they'll want to see the supporting paperwork from your archives. You know how hopeless he is; he won't have a clue where the paperwork is, so he'll be forced to ask Hattie. Then you can make a formal protest. You know he'll back down in the face of potential bad publicity. He'll sulk, but he'll back down.'

Posy shook her head, looking deeply upset. 'I wish Papa had never married Karen. Why couldn't he have found someone *nice*, someone who wasn't obsessed with money and status and who would have loved Hartington as it is? Someone who didn't criticise and make sly, spiteful comments under her breath all the time?'

'I know, darling,' Sybbie soothed. 'But unfortunately you don't have a choice. Your father married her, so you just have to put up with it and muddle through as best you can. Look, let's go round the gardens.'

Georgina was impressed by how diplomatic Sybbie was being. It was clear that she sympathised with Posy's shock at discovering the missing treasure and understood how important the Red Book was to the family and the Hall itself, but she was also trying to defuse some of the tension and avoid making the situation worse between Karen and her stepdaughters.

'Yes. I'd love to see the kitchen gardens and the ice house,' Georgina said, doing her best to back up Sybbie's efforts.

'Of course.' Posy blew out a breath. 'I'm sorry for having a hissy fit. It's just... I can't bear to think of yet another thing my mother loved being wiped out of this house. Papa's already removed all the photographs of her. I suppose I should think myself lucky that Karen hasn't tried to remodel the gardens.' She rolled her eyes. 'Especially now the Pritchards have gone.'

'The Pritchards?' Sybbie asked, sounding shocked. 'But surely they haven't retired? They can't be old enough – and anyway, they love this place as much as you do. I always thought you'd have to drag them kicking and screaming into retirement.' She shook her head. 'Brian's an excellent head gardener. He knows what he's doing, just as Maggie has the running of the house down to a fine art.'

'It's all a bit of a mess. Karen accused Maggie of...' Posy

grimaced. 'I don't believe a word of what she said, but the upshot is that the Pritchards resigned. We've had a series of temporary housekeepers ever since, and half the garden team resigned *en masse*. We're having trouble getting replacements because nobody wants to work with *her* around.'

'Not a popular woman, is she, this Karen?' Doris whispered.

Feeling slightly awkward, Georgina followed Posy and Sybbie into the garden.

'Sorry, Georgie.' Posy gave her a rueful smile. 'This really isn't how today was supposed to have been.'

'It's fine. I've done plenty of shoots where things have been a bit tricky,' Georgina reassured her. 'My job's to ignore any awkwardness and take the photos you need – or perhaps I should say "focus" on the photos you need.'

Sybbie groaned. 'That one's worthy of Bernard, Georgie. Utterly terrible.'

But it did the trick, because it broke the tension; Posy simmered down a little and smiled.

'Tell me more about the gardens, Posy,' Georgina said.

'As I said earlier, Hartington was requisitioned during the Second World War and used as a maternity hospital,' Posy said. 'That's one of the exhibitions I'd like to set up, showcasing photographs from the era and personal stories. The flower gardens were dug up and used as a vegetable plot because the walled kitchen garden didn't produce quite enough. The garden was kind of left to itself for a few years after that, but when Granny Rosa married Grandpa, she restored the gardens to how they were, using the old plans. She documented what she did, and I want to have an area either in the plant shop or above the tea rooms for an exhibition about the restoration.' She gave a wry smile. 'I loved Granny Rosa, and not just because I was named after her. She was like my mother; she always had time for people.'

'Rosa was lovely,' Sybbie said. 'She taught me a lot about

roses.' She gestured to the arbour. 'This is absolutely lovely, Posy.'

'So's the fountain,' Georgina said, taking shots from different angles.

'It costs a fortune to run. I thought you'd probably want to photograph it today, which is why I put it on earlier, but nowadays we only usually have it running during garden open days,' Posy said. 'I'm planning to change the pump to a smaller, more efficient solar pump, which will save a bit of money, but first I have to convince Papa to spend the money. Well, you know what it's like with an old house, Aunt Syb.' She rolled her eyes. 'Maintenance costs a fortune and money's always tight.'

Yet, judging from Hattie's earlier comment, the new Lady Ellingham bought a lot of designer clothes. Perhaps it was using estate money that Posy had earmarked for improving the gardens or the house, which would explain some of the tension between them.

'Tell me about that glorious oak tree,' Georgina said.

'It's a Sessile oak, and it's about four hundred years old,' Posy said. 'Sadly, if you hear any tales about this being yet another oak where Charles the First hid, it definitely isn't true. It wouldn't have been big enough at the time.'

She led them round the back of the Hall and through a worn green-painted door in the walled kitchen garden, down a narrow path towards the woods.

'This is the ice house,' Posy said. 'We think it was built in the late 1700s.'

There was a red-brick stepped gable wall with a wooden door set into it, and what looked like a short thatched tunnel which led to a cylindrical structure with a conical thatched roof.

'The inner chamber at the end is egg-shaped,' Posy said. 'And it's quite deep – about five metres, I'd say. Back in the day, they harvested ice from the lake and stored it here during winter, then took buckets of it back to the house whenever ice was needed. Apparently it lasted all year.'

Georgina took a photograph of the exterior. 'Could we have a look inside?' she asked.

'There isn't that much to see. It stopped being used by the end of the 1800s and pretty much became a rubbish dump until the 1970s. After it was cleared out, it was kept locked; Hattie and I were never allowed near it when we were small, in case we fell in,' Posy said. 'Ellen was convinced the ice house was a good spot for a bat roost though, being near water and woodland, and last winter she found evidence of them. She said she thinks they move to the woods in summer but, if there are any bats inside, they'll be hidden in a crevice somewhere. Once the surveyor's got the go-ahead, we'll install the bat bricks. In any case, we need to try not to disturb the bats.'

Posy took a bunch of keys from her pocket, selected a large iron key and slid it into the ancient lock. It wouldn't turn. 'Ellen did say the lock was sticky when she showed the bat surveyor round, earlier in the week. Maybe it's seized up,' she said, and twisted the iron latch handle. When the door opened, she frowned. 'That's strange. It wasn't locked at all.'

'Do you normally keep it locked?' Georgina asked.

'Yes. Apart from protecting the bats, it's for health and safety – in case one of our visitors to the garden gets a bit too curious, goes in and slips on the steps,' Posy said. 'If they disturb a bat, and one flies past and it makes them jump... Well, we don't want anyone falling into the ice house chamber. You'd definitely break a leg or an arm if you fell that far, and maybe do even more damage.' She frowned again. 'I'll have a word with the garden team and remind them that we need to double-check the lock first thing on the mornings when the garden is open.'

She opened the door, then took her phone out of her pocket, switched on the torch and shone it on the three brick stairs that led down to the tunnel, and which looked damp. 'Mind your footing,' she said as she walked into the tunnel. 'It's always cold here and it can get a bit sl—'

Georgina lost her footing at the bottom of the steps and instinctively pushed her arms out to the side of the tunnel to keep herself upright. 'Slippery,' she finished wryly.

'Are you all right, Georgie?' Posy asked, sounding anxious.

'I'm fine,' Georgina reassured her. 'I'm a bit clumsy.' Though she was glad that she'd hung her camera on the neck-strap rather than holding it. If she'd banged the camera against the wall, she might have damaged it.

'Bats, slippery floors and darkness? Hmm. I think I'll stay out here,' Sybbie said from the doorway.

There was no sign of bats, but there was a slightly musty, ammonia-like smell in the ice house that Georgina assumed was bat urine. There was also a sharper, metallic smell that she couldn't quite place.

'Will it disturb the bats if I take a photograph?' she asked.

'It will if you use a flash,' Posy said. 'Ellen says they don't roost here during the summer, but we need to be careful in case there are any stray ones here. Apparently they're protected by law, and even disturbing them is illegal.'

'Luckily, this is a digital camera, rather than a film one,' Georgina said, 'so I can mess about with the ISO settings, the aperture size and the shutter speed to take a photo without a flash. I promise it won't disturb any bats.'

Putting the lens between the bars at the top of the inner door of the ice house meant she could take a couple of shots of the interior domed roof and the walls; unlike the outside, the inside was lined with pale yellow bricks, laid in a gorgeous ornate pattern that she couldn't resist photographing.

'Uh-oh,' Doris said, close to her ear. 'There's a problem. You might not want to take a photograph of the bottom of the ice house.'

Georgina's skin prickled. The very first time she'd heard

Doris speak had been a warning not to go into the barn she rented out as a holiday cottage – because there had been a dead body in the barn.

Surely there wasn't a dead body here, too?

'Georgie, I mean it,' Doris said. 'There's a *problem*.'

Oh, God. It sounded as if she really did mean a dead body. Trying not to shiver, Georgina pointed the lens at the bottom of the ice house and took the shot. The screen on her camera showed a figure dressed in bright orange, lying crumpled on the floor, and a dark stain spreading next to it. Blood?

Was the person injured or were they dead? And who was it?

'Posy,' she said urgently. 'Look at my camera screen. There's a body at the bottom of the ice house.'

FOUR

'What? But – but there can't be,' Posy said, sounding shocked and a little scared. 'Nobody comes here. Ellen's in the middle of getting a survey done to make sure we can do the restoration work without disturbing the bats. They're checking the attics at the Hall, too. And, as I said, the ice house is always kept locked.'

Except it hadn't been locked just now.

'It looks like a person, to me,' Georgina passed her camera to Posy so the younger woman could see the screen.

'Oh, my God,' Posy said. 'Well, the bats are just going to have to forgive us for this. We can't leave whoever it is down there. They might be seriously hurt, or even d—' Her voice shuddered, cutting off the word.

'Hello, down there,' Georgina called. 'You're obviously not all right, but can you hear me?'

The silence felt thick and unsettling, as if the walls of the ice house were closing in on them, and Georgina shivered.

Was the person at the bottom of the shaft unconscious... or dead?

'We'd better call an ambulance,' Posy said.

'And try and get down there so we can give whoever it is first aid,' Georgina agreed.

'The rungs in the wall are broken or rusted and I wouldn't trust them with any proper weight,' Doris said. 'But obviously that doesn't apply to me, so I could use them. There's a lot of blood down there, and I couldn't see or hear the woman breathing. I think you need to prepare for the worst.'

Georgina nodded, hoping that Doris would see the acknowledgement. 'Is there a ladder kept here, or some other way to get down to the bottom?' she asked Posy, because she didn't want to explain how she knew there were rungs which couldn't be used.

'There used to be rungs in the side of the ice house, but they rusted and broke years ago. That's why Hattie and I were told not to come here, in case we fell and cracked our heads open and...' Posy shook her head. 'I don't know. Sorry. I can't think straight. I can't believe someone's down there, seriously hurt.'

'You've done this before, Georgie,' Doris said. 'You know the drill. Deep breath. Call the police and the ambulance.'

Georgina swallowed hard. So much for having a quiet life after what had happened with Roland Garnett. She'd intended to have a day out pottering around a stately home and garden and taking photographs for Hartington Hall's website and brochure, then possibly a walk by the sea and an ice cream. But it looked as if things had just got a lot more complicated. 'Let's move out from here for a minute, so we can call the ambulance,' she said, 'and then maybe you can find someone from your garden team and see if they have a ladder we can use to get to whoever's down there.'

'What's happened?' Sybbie asked when Georgina and Posy filed out of the ice house. 'I heard one of you calling. Is something wrong?'

'There's a person at the bottom of the ice house,' Georgina said. 'And something dark. I think it might be blood.' That would explain the metallic scent. 'I'm going to call the police and the ambulance, and Posy's going to find a ladder so we can get down there and see what we can do.'

'I did that first aid refresher course last month,' Sybbie said. 'When you've got the ladder, Posy, I'll go down and see what I can do.'

Georgina called the emergency services as Posy moved away.

'Which service do you require?' the call handler asked.

'Ambulance and police, please,' Georgina said. 'And maybe the fire service.' Just in case Posy couldn't get hold of a ladder.

'Can you give me your name, number and location, please?' the call handler asked.

Georgina did so. 'Someone's fallen into the ice house at Hartington Hall. They didn't answer when we called down, so I'm assuming they're unconscious.' Or dead. Not that she wanted to think about that. 'It's a big drop and we don't have a way of getting down there at the moment.'

'I'll put you through to the paramedics while we send the police, an ambulance and the fire crew out,' the call handler said.

Georgina explained the situation to the paramedic. Unless Posy came back with a ladder, they'd have to wait for the police and fire crew to arrive before they could get down to help the person at the bottom of the ice house.

'What now?' she asked Sybbie after ending the call.

'As you said on the phone, we can't do much until we can get down to whoever's there,' Sybbie said. 'We don't know how long they've been there, if they hit their head and were knocked out, if they've broken something or' – she paused, looking grim – 'if it's worse than that.'

Posy came back with Jimmy from the garden team and a rope.

Sybbie eyed it dubiously. 'Dear boy, I haven't climbed down a rope in years, but I'll give it a go.'

'No, I'll do it,' Jimmy said. 'I'm not being rude, Lady Wyatt, but it's a long way down and I'm quite a bit younger than you.'

'Call me Sybbie,' she corrected. 'And I'm a first-aider.'

'Me too,' he said with a smile, 'but I'm happy for you to direct me – just as you do when you find me pruning something. I'll see what the situation is and if whoever's down there is conscious, and then we can talk to the paramedics again if we need more help.'

He fastened the rope to the wrought-iron frame of the inner door, then carefully lowered himself over the edge.

Posy, Georgina and Sybbie waited anxiously by the doorway.

'I'm at the bottom,' Jimmy called up. 'They're definitely unconscious because they haven't moved since I started climbing down. I'm just putting the light on my phone so I can see properly.' Then his voice changed. 'Oh, my God.'

'What is it?' Posy asked.

'I... It's Her Ladyship,' he said shakily. 'Lady Ellingham.'

'What, *Karen*?' Sybbie asked.

'Yes,' Jimmy confirmed. 'And she's... she's not breathing. I think she's dead.'

'Can you check her pulse?' Sybbie asked.

'Nothing in her wrist, or her neck,' Jimmy called, a few moments later. 'I can't feel breath on my hand. And she's cold. I think she must have been here a while.'

Posy looked shocked. 'But – how can it be Karen down there? She went off to London yesterday.'

'Clearly she didn't. Or she came back and something happened here,' Sybbie said.

'Oh, my God. Karen's *dead*? I...' Looking completely at a loss, Posy raked her hand through her curls, ruffling them even further. 'I need to tell Papa. And Hattie. And get hold of Ellen.

And...' She stared at Jimmy as he hauled himself over the edge again. 'Are you *sure* it's her, Jimmy?'

'Very sure,' he said grimly. 'I shone the light on her face. It looks as if she hit her head when she fell. There's a gash on her head, and what looks like blood on the floor.' His complexion had gone very pale. 'Quite a bit of it.'

That was definitely the cause of the metallic smell, then, Georgina thought.

'Karen's *dead*.' Posy swallowed hard. 'I know I didn't get on with her and I wished her gone, often enough, but not like *this*. Oh, my God. Poor Ellen. How on earth am I going to tell her that her mother's died? And like this?'

'You need some hot, sweet tea,' Sybbie said firmly, lifting her chin and straightening her shoulders as if she was literally pulling herself together, too. 'Come on. Lock the door of this place so nobody else can go in and slip on the edge or whatever. We'll wait for the police at the Hall. You too, Jimmy – they'll want to talk to you, because you found her. And I think you could do with some hot, sweet tea, too. You look as if you're about to faint. Do you want to sit down and put your head between your knees for a minute?'

'I'll be fine,' Jimmy said, his voice a little wobbly. 'I just... I've never seen a dead body before.'

Georgina squeezed his hand briefly. 'It's a bit of a shock. Try to breathe more deeply – in for four and out for four. It'll stop your head feeling so swimmy.'

He gave her a grateful look and concentrated on breathing.

They headed back to the cottage, where Hattie was on the phone. Seeing the grim expressions on everyone's faces, she quickly ended the call. 'What's happened?' she asked as the dogs milled about their feet and Bert shoved his face into Georgina's hand. 'Boys, sit *still*,' Hattie commanded, and the dogs subsided, Bert included.

Sybbie filled the kettle, and Georgina found mugs.

'There isn't an easy way to say this,' Posy said. 'Georgina took a photograph of the inside of the ice house and there was – there was a body at the bottom. We called the emergency services, but we couldn't just leave someone down there while we waited for them to come. I went to get a ladder or something, and Jimmy found a rope and came back to the ice house with me.' She dragged in a breath. 'He went down to see who it was and how badly they were injured.' Her voice cracked. 'It's Karen.'

'Karen?' Hattie stared at her in astonishment. 'She's hurt?'

Posy slumped into one of the kitchen chairs. 'She's dead.'

'*Dead?*' Hattie repeated, her eyes widening. 'But – how?'

'It looks as if she fell and hit her head in the wrong place,' Jimmy said. 'And that's a big drop. Even if she hadn't hit her head, I reckon she would've broken a few bones.'

'But what on earth was she doing in the ice house? Nobody goes there. It's been kept locked for years anyway but, after Ellen found the bats, everyone knows not to disturb the roost,' Hattie said.

'I have no idea why she'd be there,' Posy said.

'And how did she fall? Even Karen wouldn't be reckless enough to stand near the edge of a drop when it's slippery underfoot. Especially in the sort of shoes she always wears.' Hattie frowned. 'I don't understand.'

'How are we going to tell Papa?' Posy asked. 'And Ellen?'

'We need to call them. Get them home,' Hattie said, and picked up her phone.

Neither answered. 'Maybe Ellen's in a lecture or something,' Posy suggested.

'She can't be. Term's ended. But she might be with the bat surveyor, sorting out what needs to be done for the ice house restoration,' Hattie said. 'And who knows where Papa's taken himself?' She closed her eyes. 'Oh, God. I hope he's not at a dealer.'

'Dealer?' Georgina asked. Given what Posy had told them earlier, did Hattie suspect that their father might have taken the Red Book to a dealer?

'Vintage cars,' Posy said. 'Papa can't resist them. He'll pay a fortune for a heap of rust that he'll spend months doing up.'

'To be fair to your father,' Sybbie said, 'he does have a good eye for a car. And he's meticulous when he works on them.'

'And, if he's working on a car,' Posy added to Hattie, 'that means he's not interfering in the estate. Which is a good thing.'

'We can't *afford* for him to buy another car. Not until we've got the solar water pump for the fountain sorted.' Hattie sighed. 'But you're right about the distraction. He might've stuck around today if he'd thought you were bringing the MGA, Aunt Syb, so he could spend all morning peering at the engine,' she added, referring to Sybbie's turquoise antique sports car.

'Next time you need a distraction, I'll drive it over,' Sybbie promised. 'And you could always take a leaf out of your mother's book and tell him that if he doesn't stop spending money, he'll have to sell the E-type.'

Everyone lapsed into a stunned silence. Georgina, not knowing what to say but wanting to do *something* to help, busied herself making a pot of tea, pouring it into mugs and passing them round.

FIVE

It felt like hours until the police, an ambulance and a fire engine arrived and parked on the carriage drive behind the Hall.

'We'd better go out to meet them,' Hattie said, and everyone followed her outside – including the dogs, who seemed to have picked up on the seriousness of the mood and sat patiently.

The two police officers climbed out of the car.

'Mrs Drake?' the policewoman asked.

Georgina stepped forward. 'I'm the one who called the emergency services, but I'm just a visitor.' She swiftly introduced the others.

'I'm Sergeant Leonard, and this is PC Riches,' the policewoman said. 'Jimmy – Mr?'

'Barker,' he said.

'Mr Barker,' she said. 'You're the one who went down to the bottom of the ice house. You're absolutely sure that Lady Ellingham's dead?'

He nodded. 'I checked for a pulse in her neck, her wrist and her forehead, but there wasn't one. There's a gash on her head, and it looks like blood on the floor.'

'We're going to have to treat this as a suspicious death until we know otherwise,' the young policewoman said. 'I'll call the scene of crimes team. We'll need the shoes and fingerprints of whoever's been in the ice house today, so we can eliminate you from our enquiries. I'll talk to the fire crew and paramedics; whoever gets her out will need to use gloves and forensic shoe-coverings so we can preserve the scene as much as possible. And I'll call the duty pathologist.'

'It's a bat roost,' Posy said. 'The ice house, I mean. Karen's daughter, Ellen Newman, is an ecology student. She says it's illegal to disturb bats.'

'In the circumstances, we don't have any choice,' Sergeant Leonard said gently. 'We need to retrieve the body. Can you take us to the ice house, Miss Berry? The rest of you, please stay here with my colleague PC Riches, and he'll take a witness statement from each of you.'

'Let's go back into the cottage. It'll be easier to take statements there. I'll put the kettle on again,' Sybbie said.

As they went into the kitchen, Hattie's phone shrilled.

'It's Ellen,' she said, glancing at the screen, and answered the call. 'Ellen? Thanks for calling back. Um, there isn't an easy way to say this, but there's been an accident and you need to come back to the hall as soon as possible. No, I'm sorry, I'm afraid I can't say any more on the phone. You really need to come home, though. OK. I'll see you soon.' She blew out a breath as she ended the call. 'She's on her way now. Poor girl. I think Karen's the only living relative she has.'

'What about Ellen's father? Or her grandparents?' Sybbie asked.

'Karen always refused to speak about them. We assumed her divorce from Ellen's father was pretty acrimonious and he didn't see his daughter. And Ellen's never mentioned her grandparents, so we assumed they died years ago – that, or you know how tangled family fights can get,' Hattie said. 'Now I think about it, none of Karen's family even came to the wedding. So they must have been either dead or estranged.' She frowned. 'None of her friends came, either. Or maybe she thought Papa's friends and family might be difficult with them because it was so soon after Mummy's death.'

'Is there a separate room I could use to take the witness statements?' PC Riches asked.

'Use the living room,' Hattie said. 'It's the other side of the hallway.'

'Thank you.'

'If you want to talk to us in order of who was there when we found the body, it's best to start with Posy, Georgie or me,' Sybbie said.

'Could we start with you, please?' PC Riches asked, looking at Georgina.

Georgina followed the policeman through to the living room and sat down on the sofa next to him.

'If you could tell me your name, address and occupation,' he said.

'I'm Georgina Drake, I live at Rookery Farm in Little Wenborough and I'm a photographer,' she said.

'May I ask why you're here?'

'I'm taking some preliminary photographs for Hattie and Posy. They're opening Hartington Hall to the public. As part of that, they're setting up a website and guidebook,' Georgina explained. 'Sybbie – Lady Wyatt – is their godmother and she's one of my closest friends, so she asked me if I'd help with the photographs.'

'Have you been here before?' PC Riches asked, rapidly writing notes.

'No. Today was my first visit to the Hall,' Georgina confirmed.

'Can you take me through your movements, please?'

Georgina quickly ran through the morning's events between arriving at ten and finding the body in the ice house, then Jimmy going down the shaft to discover that Karen Berry was dead. She switched on her camera to show PC Riches the photograph she'd taken. 'I can email a copy to you, if you need one, once I've downloaded the photographs to my computer,' she said.

'Yes, please,' he said, handing her a card with his details. 'Do you know what Lady Ellingham was doing at the ice house?' PC Riches asked.

'I have no idea,' Georgina said. 'Maybe it was something to do with the bats? Maybe her daughter had asked her to help with something? I'm sorry, I really don't know. I'd never met her.'

He asked a few more questions, then nodded. 'That's all for now, Mrs Drake. I'll write up your statement before I go, then ask you to review it and make any corrections before you sign it. Could you send Mr Barker in next, please?'

'Of course,' Georgina said. 'Can we get you a cup of tea or coffee?'

'Tea, just milk, quite strong, would be lovely, thanks,' PC Riches said.

'I'll get Jimmy to bring it in with him.' Georgina headed back to the kitchen.

'Jimmy, you're next,' she said. 'Wait a second, though. I promised PC Riches some tea.' She tested the pot. 'Still hot. Good. It shouldn't be stewed, just nicely strong.' She deftly poured tea into a mug, added milk from the jug and handed it to Jimmy to give to the officer.

'So what happens now?' Hattie asked.

'We all give our statements, then I imagine the police will investigate what happened, there will be an inquest and then they'll release the body so you can bury her,' Georgina said.

'I loathed the woman, but I didn't want her to *die*,' Hattie said. 'I just wanted Papa to realise what she was really like. All sweetness and light to his face, and sly as anything when he wasn't there, and always blaming others for things they hadn't even said or done.'

Georgina could almost hear Stephen's voice in her head. '*Look like the innocent flower /But be the serpent under't,*' she couldn't help saying.

'*Macbeth*? I did that for GSCE,' Hattie said, clearly recognising the quote. 'And that's just how Karen was. I know you're not supposed to speak ill of the dead, but she really has turned out to be the most horrible woman I've ever met.' She grimaced. 'And everything with her came down to money.'

'Darling, I know Posy hasn't had a chance to tell you yet, but you also need to know that the Red Book's missing,' Sybbie said quietly. 'Posy thinks Karen might have taken it to a dealer or an auction house in London.'

Hattie sucked in a breath. 'Oh, no. Please, don't say anything about that to the police, or they'll think Posy bumped her off, and – well, I *know* my little sister. She didn't like Karen either, but she'd never kill her.'

Colin – the detective inspector who'd investigated the case of the body at Rookery Farm, Georgina's holiday cottage – had once said to Georgina that, given the right circumstances and the right motivation, most people would be capable of murder. And Posy had been very upset indeed about the Red Book going missing, probably because it had meant so much to her late mother. She'd even threatened to kill Karen, though at the time Georgina had thought Posy was just letting off steam.

If Posy had known about the book going missing before she took Georgina and Sybbie to the library, and thought Karen had taken it, could she have lured her stepmother to the ice house and pushed her off the edge?

But that theory also assumed that Posy was an excellent actor. Georgina had spent a lot of time around actors, with her daughter being an actor and her late husband being an actor-director, and she was pretty sure that Posy's shock at discovering the body had been genuine.

'It was probably an accident,' she said. 'I slipped in the ice house entrance, despite Posy warning me. Maybe Karen slipped and fell.'

'But why would Karen go to the ice house in the first place?' Sybbie asked.

'No idea. She hates bats and I've heard her having a go at Ellen about why she had to specialise in nasty, dirty creatures instead of the beautiful deer in the park. It was a common complaint, along with why does she have to dress in black all the time and dye her hair black and wear so much eyeliner and clompy boots instead of pretty shoes,' Hattie said, unconsciously slipping into a savage mimicry of Karen. She sighed heavily. 'I'll try Papa again.'

When there was no answer, she left a voicemail. 'Papa, please call me. It's urgent. The police are here and you need to come home.' She sighed again and swiftly tapped out a text message. 'I don't know where the hell he is.'

SIX

Jimmy came back into the kitchen. 'He wants to speak to you, next, Lad— Sybbie,' he corrected himself.

'Thank you, Jimmy.' Sybbie smiled at him and left the kitchen.

'Let me put the kettle on again,' Hattie said, refilling it with water and switching it on. 'Jimmy, did you want tea or coffee?'

'I ought to be getting back to work,' Jimmy said. 'But PC Riches said to wait until he'd done my statement, so I could read it through and sign it.'

'I wouldn't expect you to go back to work today anyway,' Hattie said. 'Not after you found a dead body. It's too much of a shock.'

'I don't want to sit around thinking about it,' Jimmy said. 'I'd rather keep myself busy.' He raised his eyebrows. 'Why was she in the ice house, anyway?'

'Your guess is as good as mine,' Hattie said dryly.

'My grandad said it used to be a lovers' meeting pl—' He stopped, wincing. 'Sorry. I didn't mean to imply...' He flushed, looking hugely embarrassed.

'It's all right,' Hattie said. 'I don't think she was cheating on Papa.'

But she clearly suspected Karen of something, Georgina thought. There had been a flicker of an expression on her face, gone too quickly for Georgina to identify it.

'Do you think someone pushed her?' Jimmy asked.

'But who'd do that?' Georgina asked.

Jimmy snorted. 'There'd be a list as long as your arm. She's not exactly popular round here,' he said. 'She weren't nothing like Lady Millie. She wouldn't give you the time of day – well, not unless she wanted something from you.' He stopped and grimaced. 'Sorry. You shouldn't speak ill of the dead.'

'It's no secret that Posy and I didn't like her, either,' Hattie said. 'I could live with the fact that Papa moved her in so quickly after Mummy's death, if I at least thought she loved him and made him happy. But she didn't. She's had more rows with him in the last six months than my mother had with him in their last ten years together. As soon as they got married, she started making his friends feel unwelcome. None of them come here, anymore. Aunt Syb's the only one of Mummy's friends who still comes here, and that's to see us rather than Papa.'

'And there's what she did to you, Hattie,' Jimmy said. 'Everyone knows she pushed you and Posy out of the house.'

'We chose to move,' Hattie said.

His raised eyebrows said he didn't believe it, and neither did any of the rest of the staff.

'Moving out to the cottage saved a lot of rows,' Hattie said with a sigh. 'Oh, God. I don't know what to say to poor Ellen.'

'You'd never believe Ellen was Her Ladyship's daughter,' Jimmy said. 'No airs and graces, no side to her. She doesn't mind getting her hands dirty and she mucks in with everyone else.'

'She's a nice kid,' Hattie agreed. 'She doesn't deserve—'

But whatever Hattie was going to say was broken by Posy arriving.

'The body's definitely Karen,' she said. 'The pathologist's been, and she went into the ice house to do some tests. Between them, the fire crew and the paramedics brought her up.' Her face was grim. 'She was wearing that orange trouser suit. The designer one she was so pleased with. And the Louboutins, though one of them's broken where she landed.' She dragged in a breath. 'I identified her formally. It wasn't very...' Her face crumpled. 'At least that'll save Ellen having to face the worst bit.'

'Oh, Posy.' Hattie gave her sister a hug. 'Ellen's on her way back. I still haven't managed to get in touch with Papa. I've left him a voicemail and a text.' She looked at Sergeant Leonard. 'He can't be bothered with mobile phones. My mother pushed him into being a bit better at answering, but since she died he's lapsed back into ignoring his phone most of the time. I'm so sorry.'

'Not your fault, Miss Berry,' Sergeant Leonard said.

'What happens now?' Hattie asked. 'How do I tell Ellen that her mum's dead?'

'We can do that,' Sergeant Leonard said. 'Because it's an unexpected death, I'm afraid we have to treat it as suspicious until we've determined the cause of death and what happened. That's why I called the pathologist. Do you know who Lady Ellingham's doctor was?'

'The same as Papa's. We all use the village practice.' Hattie found the number in her phone and gave it to Sergeant Leonard. 'If she's dead, why would you need the doctor?'

'If the deceased had seen a doctor recently and received treatment, it might be relevant to the cause of death,' Sergeant Leonard explained.

'So Karen's body goes for a post-mortem now, and the

coroner makes a judgement on the cause of death from the pathologist's report?' Georgina asked.

'That's pretty much it.' Sergeant Leonard raised her eyebrows at Georgina. 'Do you work in that area, Mrs Drake?'

'No. One of my guests...'

'Don't mention the m-word,' Doris whispered urgently.

'... died in my holiday cottage, a couple of months ago,' Georgina said. It was the truth – just not the whole truth. And Doris was right: talking about a murder would only complicate things. 'So I'm familiar with the procedure for an unexpected death.'

'I see,' Sergeant Leonard said. 'The ambulance is taking the deceased to the pathology centre now for the post-mortem. We can arrange for Lord Ellingham and Miss Newman to see her after the post-mortem, though I'd advise against it. It can be very upsetting, even though the pathologists are very careful.'

The SOCO team were next to arrive, and Sergeant Leonard briefed them.

And then a grey saloon car Georgina recognised parked next to the SOCO team's car.

'A familiar face,' Sybbie remarked.

'Indeed,' Georgina said wryly.

Two seconds later, Detective Inspector Colin Bradshaw climbed out of the car, followed by his sergeant, Mo Tesfaye.

Georgina walked out with Posy to meet them.

Colin raised his eyebrow. 'A dead body, and *you* were the one to find it, Georgie?'

'Don't forget me,' Sybbie said with a smile, joining them. 'I was there, too.'

Colin groaned. 'I should have guessed you'd be involved in this. Jodie and Cesca here as well, are they?'

'Not this time,' Sybbie said, 'though, if you're a good boy, you might get a bit of Cesca's *nonna's* apple cake.'

'I'm very good,' Colin drawled. 'Aren't I, Georgie?'

'Oh, for pity's sake, stop flirting,' Georgina said, feeling the colour slide into her cheeks when Doris teased, 'Ooh, he's in full on Darcy mode. Be still, my beating heart. Where's the nearest lake?'

The speculation on Posy's face made Georgina add swiftly, 'Colin and I are friends.'

'As in "just good".' Sybbie added speech marks with her fingers, and Georgina saw the answering colour slide into Colin's cheeks, while Doris laughed softly.

Bert came barrelling over and leaped up happily at Colin, as if he hadn't seen him for weeks instead of merely the previous evening.

'Bert, *sit*,' Colin said, and Bert did so, wagging his tail madly among the shingle and causing a cloud of dust to rise. 'We'll have some quadruped exercise later,' Colin said, scratching behind the dog's ears.

'Ah. Bert's a dog who can spell a certain four-letter word starting with the letter after V?' Posy asked. 'Our lot can, too.'

'He's a good boy,' Colin said, and Bert shuffled closer, happily leaning against Colin's leg and closing his eyes in bliss at the ear-scratching. 'At least tell me you had a witness this time when you found the body, Georgie.'

'He means one he can actually see and hear,' Doris murmured, echoing Georgina's thoughts.

'Yes, I did. Posy – Miss Rosalind Berry – was with me,' Georgina said. 'Posy, this is Detective Inspector Colin Bradshaw.'

'And this is my detective sergeant, Mo Tesfaye.' Colin introduced them and shook Posy's hand. 'My condolences, Miss Berry.'

'Do call me Posy,' Posy said. 'Please come in, both of you. Let me get you a cup of tea, and then we can answer any questions you might have.'

'That's kind of you to offer,' he said, 'but I really need to see where Lady Ellingham was found, first, and speak to the SOCO team and to the officers who came out to see you first. Perhaps we can have a chat afterwards?'

'Of course. I don't think any of us are planning to go anywhere,' Posy said, a note of weariness in her voice.

Sybbie put her arm around Posy's shoulders. 'We're certainly not. And I can stay over tonight, if you need me.'

Posy looked gratefully at her. 'I might just take you up on that, Aunt Syb.'

* * *

Colin and Mo put on forensic suits and boots, and Sergeant Leonard led them, together with the SOCO team, to the ice house. Making sure not to touch anything, Colin went through the first door into the passageway and was careful where he placed his feet. The place smelled damp and, apart from the fact that he didn't want to damage evidence, he didn't want to risk slipping on moss or whatever and falling over the edge himself.

The light from his torch showed him an egg-shaped area at the end of the tunnel with a five-metre drop from the doorway; there was a dark patch of what he suspected would turn out to be blood at the bottom of the ice house.

A fall of just two metres could be fatal or cause a life-changing injury, depending on what part of the body hit the ground first. A five-metre drop would cause significantly more damage.

'What are your thoughts, Sergeant?' he asked.

'That's one for the post-mortem to decide, sir,' Sergeant Leonard said. 'Lady Ellingham might have slipped on the edge, or she might have been pushed. According to Posy Berry, the ice house is usually kept locked. Lady Ellingham's daughter, Ellen, says the ice house is a bat roost, which means it's legally protected.'

'So we have to be careful how we investigate, too,' Colin said. 'All right. We need to find out why Lady Ellingham was here. It doesn't seem like a place you'd visit, even as part of a stroll, given that it's a bat roost – not unless you were very interested in bats. Was she meeting someone there? If so, who? And why?'

'Jimmy Barker – the one who went down on a rope to see if he could give first aid – says that this place used to be a known spot for lovers to meet,' PC Riches said.

'Nothing romantic about this place,' Mo said. 'And if she *was* having a fling, would she really risk her husband or his daughters spotting her?' He shook his head. 'No, I can't see that as a reason for her being here.'

'She doesn't seem to have been very popular,' PC Riches added. 'There are definitely some, er, family tensions.'

Sybbie could probably fill him in on the background to the family before he spoke to them, Colin thought. She was straightforward and wouldn't mince her words.

'Has the body gone to Sammy Granger's – the pathologist's – lab?' he asked.

'Yes,' Sergeant Leonard confirmed. 'Though I took a photograph of the body where it lay at the bottom of the ice house, in case you wanted to see it.'

'Thank you. Would you mind emailing it to me, please? I'll leave the SOCO team to examine the area. And obviously please take careful account of health and safety as well as of the bats,' he said.

'Yes, sir,' Sergeant Leonard said.

And Colin wondered all the way back to the cottage: was this an unfortunate accident, or was it deliberate? Was it murder?

SEVEN

Hattie's phone shrilled, and she snatched it up. 'Papa? Oh, thank God. There's been an accident. You need to come home, please. Yes, right now.'

Sybbie and Georgina exchanged a nervous look.

'Papa, the police are here and they need to talk to you. No, I'm afraid I can't tell you anything on the phone – you need to be *here*. How long shall I tell them you'll be? All right.'

When the call ended, she put the phone back on the table. 'He thinks he'll be about another hour, I'm afraid,' she said to Colin.

Colin nodded. 'Thank you, Miss Berry.'

'Do call me Hattie,' she said.

'At the moment, we're making enquiries to find out what actually happened to Lady Ellingham,' Colin said. 'We're keeping an open mind about whether it was an accident. To help us with our enquiries, we need to know some background information. I know you've all given statements to PC Riches and signed them, but if there's anything you can think of that might be useful – even if it doesn't seem connected – I'd very much appreciate you telling me now.'

The missing Red Book and Posy's suspicions, Georgina thought. But it would be much more tactful to tell him about those later. And she'd get Sybbie to fill in the family background at the same time.

The kitchen door opened abruptly, and a young woman stood there. Her black hair, clearly dyed, was pulled back into a low-lying ponytail by an elastic hairband; she was wearing a baggy black long-sleeved T-shirt, despite the warmth of the day, over loose-fitting black jeans, and Dr Martens boots. And, just as Hattie had mentioned earlier, she wore a lot of black eyeliner. Underneath it, Georgina thought her eyes might be light blue.

She looked around the busy room, until her eyes found Hattie. 'You said there was an accident. What's going on?'

Hattie nodded. 'Come and sit down, Ellen.'

Ellen shook her head and folded her arms. 'I don't need to sit down.'

'Please sit down, Miss Newman,' Sergeant Leonard said. 'I'm Naomi Leonard.' She gestured to her uniform. 'Obviously I'm from the police.'

'What's happened?' Ellen asked, slumping into the chair next to Hattie.

'There isn't an easy way to tell you this, and I apologise for the abruptness,' Sergeant Leonard said, 'but I'm afraid your mother was found in the grounds of the Hall this morning. We think she fell. And I'm so sorry, but she didn't survive the fall.'

'My mother's *dead*?' Ellen stared at Sergeant Leonard as if she couldn't quite comprehend what she'd just been told. 'But... she can't be. How? What do you mean, fell? This bit of Norfolk's practically flat! There isn't anywhere for her to fall, except maybe over a tree root in the woods.'

'She was found in the ice house,' Sergeant Leonard said.

'What?' Ellen frowned. 'But – how? What was she doing *there*? It's a winter bat roost. We keep it locked to stop people going in and disturbing them.' Her frown deepened. 'It doesn't make any sense. Mum hates the bats. Why would she even go there?'

'At this stage, we don't know,' Sergeant Leonard said. 'But she was found at the bottom of the ice house. The pathologist says it looks likely that she hit her head when she fell. If it helps, she would've been unconscious before she reached the bottom of the shaft.'

'I...' Ellen shook her head. 'There must be some mistake. It can't be her.'

'I'm sorry, Ellen. When they brought the body up, I identified her for the police,' Posy said. 'I know it's your place to do it, as her next of kin, but I didn't want you to have to face...' She gulped.

Ellen stared at her. 'Well, you've got your own way now, haven't you? She's gone. You hated her. Both of you.'

'Ellen – please,' Hattie said. 'Nobody would've wanted anything like that to happen to your mother.'

'Didn't they?' Ellen stood up, her lip curling and her chair scraping harshly against the tiled floor. 'Well, she's *dead*, so someone did. Right now, I don't want to be anywhere near here.' She turned abruptly and left, banging the kitchen door behind her.

'I'll go after her,' Sergeant Leonard said.

'If you can,' Colin said, 'ask her to talk to me or get a witness statement from her, please. And we need to get a family liaison officer here.'

'I'll sort it out,' Sergeant Leonard said.

'Ellen's upset, obviously,' Hattie said, looking at Colin. 'She wasn't actually accusing us of pushing her mum off the edge of the ice house, just now. She was lashing out.'

'Were there family tensions?' Colin asked, careful to keep his voice expressionless.

Posy sighed. 'Yes. Our father married Karen – Ellen's mum – six months after our mother died.'

'When was that?' Colin asked.

'The wedding was about four years ago,' Hattie said. 'Papa's not good at emotional stuff or at dealing with things on his own. We understand that.'

'But Karen had, um, different ideas about how things should be handled. With the Hall, I mean,' Posy said.

'So you argued?' Colin asked.

'Quite a lot,' Posy admitted. 'Not with Ellen, but with Karen and Papa.'

'The last few months, it's been even more difficult. That's why we moved out of the Hall and into the cottage, three months ago,' Hattie said. 'The old workers' cottages were all supposed to be rented out as holiday accommodation. But the two of us moving into this one meant it was easier for everyone.' She grimaced. 'There was less tension.'

'What about your relationship with Ellen?' Colin asked.

'Normally, it's all right,' Posy said. 'She'll sit here in the kitchen with us and tell us about her bats and show us her photographs. When she told us she wanted to do a degree in ecology, she said she was sure there were bats in the ice house and maybe in the attic of the Hall, and she wanted to use the estate as a case study for her degree. We supported her.'

'She mentioned that Lady Ellingham didn't like the bats,' Colin said mildly.

Hattie winced. 'Karen was a bit over the top about it. She went on and on about bats being dirty, disgusting creatures, and why couldn't Ellen study the deer in the park instead?'

'Did Karen think you supported Ellen over the bats just to get at her?' Sybbie asked.

'Probably,' Posy agreed. 'Though that wasn't actually why we supported Ellen. She's a nice kid. She's a bit shy, and it must've been hard for her, coming from London to live here in the middle of nowhere. Especially at the age of sixteen. All her friends were miles away – *hours* away, even by car – and there was nobody her own age nearby, really. So we tried to do what we could to... to make her feel welcome here, I suppose. We're, what, eight and ten years older than her. We could remember what it's like, being sixteen and feeling all over the place.'

'When she started talking about the bats, we liked the fact that she was taking an interest in the estate,' Hattie said. 'Of course we'd encourage that.'

Colin made notes. 'Is there anyone else Lady Ellingham had a difficult relationship with?'

'Our housekeeper – *ex*-housekeeper,' Hattie amended. 'Maggie Pritchard had worked here for more than thirty years, since before our parents got married.'

If Mrs Pritchard had been close to the first Lady Ellingham, she might have resented the second marriage, Colin thought, not wanting anyone to take the first Lady Ellingham's place. 'Anything in particular they disagreed on?' he asked.

'Karen wanted to change the way Maggie had always done things. It didn't go down well – and, to be honest, it did feel as if Karen was just making change for change's sake,' Hattie said. 'We already did things the most efficient way.'

'And then Karen accused Maggie of stealing some earrings – which of course she didn't. Maggie wasn't a thief,' Posy said. 'But Papa insisted on searching the Pritchards' cottage. The earrings were found in their kitchen, hidden in the dresser.'

'We're pretty sure Karen planted them,' Hattie said. 'It's the sort of sly thing she'd do.'

'Did Lady Ellingham have a key to the Pritchards' cottage?' Colin asked.

'She had access to the keys in the estate office,' Hattie said. 'Which are all labelled. They're kept in a locked cabinet, but she also could've used Papa's key to open the cabinet at any point.'

'Who else has a key to that cabinet?' Colin asked.

'I do,' Hattie said. 'And my keys are always kept with me.

Papa's nominally in charge, but I'm the one who actually runs the estate. The house and the finance side, I mean. Posy manages the grounds, the pop-up teas and the plant shop. We're a team.'

He made a note. 'Did your father ask the police to investigate the alleged theft?'

'No. Maggie resigned, and Papa said they wouldn't take the issue any further because the earrings had been returned,' Hattie said. 'We only found out about that after the Pritchards left. Her husband resigned, too. Brian was our head gardener.'

'Half the gardening team resigned in protest at the way the Pritchards were treated,' Posy said. 'Which is why the garden's looking a bit shabby at the moment. Even though Hattie and I are both pitching in, we don't have enough staff to manage the grounds properly. Papa's in the process of interviewing for replacements.' She grimaced. 'Though we haven't had many applicants. Word gets around. The Pritchards are a bit set in their ways, but they're good people and they're well-liked by everyone in the village.'

The inference was clear: unlike Karen Berry.

'What about the housekeeper?' Colin asked. 'Do you have a new one?'

'We've had a series of temps,' Hattie said with a sigh. 'We haven't found a full-time replacement for Maggie yet.'

'When did you last see Lady Ellingham, Posy?' Colin asked.

Posy frowned. 'Yesterday morning. Though I didn't really see her. I heard her,' she corrected. 'I was going to check something with Papa about the house opening, and I could hear raised voices. Not the actual words, but the volume told me they were having yet another row. I started to back off, because I didn't want to get dragged into it – Karen likes playing the blame game, and I hate all that kind of nonsense. You know, all the he-said-she-said palaver. Then I heard a door slamming, and silence. Even if the row was over, I knew my father would need a bit of time to simmer down, so I came back here.'

'And you, Hattie? When did you last see Lady Ellingham?' Colin asked.

'Saturday afternoon,' Hattie said. 'I went to tell Papa that Aunt Syb would be coming today, bringing her photographer friend.' She bit her lip. 'Karen was grumbling that you'd be banging on about Millie all day, Aunt Syb.'

'Indeed,' Sybbie said dryly. 'I'm well aware that I'm not Karen's favourite person. She's not mine, either. And no, Colin, before you suggest it, I haven't seen her for weeks, and I certainly didn't push her into the ice house.'

'I wouldn't dream of suggesting it,' Colin said mildly. 'Though no questioning the witnesses this time, hmm?'

Sybbie gave him a wry smile of acknowledgement; that was exactly what she'd done when she, Georgina, Francesca and Jodie had needed to clear their names earlier in the summer. 'Best behaviour. Promise.'

'I need some air,' Posy said. 'Detective Inspector Bradshaw, would you mind if I just took the dogs for a turn round the garden?'

'Of course,' he said.

'Go with her,' Doris whispered into Georgina's ear.

'Why don't I come with you, Posy?' Georgina asked. 'Maybe I can take some more shots of the garden for you. And Bert could do with going outside, too.'

To her relief, Posy gave her a wan smile. 'Thanks, Georgie. The company would be appreciated. Come on, boys.'

Posy and Georgina walked round the formal gardens; the dogs ran around playing chase, while Georgina took photographs. But then Georgina realised that there were only three spaniels playing together. Bert was missing.

'Bert?' she called, slightly anxious. When there was no

response, she tried her usual two-tone call of his name. 'Be-ert! Here, boy!'

A few seconds later, the spaniel appeared from behind the large, ancient oak tree. Georgina's relieved smile was short-lived as she saw the state of his nose and paws.

'Bert! Have you been digging?' She shook her head. 'I'm so sorry, Posy.'

'Our three are diggers, too, given the chance,' Posy said. 'It's fine.'

'In my garden, maybe – but yours is open to the public. The last thing you need is a massive hole in the middle of the lawn or the borders. I'd better go and check he hasn't done any serious damage,' Georgina said, and headed over towards the oak tree.

As soon as she saw the scattering of earth over the roots where Bert had been digging, she could see there was a problem.

'Posy!' she called.

Posy jogged over to her. 'What is i—? *Oh*,' she said, seeing the bones sticking out of the earth. 'Oh, no.'

EIGHT

As they stared down at the grim pile of disturbed earth and bones, Georgina said, 'They look human to me, maybe leg bones. I have no idea how old they are, but...'

'I think you're right. Oh, God. I can't believe we've found two dead bodies here, *and* on the same day.' Posy shook her head. 'One's too many. Two... well, it feels as if the world's just gone mad.' She sighed. 'One of us had better stay here – no, thinking about it, *both* of us had better stay here, in case we need an alibi,' she corrected, and took her phone from her pocket. 'Hattie? Can you get the police to come and have a look by the Great Oak? Bert's just found some bones. Georgie and I think they might be human.'

A couple of minutes later, Georgina saw Colin and Mo walking across the gardens towards them.

Colin glanced at the hole by the roots of the oak tree, near to where they were standing. 'So you've found yet *another* body?' he asked Georgina.

'Bert found the bones,' she said, though she had a feeling that Doris might have had something to do with this. Why else would Doris have been so keen for her to go to the garden?

'All right. Walk me through how it happened,' he said.

'We were talking,' Posy said. 'Not about anything in particular. Just the garden. Georgie took some more photos – the roses are looking particularly nice right now. And then we realised we'd lost a dog, so Georgie called Bert.'

'How did you know Bert was the missing one?' Colin asked.

Posy coughed and indicated the four dogs. 'There were three black-and-white ones in view.'

'And Bert's liver-and-white, so he was obviously the one who'd gone off. OK. Just confirming the details,' he said. 'So you called him, Georgie? What then?'

'He came back – and he'd got earth round his face and his paws,' Georgina said. 'I went to see how big a hole he'd dug and if I'd need to borrow a spade or something to fill it in. And I could see a couple of bones sticking out of the ground. They look human, to me.' She gestured towards them.

'It's illegal to disturb human remains,' he said, 'so, as his owner, you did the right thing to stop him digging. If they're more than a hundred years old, they'll be classed as archaeological remains, and not of interest to the police. But I'm not an expert on dating bones.'

'What happens if the bones are less than a hundred years old?' Posy asked.

'Then we'll need to investigate further,' Colin said. 'I'm sorry, Posy. This must be difficult for you.'

'Two bodies – well, a skeleton and a body,' she said with a sigh. 'It's beginning to feel as if someone doesn't want us to open the house. Maybe it's Lavender.'

'Lavender?' Georgina asked.

'The family ghost,' Posy said.

'Most old houses have a ghost story attached to them,' Colin said.

'Or a real one,' Doris said, echoing Georgina's unspoken thoughts.

'What's the story with your ghost?' Georgina asked.

'She appears whenever there's a death in the family,' Posy said.

And there had been a death in the family, this weekend.

'Has she been seen recently?' Georgina asked.

'It's not so much seen,' Posy said. 'It's the scent of lavender – that's why we call her that. One of the pop-up tea room volunteers mentioned she could smell lavender really strongly the other day, but I assumed she meant in the knot garden. We've got six different varieties.' Then she looked at Georgina. 'Though you smelled lavender in the library, today.'

'Along with beeswax. I assumed it was polish, or from the garden,' Georgina said. The family ghost story explained why Posy had reacted so strangely to her comment about smelling lavender, earlier. 'So it's not specific to someone in the family sensing a ghost, like Sybbie's ghost at Little Wenborough Manor?'

'No.' Posy swallowed hard. 'The day Mum died, even though it was December and lavender doesn't bloom then, I remember smelling lavender. Hattie did, too. But we were both upset, and grief can do funny things to you.'

Georgina took her hand and squeezed it. 'I know,' she said gently. 'My husband died, two years ago. I still miss him.'

Posy's eyes welled up with tears. 'I miss my mother. Every single day. She was the heart of this place.'

'We'll need to talk to the Finds Liaison Officer or the County Archaeologist and ask their advice about the bones. In the meantime,' Colin said, 'I'll ask the SOCO team to rig up some protective covering to secure the area, and can you make sure your garden team keeps away from the area until we've finished investigating and exhuming the bones, Posy?'

'Of course,' Posy said.

'Thank you,' Doris said softly. 'And she's right about the lavender.'

She and Doris *definitely* needed a chat, later, Georgina thought.

Colin made a couple of phone calls as he followed them back to the kitchen, while Mo made notes on his phone. 'I've left a message with the Finds Liaison Officer, and the SOCO team are coming over now to have a look and then secure the area,' Colin said.

'That's good,' Georgina said.

When they got back to the kitchen, Henry had arrived. He was tall and well-built, with the kind of iron-grey hair that suggested it had been black when he was younger. He was wearing a white Oxford shirt with a sky-blue silk scarf tucked inside the collar, and he had a stubborn set to his clean-shaven jaw.

He was sitting at the table and Hattie had clearly just told him of Karen's death because he didn't even look up when Georgina, Posy, Colin and Mo came into the room.

'It *can't* be her,' he whispered brokenly. 'She can't possibly be dead.'

'Papa—' Hattie put a comforting hand on his shoulder.

He shook her off. 'You never liked her. Don't start pretending now.'

'I'm not pretending anything, Papa. You're hurt, and I love you,' Hattie said.

Though it was obvious to the rest of the room that she hadn't protested that her father was wrong and of course she'd liked Karen.

His lip curled. 'Karen was right about you and your sister. You're a pair of moneygrubbers.' His eyes narrowed. 'I wish I'd sold the Hall now, like she asked me to.'

Hattie and Posy both looked utterly shocked at their father's words; Georgina wasn't sure whether the accusation of greed had upset them most, or the revelation that he'd seriously considered selling their home.

Posy was the first to recover. 'Papa, you *know* we're not moneygrubbers,' she said. 'We're the custodians of Hartington for the next generation – just like you are, for us, and Grandpa was for you.'

'We should've tried for that baby,' Henry said, and his daughters both flinched.

Clearly that was news to them, too, Georgina thought.

'Lord Ellingham, you've just had a horrible shock,' Colin said. 'I'm Detective Inspector Colin Bradshaw. Perhaps we can go somewhere quiet and have a chat – you, me and my Detective Sergeant, Mo.' He widened his eyes at Georgina, and she got the message: he wanted her to keep a mental note of whatever Posy and Hattie said while he was out of the room, and fill him in later.

Lord Ellingham – who hadn't acknowledged Sybbie or Georgina's presence – let Colin usher him out of the kitchen, his back slightly bowed and his face lined with pain.

'I know he's just lost his second wife, and I'm sorry for that, but honestly I could shake your father until his teeth rattle,' Sybbie said. 'Don't listen to a word he just said to you. It's grief talking.'

'Is it?' Hattie asked grimly. 'I was brought up knowing that I'd be expected to run the estate when he got too old to do it himself. To be honest, he's never been hugely interested in the estate. He'd rather tinker with his cars. Mummy and Granny Rosa taught me everything I know. I could've earned a decent salary after uni, but I came home to work for nothing at Hartington – because it's my *duty*. And he's just thrown it all back in my face.' She dragged in a breath. 'I didn't know he was even thinking of selling the Hall.'

'Any solicitor worth his salt would've stopped him doing that,' Sybbie said firmly.

'Isn't the estate entailed?' Georgina asked.

'No. The title goes to the next male blood relative – ours is a distant cousin I can't ever remember meeting, and to be honest nobody cares about the title – but the entail on the estate was broken years and years ago. Papa can leave the Hall to whoever he wants,' Posy said. She bit her lip. 'And that also means he has the right to sell it, if he wants to.'

'I thought we'd always live at Hartington, and bring up our own children here in years to come,' Hattie said softly. 'Except that's obviously not what Papa wants anymore, is it?'

'He's lashing out and it's not fair of him to take it out on you,' Sybbie said. 'Don't take it to heart. I'm sure he didn't mean it.'

'Was he really planning to have a baby with her?' Posy asked. 'I mean, Ellen's twenty. Karen's forty-three.'

'They probably would have had to go through IVF for Karen to get pregnant,' Hattie said, 'and there aren't any guarantees that IVF would work. The older you are, the more the odds are stacked against you. But it's possible.'

'Highly unlikely, though, and your father knows that. Don't take any notice,' Sybbie said again. 'When he's had time to calm down and think about it, he'll apologise.'

Both girls gave a humourless laugh.

'This is Papa we're talking about,' Hattie said. 'If he had his way, the family motto would be *Nunquam deprecarentur*.'

Never apologise, Georgina translated mentally, and winced. Henry Berry clearly didn't have a particularly good relationship with his daughters, and that might even have been true before their mother's death.

'Because he's a middle-aged, entitled – in all senses of the word – white man,' Sybbie said crisply, and laughed. 'Which I, as a middle-aged, entitled white woman, can say with utter impunity.'

Hattie reached over to squeeze her hand. 'Aunt Syb, thank you.' Her face was still pinched with hurt, though. 'Moneygrubbing. I can't believe he said that. That's not who I am – or Posy.

For pity's sake, we don't even take a salary from the estate! We live off our trust funds, and that's thanks to Mummy's family. It never mattered until now, because we're part of Hartington and it's what we're supposed to do. Work hard, keep the house going, find a way to make it self-sufficient and preserve it for the future.'

'I know, darling,' Sybbie said.

'It's *her*,' Posy said. 'Karen's the kind of person who knows the price of everything, but not its value. To her, the Hall is something to be sold on the open market for millions. She doesn't see it as being part of the community, or part of the history of this area, or even just loved for its own sake because the building and the gardens are so gorgeous. It's just cold, hard cash to her.' She blew out a breath. 'Papa was never this bad until he met her. He could be a bit scratchy at times, yes, but every day he's been with her he's become a bit more difficult.'

'You feel Karen drove a wedge between you?' Georgina asked.

'Not just us,' Hattie said. 'He's fallen out with most of his old friends since he married her. He doesn't see them anymore. I was actually starting to wonder if he might be ill, because the way he behaves has changed so much since he married her. Especially in the last two years. I wondered if it might be depression, Parkinson's, or even the beginnings of dementia?' She shook her head, looking frustrated. 'But what would I know? I'm not a medic, and the internet can't diagnose him properly.'

NINE

'When did you last see your wife, Lord Ellingham?' Colin asked. Henry Berry was a large man, but he looked as if someone had knocked all the stuffing out of him and he was struggling to hold himself together. At the same time, the way he was dressed... It was nothing like Bernard, Sybbie's husband, who managed to look stylish and completely at ease, whether he was wearing an Italian handmade suit and highly polished shoes to a function, or jeans, wellies and a Barbour jacket on the farm. Henry Berry, with that Oxford shirt, formal trousers and shoes and the silk scarf, looked more as if he was trying to live up to an image of what someone else thought an upper-class man would wear. Karen Berry's choice, perhaps? Colin wondered.

'Yesterday,' Henry said. 'We had a bit of a row, and she stormed off. I assumed she'd gone off to London and was buying dresses or trinkets to cheer herself up, the way she always does, and she'd be all right when she came back.'

'What was the row about?' Colin asked.

'I can't remember. Nothing important.' He shook his head,

as if to clear it. 'We bicker. Everyone does.' He stared at Colin. 'I can't believe my wife's dead. How did it happen?'

'We're investigating that,' Colin said. 'The pathologist will do a post-mortem. Do you know if your wife saw your family doctor at any point in the last couple of months?'

'I don't think so,' Henry said. 'I know she went to the surgery, because she picks up my prescriptions and they have a pharmacy there. Blood pressure, you know, a bit of a dodgy ticker, aches and pains in my bones. It's a damned nuisance, getting old. Having to take so many pills every day, you practically rattle, and it doesn't do a bit of good.' He flapped a dismissive hand. 'But as for when she last saw the doctor... no, I really couldn't tell you.'

Colin glanced at Mo, who gave a slight nod, and Colin knew his DS would've made a note to check with the GP whether Karen Berry had any medical issues.

'Can you think of any reason why she might have gone to the ice house?' Colin asked.

Henry looked blank. 'No. No, I can't. She hated the country, wasn't one for taking walks around the grounds.'

Yet she'd chosen to live in Hartington Hall – a country house on an estate on the edge of a small village in deepest rural Norfolk. And Henry Berry, knowing that his wife didn't like it here, insisted on staying. Why?

'Hated Ellen's bats, too,' Henry added.

Which made it even less likely that Karen would go to the ice house, in case she encountered the bats. They were missing something crucial, Colin thought. He considered the old rumour about the ice house. 'Could she have met anyone there?'

Henry shrugged and spread his hands. 'Who? She hasn't really settled here, you know. Finds it difficult – too many people around who knew Millie, my former wife. They compare them and find Karen wanting, even though she's done nothing wrong except fall in love with me,' he confided. 'She wanted to move back to London, you know. Said if I sold the Hall, we'd have enough to get somewhere decent in Mayfair. And I thought, if it makes her happy, then I'll do it. I've been speaking to an estate agent on the quiet.' He tapped the side of his nose.

Colin remembered the expression on his daughters' faces when Henry had mentioned selling Hartington Hall: the initial shock and disbelief had been quickly followed by a tinge of anger. Selling up would mean they'd lose the home they'd shared with their late mother – and that would be quite a strong motive for getting rid of their new stepmother, the woman who was influencing him to sell.

But they'd also said that Henry had married Karen four years ago. Why had Henry left it so long to even consider moving, knowing his wife didn't enjoy life in the country? And why hadn't Karen left before now, if she was so unhappy here?

'How long did it normally take Lady Ellingham to calm down, after a row?' Colin asked.

'Depends. Usually until she's bought enough to make her happy,' Henry said. 'She likes smart clothes and shoes.' He closed his eyes. 'Always so bright. That orange trouser suit she loved so much, especially with the pink high heels. But I can afford them, so why shouldn't she have them?'

Which wasn't quite what Colin had asked, but the answer was illuminating. Henry had accused his daughters of being moneygrubbers, but his wife was the one who bought expensive designer stuff and his daughters were the ones who seemed more concerned about keeping the estate's finances on an even keel. 'Did you exchange any texts or phone calls with her after your row?' he asked.

'No.' Henry wrinkled his nose. 'I don't like those blasted mobile phones. You can never get away from them. I turn mine off, half the time.'

That would be easy enough to check, Colin thought. But

what he really wanted to know was why Karen Berry had ended up dead at the bottom of the ice house, a part of the estate that she clearly disliked and had no reason to visit, when she was thought to be in London. And had she simply fallen, or was she pushed?

So far, Henry Berry hadn't been particularly helpful.

'She didn't message you?' he enquired. 'And you weren't concerned by her silence, even though as far as you know she left the house yesterday?'

'I thought maybe she'd left her charger behind and her phone battery had died,' Henry said. 'It wouldn't have been the first time. Half the time when she goes to London, her phone dies.'

'Does she go to London often?' Colin asked.

'Is that relevant?'

'It might be,' Colin said, noting that Henry's tone had suddenly become defensive and his eyes had narrowed.

'A couple of times a month,' Henry said, flapping his hand dismissively.

'For how long?'

'I don't know. A couple of nights.'

Even at budget hotel rates, four nights a month in London wouldn't be cheap, and Colin had the impression that Karen would've chosen much more luxurious establishments. 'Did you go with her?'

'Not always.' He glared at Colin. 'Are you trying to insinuate something?'

'I'm just clarifying the facts,' Colin said. 'Do you know where she normally stayed?'

'Somewhere in Mayfair.'

It was obvious they weren't going to get any further with him at this point. 'I might have more questions for you later, Lord Ellingham,' Colin said. 'My condolences on your loss.'

'I thought Karen would be with me in my old age,' Henry said piteously.

It reminded Colin of something. Shakespeare, he was sure. Georgina would know.

'She was twenty years younger than me,' Henry continued. 'I thought she'd give me a new lease of life.'

'My condolences,' Colin repeated politely. 'I'll let you be with your family.' He nodded to Mo, and they left the room.

Colin checked his phone. 'We might as well head back to the office. There isn't much more we can do here until we've heard what Sammy Granger and the SOCO team have to say.'

'Do you think her death was an accident?' Mo asked.

'Why would someone who dislikes bats and hates the countryside go to an ice house near the woods, where bats are known to roost, and which is usually kept locked?' Colin asked. 'If we can answer those questions, then I can answer yours.'

'Gut feeling, guv?' Mo asked quietly.

Colin narrowed his eyes and shook his head very slightly.

'I agree,' Mo said.

Colin's phone beeped to signal an incoming text. He scanned it quickly. 'SOCO's looked at the second body,' he said. 'The Finds Liaison team needs to confirm it, but they think it's probably not something we'll need to handle.'

'One less complication, then,' Mo said.

They walked back into the kitchen. 'Thank you for your patience,' Colin said to Posy and Hattie. 'The SOCO team are securing the area by the oak tree. They think the bones will probably be classed as "bones of antiquity" and you won't need to do anything more than to arrange a reburial in consecrated ground, but we'll need the experts to check it out first. I'm afraid I can't do anything more here until I've seen the pathologist's report about Lady Ellingham, but I'll leave you my details in case there's anything you can think of that might be relevant, no matter how small.'

'I've just spoken to Bernard. I'm staying here, tonight, to help the girls and Henry,' Sybbie said. 'I assume the grounds need to stay closed to the public, this week?'

'That would be a good idea,' Colin said.

'I'd better get something up on the website, and contact anyone who's bought a ticket so I can refund their money,' Posy said. 'And we had a garden tour coming on Friday. I'll have to cancel and see if they can reschedule.'

'It might be wise to keep things vague about why you're closed,' Colin said. 'Talk about unforeseen circumstances, or something like that.'

Posy nodded. 'Got it.'

'I think the best thing I can do is go home and sort out the photographs for you,' Georgina said. 'I'll take my leave, too.' She hugged Posy and Hattie in turn. 'I'm so sorry. This must all be very difficult for you. If I can do anything to help, you have my number.'

'Thank you.' Posy gave her a wan smile. 'And thank you for all you've done today.'

'Colin, Mo. I'll see you later,' Georgina said, smiling at them both, and clipped Bert's lead to his collar. 'Come on, Bert. You'll sleep for a week after all that running around.' She looked at Posy. 'Sorry again about the digging.'

'It's honestly not a problem. We're used to it with our three,' Posy reassured her.

Colin had a brief word with Sergeant Leonard and PC Riches, thanking them for their help, and then with the SOCO team, and finally sent a swift text to Georgina.

> Can I buy you and Bert dinner tonight?
> Feathers at 7 work for you? C x

Then he climbed behind the wheel of his car and drove himself and Mo back to Norwich.

* * *

'Are you in the front with me or in the back with Bert?'
Georgina asked as she drove back down the long tree-lined
driveway. She'd left both car doors open while she'd secured
Bert's harness to the seat belt.

'Front,' Doris said. 'Bert's going to have a nap now – aren't
you, Bert?'

The spaniel gave a soft wuff of agreement and wagged his
tail.

'I assume you knew about the bones under the tree and you
instigated the digging?' Georgina asked.

'I hope you don't mind,' Doris said. 'They belong to Anne.'

'Is Anne the ghost Posy talked about, the one who smells of
lavender?' Georgina asked.

'Yes. She was a housemaid at Hartington Hall. Her
favourite task was making lavender sachets for the wardrobes, so
that's why they can smell lavender whenever she's about.'

'Which, according to family legend, is when somebody
dies,' Georgina said. 'When did Anne...' She searched for the
right phrase. 'Pass over?'

'As far as I can work out, a good hundred and fifty years
ago,' Doris said.

'In that case, the experts will definitely say the skeleton's
classed as "bones of antiquity" and the police won't investigate
further,' Georgina said.

'The police won't take it further anyway,' Doris said, 'but I
can. Well, with your help,' she amended.

'How much do you know?' Georgina asked. 'And how come
Anne could contact you? I thought you were... well...'

'On my own?' Doris asked. 'I was. But my life's changed an
awful lot since I met you. Not only can I go where you go – and
it's amazing to see how much the world around here has
changed – I can also talk to people. People like me, that is, ones

who are stuck. *Not* Stephen, before you ask,' she added hastily. 'But Anne's been waiting for the truth to come out about her death for decades.'

Like Doris herself; Georgina still hadn't quite got to the bottom of what had really happened on the night she'd died, St Valentine's Day, 1971. She hadn't yet been able to track down Doris's boyfriend, Trev, who might've been able to shed light on the matter. 'And she spoke to you today.'

'When we went on the tour of the house – when you smelled the lavender. That's why I asked Bert to dig in that spot. Because Anne told me she was buried there, and she asked me to help.'

'Was she murdered?' Georgina asked.

'We're not sure. Right now, she can only remember bits of what happened,' Doris said. 'Like me. But if we can find the paper trail, it might help.'

'All right,' Georgina said. 'We'll have a look at the computer later this evening. And I haven't given up on finding some information about Trev, either. I promised you I'd find out what happened to you, and I will.' She paused, thinking about this new development. 'Since you can talk to people, do you know what happened to Karen Berry?'

'No. I was there with you when Jimmy went down the rope, so I know what he said about it,' Doris said. 'But Karen Berry isn't talking to me or asking for my help. Just Anne. And, at the moment, I don't think I can contact her. The way it seems to work is that the person needing help has to make contact with me.'

'Got it,' Georgina said. 'Are you all right? Because hearing about someone falling and hitting their head... it must be really upsetting for you.' It was what had happened to Doris, or so they'd pieced together so far. Doris Beauchamp, aged eighteen, had fallen down the stairs at Rookery Farm and hit her head in the wrong place. And then she'd died.

Just like Karen Berry had fallen off the edge of the ice house, hit her head and died.

'I've had long enough to get used to the facts,' Doris said. 'It's the missing stuff that I need to remember. I'm hoping that helping Anne might shift something in my head and make me remember. Plus she asked me for help, and it's nice to feel I can actually do something. That I'm not just this pathetic wraith, drifting around uselessly.'

'You are absolutely *not* pathetic or useless,' Georgina said fiercely.

Doris coughed. 'Thanks for the vote of confidence, but I haven't got very far in the last fifty years, have I?'

'Only because you haven't had the chance,' Georgina said. 'Now, as Sybbie isn't in the car with us, did you want to go back to that audiobook, or do you want something to sing along to?'

'*Jane Eyre*, please,' Doris said. 'We're at the bit where Jane's just met Rochester.'

'Don't worry, it's bookmarked,' Georgina said, and hooked up her phone to her car's hands-free system. 'Oh. There's a message from Colin. He's suggesting buying Bert and me dinner tonight at the Feathers.'

'He really likes you,' Doris said. 'And you like him. We can do the internet sleuthing stuff later, so don't use that as an excuse. Say yes.'

Georgina smiled. 'I will.' She sent a text back, accepting the offer of dinner, and switched from the radio to the audiobook.

Just before the book started playing and she drove off, her phone came up with another message from Colin.

Excellent. Pick you up at ten to.

TEN

At precisely ten minutes to seven, Colin knocked on Georgina's kitchen door and walked in. He was a familiar visitor to the house; they'd been seeing each other for three months now, taking it slowly, and for both of them it had been a shift away from the sadness of the past and towards the hope of happiness.

'Hello, you.' She got up from the table, where she'd been making notes on a pad about what she'd need to know to start researching Anne's case, slid her arms round his neck and kissed him.

He kissed her back. 'Hello. Mmm. You've just made a not-so-nice day feel a bit better.'

'Good.'

He stooped to ruffle the top of Bert's head. 'And you. *Both* of you finding a dead body. And on the same day. Who could've predicted that?'

Bert wagged his tail happily.

'When will you hear about Karen Berry and A— the unknown skeleton?' Georgina corrected herself. Colin didn't know about Doris; if she told him that she knew the skeleton's name, she'd have to reveal *how* she knew, and she wasn't ready yet to risk telling him. He'd told her before that he didn't believe in ghosts: just in memories, regrets and guilty consciences. None of which explained Doris.

'Hopefully the pathologist can give me some information about Karen tomorrow,' he said. 'As for the skeleton under the oak – a lot depends on when the Finds Liaison Officer can come out to see the bones, but you heard me say what the SOCO team thinks. In their opinion, the bones look more than a century old.'

'Underneath the roots of a tree is a pretty unusual place to bury someone,' Georgina said. Even if Doris hadn't told her that Anne had asked for help, that fact alone would've made her suspicious. 'To me, it feels as if someone was trying to hide a death.'

'I agree. It might have been accidental and whoever was involved was terrified of being hanged for a crime they didn't commit; or it might be an old, old murder. Sadly, it's a case I don't have the slightest chance of solving,' Colin said. 'I might not even be able to find out who the bones belong to, let alone why the body was buried under the tree or who else was involved. But I can at least make sure the remains are treated with respect and reburied.'

'There might be a paper trail,' Georgina said.

'In which case, your Bea can probably help.' Georgina's daughter, Beatrice, was an actor based in London, but when she was 'resting' she worked for a probate genealogy company. 'But I still can't investigate a case that cold, Georgie. I don't have the budget and my team already has enough to do. Come on, I'm hungry – and Bert is, too. Time for dinner.'

'Bert's *always* hungry,' Georgina said as the spaniel wuffed at the D-word.

After lasagne, salad and a long cold drink at the Feathers in Great Wenborough, the next village – and two sausages cooked especially for Bert, because the chef in the kitchen adored him –

they went back to Rookery Farm. Georgina made them both an iced coffee, and she and Colin sat on the cushioned wrought-iron bench on the patio with Bert stretched out at their feet, listening to birdsong and looking out over the summer flowers in Georgina's garden. She'd persuaded Young Tom, who looked after her garden, to plant a section of the garden behind the greenhouse especially for butterflies, bees and other insects; the chaotic mass of wildflowers looked incredibly pretty, a froth of cornflowers, poppies, corn cockles, chamomile and love-in-a-mist.

There was a sudden harsh cawing, and several rooks fluttered up over the oak trees at the bottom of the garden.

'Something or someone's disturbed them,' Georgina said.

'Or they're going to show off and do a murmuration for us,' Colin said, sliding an arm round her shoulders. 'We can sit back and enjoy the show.'

She smiled. 'I think you're going to be disappointed. You might get a big group of rooks flying together, but only starlings do those glorious wave-like murmurations.'

'What's the name for a group of rooks?' he wondered idly.

'A parliament,' she said.

'I'm sure that's a group of owls,' he said.

'Not just owls. There's Chaucer's *Parlement of Foules,*' Georgina said. 'Let me look it up on the net.' She checked her phone. 'Apparently there are four collective nouns for rooks. A parliament, a building – which I'm guessing is something to do with how huge and deep their nests are – a storytelling, and the best one, I think, is a clamour.'

'Clamour certainly suits yours,' he said with a smile. 'I love your garden. Including the rooks, even when they're cawing their heads off.'

'It's a good place to just *be,*' she agreed. 'Colin, was Karen Berry's death an accident?'

Colin sighed. 'Strictly speaking, you know we shouldn't even be talking about this.'

'Isn't there something about conversations between partners having legal privilege?' she asked.

'If you want to invoke the privilege of marital communications,' he said, 'you have to prove that the communication was made in confidence, that it was intentionally to convey a message from one to the other, and that it was made during a valid marriage.'

'Two out of three ain't bad,' Georgina quipped with a grin.

Colin gave her a speaking look. 'I think I prefer you quoting Shakespeare and Chaucer at me rather than Meat Loaf. All right. I admit, you were helpful in solving Roland Garnett's case; and, when Mo and I took Lord Ellingham into the living room for a chat, his daughters probably had a bit to say that might be helpful to us.' He turned to face her, making sure that his face was in the light so she could lipread him if she needed to. 'What's your theory?'

'I don't have one at the moment,' Georgina admitted. 'But it seems odd to me. Karen Berry has an argument with her husband and everyone thinks she's gone to London in a huff. Then, the next day, she's found dead at the bottom of the ice house.'

'She was certainly dressed for London, from the photographs,' Colin said. 'Orange trouser suit, pink high heels.'

'Which isn't the sort of thing you'd wear if you were going to a building like the ice house,' Georgina said. 'Surely you'd wear something casual, and flat shoes you're not likely to slip in? It's obvious that high heels and slippery floors don't go together.'

'An accident in the making. Or so it would seem,' Colin said. 'Would Karen have had a handbag?'

'If she didn't have pockets in her trouser suit, she'd need something to hold her phone and keys – and a purse, unless she could use her phone or a watch to pay for things,' Georgina said. 'Wasn't her bag with her at the bottom of the ice house?'

'No. There was no sign of a mobile phone, either,' Colin said. 'Which is odd.' He grimaced. 'And I didn't tell you that.'

She pressed her palm briefly to his face in a gesture of reassurance. 'Colin, I'm not going to blab all over social media or call one of my mates in the press.'

'I know.' He sighed. 'Sorry. I'm always a bit twitchy at the start of an investigation.'

'Why?' she asked softly.

For a moment, there was something in his grey eyes and Georgina thought he was going to open up to her, but then the shutters went up. 'You were telling me your theory,' he said instead.

'It's the location that troubles me most. The building's apparently always kept locked – because of the bats, and for health and safety reasons – but it was unlocked when Posy and I went there, which is also odd. Plus Karen was known to hate bats. Why would she even go to the ice house in the first place?'

'Let alone fall off the edge into the chamber, apart from the fact that she was wearing completely unsuitable shoes – the sort that she didn't like getting dirty in the first place?' Colin said. 'Good questions. Which, at the moment, I can't answer – along with why the door was unlocked.'

'The passageway is definitely slippery. Posy warned me about it before we went in, and I still nearly fell over,' Georgina said. 'I think the fall itself could have been an accident, especially as she was wearing those spindly high heels.'

'It's more than just *where* she died that bothers me. It's who was there. If Karen went to meet someone at the ice house, slipped and accidentally fell over the edge,' Colin asked, 'then why didn't that person go and get help?'

'Maybe Karen got to the ice house first. Maybe she had the key to unlock the door,' Georgina suggested.

'I need to know how many keys there were to the ice house, where they were kept and who had access to them,' Colin said, making a note on his phone. 'Hattie said keys are kept in a locked cabinet in the estate office, and Karen had access to them via Lord Ellingham. But who else did?'

'The senior staff on the garden team?' Georgina suggested.

'I'll check.' He paused. 'In your scenario, what happens next?'

'Say she slips on the edge and hits her head as she falls – Sergeant Leonard told Ellen that the pathologist said she hit her head on the way down, and implied she was unconscious,' Georgina said. 'If she's knocked unconscious, either on the way down or when she hit the bottom, then she won't be able to call for help. Or, because the walls are so thick, anyone outside wouldn't hear her calling. And then, if the person she's meeting is late, they might not realise that she's already inside the ice house and has fallen in. They might wait outside for her, not even bothering to try the door because everyone knows it's kept locked. When she doesn't turn up, they might decide she's either got fed up waiting for them and left, or she's changed her mind about meeting them and hasn't turned up in the first place,' Georgina suggested. 'So they'd leave without even knowing that Karen was hurt – or dead – in the ice house.'

'Both theories work,' Colin agreed. 'Though it's still an odd place to meet someone.'

'Or maybe it's the best place to meet someone secretly,' Georgina said. 'Given Karen's public antipathy to bats, the ice house is the last place anyone would expect her to go. Plus it's set behind the walled garden, so nobody would see her going there – either from the house or from the garden.' She wrinkled her nose. 'But she was wearing that bright orange outfit. She'd stand out a mile; someone must've seen her.'

'I'll need to get Mo to walk there with a high-vis coat on or something, so we can work out whether she would've been seen from the house or the garden,' Colin said. 'But, if she couldn't be seen even when she was wearing bright clothes, that's a good point. The ice house would be perfect for a secret meeting.' He frowned. 'If Sybbie hadn't decided to stay at the Hall tonight, I would've suggested she and Bernard joined us at the Feathers and asked her to fill me in on the family background.'

'Actually, I can do some of that,' Georgina said. 'The first Lady Ellingham, Millie, was Posy and Hattie's mother; she was Sybbie's best friend, and she died from breast cancer four and a half years ago. From what Sybbie and the girls have told me, Henry seems to be the type who isn't good at coping with emotional things. He married Karen quite quickly after Millie's death.'

Georgina had lost her husband, Stephen, to a heart attack, more than two years ago, and she still wasn't sure if she was ready for a relationship. She and Colin were keeping things very low-key between them, seeing where it went; though Georgina really liked the man she was getting to know. She liked his intensity, his attention to detail and the way his grey eyes crinkled at the corners when he smiled.

But, even if they did get to the point where they wanted to make their relationship more permanent, she wouldn't do anything without checking that her children – or Colin's daughter, Cathy, whom she hadn't yet met – were happy about them moving their relationship forward. Henry Berry seemed to have rushed into marriage with a woman he hadn't known for very long, without thinking of how it might affect his daughters.

'Do you know how he met Karen?' Colin asked.

'That's a question for Sybbie, or for Henry himself,' Georgina said. 'I never knew Millie, but it seemed she was very well loved. I think it would've been hard for anyone to step into her shoes – and I get the feeling that Karen struggled.'

Colin nodded. 'From what I've heard today, the new Lady Ellingham doesn't seem to have been popular with anyone.'

'Most of Henry's friends have apparently stopped going to the Hall, because they don't feel welcome. Sybbie is the girls' godmother, and she's the only one of Millie's friends who still visits,' Georgina said. 'And you know Sybbie. She's very loyal. She's not going to dump the girls just because their stepmother makes her feel unwelcome.'

'I'd say it's unlikely that Karen was a family friend before Millie died, then, otherwise Millie's old friends would also be in her circle of friends and they'd still visit the Berrys,' Colin said.

'I already told you that Posy and Hattie moved out of the Hall into one of the holiday cottages, three months ago, because of all the family tensions.' Georgina bit her lip. 'I probably shouldn't tell you this.'

'That sounds as if you *definitely* should tell me,' Colin said.

'It seemed Karen planned to sell things from the house. Things that should've been kept at the Hall because they were heirlooms.'

He looked surprised. 'How do you know? And what sort of things?'

'Posy and Hattie overheard her talking about selling the antique copper pans. So they took them and put them in their kitchen to stop Karen flogging them off in an auction.'

'Which is their side of the story; we'll never know Karen's, now, so we can't have a truly balanced view of the situation,' Colin pointed out, and took a sip of his iced coffee.

'That's true,' Georgina admitted. 'I get the impression that, because Henry remarried very quickly, his daughters didn't have a chance to grieve properly for their mother. They resented Karen taking what they saw as Millie's place – which is understandable, just as it's understandable that Henry couldn't handle being on his own and needed a partner in his life. Karen resented his daughters for resenting her, and it became a vicious spiral.'

'Leaving Henry Berry caught in the middle,' Colin said.

ELEVEN

'The first time I met Henry was when you did,' Georgina said, 'but I trust Sybbie's judgement, and I'm under the impression that she didn't have a huge amount of time for him even when Millie was alive. I know he was probably still in shock after learning about Karen's death, but he really was cruel to his daughters today. Stephen would never have talked to Will or Bea like that.' She wrinkled her nose. 'I think Stephen would've cast him as Lear. You know, the kind of man who sees his children rather than himself as the problem. *How sharper than a serpent's tooth it is/ To have a thankless child!*'

'That's reminded me. Earlier, Henry said something that made me think about Shakespeare – something about spending his old age with Karen,' Colin said.

'That'd be *Lear*, all right. *I loved her most and thought to set my rest/ On her kind nursery,*' Georgina quoted. 'Though Lear said that about his daughter, not his wife. We don't know anything about Lear's wife in the play. And that quote is the line immediately before Lear banishes Cordelia; he acts like a petulant little boy having a tantrum because he hasn't got his own way.'

'Aren't we supposed to feel sorry for Lear?' Colin enquired.

'Stephen had a theory that Lear had dementia, which would explain his behaviour,' Georgina said thoughtfully.

'And you don't agree?'

'It's one interpretation,' she said. 'But if nobody ever says no to you or teaches you boundaries, you never have to face the consequences of your actions. In Lear's case I think it's classical hubris and he's the author of his own downfall. He wants his daughters to give him public adoration, throws a hissy fit when they don't, and then expects them to host his retinue even though they're drunk, disruptive and abuse the staff.'

'And in return he gave the two oldest daughters half his kingdom each,' Colin pointed out.

'It's not really about the money, though, is it? It's about respect and boundaries.' She looked at him. 'That's something else Posy said about Karen: that she knew the price of every-thing and the value of nothing. It seems Karen was all about the money, whereas Posy and Hattie see themselves as looking after the Hall for the next generation and they want to keep the place going.' She wrinkled her nose. 'Well, you already know that. You were there when Henry said Karen had wanted him to sell the Hall.'

'And have another baby.' Colin nodded. 'Could he have done that?'

'Sold the Hall, yes – I asked that when you weren't there, and Posy said it's not entailed so her father could do whatever he wanted with it. The baby, I don't know.' She frowned. 'It sounds to me as if Karen helped to deepen any rifts between Henry and his daughters. Maybe she thought if she stirred it up and he was angry enough with them, then it would help to salve any guilt he felt about selling the Hall and he'd be more likely to do what she wanted. He'd see it that his family wasn't supporting him, so why should he support them?'

'Back to being like King Lear, with his tunnel vision,' Colin said. 'But does that make Ellen Cordelia?'

'Only in that she's the youngest child. Posy and Hattie both seemed to like her and sympathise with her,' Georgina said. 'And Jimmy from the garden team said the same. Nobody had much time for Karen, because she didn't treat people very well, but Ellen got her hands dirty and was part of the team.'

'According to the statement he gave to PC Riches, Jimmy said that the ice house was known as a meeting place for lovers, years ago,' Colin mused.

Georgina scoffed. 'You'd have to be pretty desperate to meet a lover there, don't you think? It's cold, damp and dark – not to mention the risk of slipping and falling into the ice house chamber. It's certainly not my idea of a romantic trysting place.'

'Nor mine. But could Karen maybe have met a lover there?' Colin asked. 'Has Sybbie ever said anything to you about Karen being unfaithful?'

'Sybbie doesn't gossip like that,' Georgina said. 'I wouldn't know.'

'There's a big age gap between Henry and Karen,' Colin mused. 'Which doesn't necessarily mean they were unhappily married. But if you're from different generations, there's often a big difference between the way you see things.'

'Could she have met someone else, for a different reason?' Georgina asked.

'Such as?'

'It's hearsay,' Georgina said, 'but there's definitely gossip of another sort in the village, and Posy thinks that's why they're having trouble recruiting staff.'

'Which is?'

'You were there when Posy told us. Karen accused Maggie Pritchard – the housekeeper, who'd been working there for thirty-odd years, and was close to Millie and the girls – of stealing some earrings. The earrings were found at the

Pritchards' cottage, and Posy thinks Karen planted them as an excuse to get rid of Maggie. The Pritchards resigned before they could be sacked,' Georgina reminded him. 'But Maggie's husband was the head gardener, and half the garden team resigned as well, in protest.'

'Why do you think Karen wanted to get rid of the housekeeper?'

'I might be leaping to conclusions, here,' Georgina warned. 'But, given what Hattie said about the pans – that Karen was planning to sell them in an auction room – I wonder if Karen might have been taking other things from the house and selling them, too, and she didn't want anyone to realise what she was doing. With the housekeeper gone, the girls moved out of the house, Henry distracted with his cars, and the help in the house all being temps who wouldn't know where things were normally kept, who would notice if things went missing?'

'That's a very big leap, and you're right; at the moment it's all based on hearsay. There's no evidence of Karen Berry taking things and selling them,' Colin said.

'I know,' Georgina said, feeling guilty. 'Plus it's unfair to make judgements about a woman I'd never met and didn't know. And, for that matter, about someone who's dead and can't speak for herself.'

Colin brought her hand to his mouth, pressed a kiss into her palm and folded her fingers over the kiss. 'You're not the judgy sort, Georgie. So what aren't you telling me?'

Of course he'd pick up that she was holding back on something. Georgina chuckled wryly at being caught out. 'I was going to tell you. There's something called a Red Book – something to do with a landscape designer called Humphry Repton. Sybbie can tell you more about that,' Georgina said. 'The Red Book's worth a lot of money; but it also has a lot of sentimental value to Posy and Hattie, because it's connected to their mother. Henry apparently wanted to sell it years ago, to help pay death duties when his father died, but Millie stopped him because it was important for the house. Posy was going to show it to me earlier so I could take photographs for their guidebook, but she discovered it had gone missing.'

'Temporarily mislaid? Or,' Colin said thoughtfully, 'Henry might have chosen to sell it without telling his daughters. Just as he didn't tell them that he was thinking of selling the house and estate.'

'Posy thought Karen was behind its disappearance – possibly because she disliked Karen. But what if,' Georgina asked, 'Karen was meeting a dealer rather than a lover at the ice house?'

'Apart from the fact that there's no trace of this Red Book, and I'm sure the SOCO team would have found it if it was anywhere near the ice house,' Colin said, 'surely she'd be more likely to meet a dealer in London?'

'Where she'd leave a trail on CCTV and the like? If she was selling the book without Henry's knowledge,' Georgina said, 'then wouldn't she arrange to meet someone at a place where nobody would expect her to go, where nobody was likely to see her, and where there was no CCTV? Though again,' she added, 'if you don't want to be seen, why would you wear a bright orange trouser suit?'

'Her death *could* have been a simple accident,' Colin said.

'In which case, you still need a reason for Karen being at the ice house. Which you said you haven't established yet.' Georgina looked at him. 'And you don't actually think it's an accident, do you? Especially with her phone and her handbag being missing. Supposing she met this alleged dealer, they argued over the price of whatever she'd taken from the house, and the dealer grabbed her bag to take the item from her anyway? Then, during the tussle, she lost her balance and fell backwards?'

'Either the strap would've snapped as she fell, or she

could've dragged the alleged dealer over with her. At the bare minimum, there would be signs of a scuffle and someone trying to grab a handhold,' Colin said. He sighed. 'Until I have the pathology report, I'm keeping all options open. As you know from what happened at Rookery Barn, if there's an unexpected and unexplained death, then we need to secure the area where the body was found, in case we need to investigate it further.'

'If the report shows that Karen's death wasn't an accident, I really don't think Posy or Hattie would've been involved,' Georgina said.

'That's because they're the goddaughters of one of your close friends and you want to think the best of them,' Colin said. 'You have to take the emotion out of it and keep an open mind, Georgie. Think about it. They had a motive. They both resented her. Karen was putting an emotional wedge between them and their father – or making the situation worse, at least; she was pushing their mother into the background; and she wanted to sell their home—'

'—which they didn't find out until after her death,' Georgina cut in.

Colin ignored her comment. 'And they suspected she'd taken something that they associated with their mother, even though they didn't have any proof that she'd done it. Those are all strong motives for wanting to be rid of someone.'

'Again, they didn't find out about the missing book until after Karen's death. What about the Pritchards? Because of Karen, they lost their jobs and their home at the Hall, and she'd tried to smear their reputation. Bea once asked you why people killed, and you said it was usually for love, money or revenge,' Georgina pointed out. 'Would they want revenge? And the Pritchards would've known about the ice house. As the head gardener, Brian Pritchard might even have had his own key to the place.'

'All three motives fit Posy and Hattie too,' Colin said

thoughtfully. 'They loved their mother. Any property wrangle will by definition involve money; and if the new Lady Ellingham had made their relationship with their father more difficult than usual as well as taking their mother's place, wouldn't they want revenge?'

'Well then, what about Henry?' Georgina asked. 'They had a huge row yesterday. In fact, Posy says he was always arguing with Karen. More than he ever argued with Millie. And Hattie said Karen was big on retail therapy; she flounced off to London and spent a fortune whenever they had a fight.'

'Hearsay,' Colin said. 'The only people who ever really know what goes on in a marriage are the people in it.'

'Didn't Henry admit to the row when you talked to him?'

'I can't answer that,' Colin reminded her.

'All right. But what we were saying earlier about King Lear having dementia – that reminds me of something Hattie said. She thought her father's behaviour had changed a lot since he married Karen, and she wondered if it might be early-onset dementia, or another medical condition that causes a personality change.'

'I need to talk to the family doctor anyway, to check whether the deceased had any medical conditions,' Colin said. 'Since we're looking at Henry as a possible suspect, if he was prone to flying into a rage, might he have pushed Karen off the edge of the ice house after their row, and made everyone think she'd gone to London?'

'But why would she have gone to the ice house with him, particularly if he was angry?' Georgina asked. 'Surely she would've just carried on the fight in the house?'

'At the moment, I don't know,' Colin said.

'I'm just saying that Posy and Hattie aren't the only ones with motives to get rid of Karen,' Georgina pointed out. 'How did she get on with her daughter? We know Karen didn't like

Ellen studying the bats. From what Hattie said, she sounded very critical of Ellen's clothes and interests.'

'Which Ellen might be doing partly as a late teenage rebellion,' Colin said. 'There was nothing that stood out in the statement she gave Naomi Leonard.' He sighed again. 'Depending on the post-mortem report, I might have a lot of questions to ask.' He drew her closer. 'And any conclusions I draw have to be based strictly on evidence. But thank you for everything you've given me to think about. I know you've already given a witness statement about finding the body – *both* bodies,' he amended, 'but I might need another formal chat with you at some point.'

'Depending on the post-mortem,' Georgina said. 'All right. If you need to speak to me, you'll probably need to speak to Sybbie as well. I could always bring her with me to your office at some point in the next week.'

He raised an eyebrow. 'That sounds as if you're trying to find an excuse for a trip out.'

'There is this exhibition in the city we'd both like to see,' Georgina admitted with a grin.

'I *knew* it.'

'Of course you did, you being a super-sharp detective, and all that,' Georgina teased.

He laughed and kissed her. 'Right. I'd better get back. I'll call you tomorrow.' He made a fuss of Bert. 'Goodnight, lovely boy. I promise we'll have a proper quadruped constitutional later in the week.'

'North Norfolk – the s-e-a-s-i-d-e?' Georgina spelled out, knowing that Bert understood the word 'seaside' and would start racing round the garden in delirious circles if she dared to say it in full.

Colin smiled. 'Perfect.'

TWELVE

'Colin really is lovely,' Doris said as Georgina brought the glasses back into the kitchen.

'Yes, he is,' Georgina said. Though he was also damaged, and she thought it would be a while before he could completely trust her with his past. Then again, she was still dealing with the pain of losing Stephen. She and Colin were muddling through it together as best they could. But, in the three months they'd been seeing each other, she'd felt happier than she had in the two years since Stephen's death. Colin, too, seemed more contented than when they'd first met.

'I think you're good for each other,' Doris said.

'I agree, but it's still early days and we're taking it slowly,' Georgina said. 'Now, I'll get my laptop and a mug of tea, and then I want to know more about Anne.'

The kitchen at Rookery Farm was her favourite room in the house: the cream Shaker-style cupboards; the oak table with its mismatched chairs; the oak dresser covered in ladybird-themed crockery given to her by family and friends over the years acknowledging Stephen's nickname for her, 'Shutterbug'; the monkey-tail latches on the casement windows; the deep rich red of the pamment-tiled flooring. The room always felt like the heart of the house, particularly when it was filled with family and friends.

Georgina switched on the kettle, made herself a mug of tea, turned on the overhead light as dusk was starting to fall outside, then took her laptop from the dresser drawer and opened a new word-processing document. Bert curled up under the table, settling his head on her feet.

'Anne. Is that with or without an E?' Georgina asked.

'I'm not sure,' Doris said.

'OK. It'll probably bounce between the two in any documents, anyway, or maybe even show up as Anna; Bea says historic spelling of names is always pretty fluid, and you have to double-check transcriptions against the originals wherever you can – and against other names in the same handwriting, if you're not sure of some of the letters,' Georgina said. 'What else can you tell me?'

'She was a domestic servant at Hartington Hall,' Doris said. 'She's a bit shaky about the year, but she knows Victoria was on the throne.'

'After 1837, then,' Georgina said. 'With any luck, we'll pick her up on one of the census returns. What's her surname?'

'She didn't say – and I didn't ask,' Doris admitted.

'Age?'

'Eighteen – as she put it, the same age Victoria was when she became queen.' Although she didn't say it, Georgina knew they were both thinking it: it was the same age Doris was when she died.

'OK. We'll look at all the census returns for Hartington Hall between 1841 and 1901 to see if we can find someone,' Georgina said. 'What else do you know?'

'She was in love with William. They were going to marry, and he was planning to get a special licence.'

'Why get married by licence rather than banns?' Georgina

asked. 'A licence was quite expensive, especially if William was a servant as well. So there must've been a reason why they wanted to get married quickly or privately.'

'Maybe she was pregnant,' Doris said.

Was that why Doris had been able to connect with Anne's ghost – because she, too, had been pregnant when she'd died? Georgina wondered. Or maybe she was overthinking things. Georgina certainly wasn't pregnant when she'd first started to hear Doris.

She clicked onto one of the websites Bea had told her about. 'Reasons why they'd want a licence, to marry quickly or privately...' She skimmed the page. 'As you said, being pregnant; if the groom was on leave from the army or navy; if there was a big age gap between them – which I guess would lead to gossip; if their social statuses were very different; if they didn't have the same religion, or they were Nonconformists or Roman Catholics; or if they were over the age of twenty-one and the families opposed the marriage.'

'So if they were both under the age of twenty-one?' Doris asked.

'They'd need consent from a parent or guardian,' Georgina said. 'Let's start with the 1841 census return for Hartington Hall and the surrounding area, and we can see if that gives us any leads.'

There were two Williams listed on the census return.

'There's the butler – but he's nearly forty years older than Anne is,' Doris said, clearly reading the screen over Georgina's shoulder. 'Though you did say that a big age gap was a reason to get a licence, and butlers earned more than general servants so he would've been able to afford one.'

'And he's single, whereas the other William's married and lives with his wife, and it looks as if a couple of their grandchildren were staying overnight in their cottage,' Georgina said. 'I think Anne would be more likely to see William the butler in the course of an average day than she would William the agricultural labourer.'

'I got the impression that William was nearer her age,' Doris said. 'And I can't see any Annes.'

'Let's try the 1851 census,' Georgina said. 'This is more promising. Anne Lusher, aged fifteen, housemaid.'

'She's the only Anne,' Doris said. 'The two Williams from 1841 are still there – but look at the third line from the Hall itself. The Honourable William Berry, aged nineteen. He's nearer her age. I wonder if he's our William?'

'Relationship to head of house: son,' Georgina read. 'Which would make a marriage licence more likely – there's the social difference between William and Anne. Though, because they're both under twenty-one, they'd both need their parents' consent to get married.'

'Surely, at fifteen, Anne would be too young to get married?' Doris asked.

'Actually, no,' Georgina said. 'After the 1836 Marriage Act, girls could get married at twelve and boys could get married at fourteen, as long as they had their parents' permission.'

'Seriously? That young?' Doris sounded shocked. 'That's terrible!'

'It's worse than you think. Legally, it was like that until 1929, when the law changed to say you had to be at least sixteen to get married,' Georgina said. 'And then this year the law changed again so you have to be at least eighteen. Bea says in practice, in the 1800s, women tended to get married after they turned eighteen.'

'By the time Anne was eighteen, in 1854, William Berry would've been twenty-three – old enough not to need his parents' consent,' Doris said.

'Exactly. As long as Anne's parents gave permission, they could get married. And having a special licence meant that they could get married anywhere – they didn't have to stay in their parish and have William's parents glaring at them from the pews,' Georgina said. 'I wonder why William wasn't on the 1841 census?'

'Maybe the Berrys had another house somewhere else,' Doris suggested, 'or he was away at school.'

In the 1861 census, neither Anne nor William were listed at Hartington Hall. Neither was William's father, Edward Berry, Baron of Ellingham. The census listed Henry Berry as the Baron of Ellingham; he wasn't listed as living at the hall on the 1851 census, even without the title.

'If Edward Berry had died between 1851 and 1861, I would've expected William to inherit the title,' Georgina said. 'So why didn't he? And Henry's quite a bit older than William. I wonder if Henry might have been Edward's brother, or maybe a cousin?'

'Maybe you could ask Posy or Hattie,' Doris suggested.

'Good idea. Though I'll see what's in the birth, marriage and death records first.' Georgina tapped a few more keys. 'William seems to be Edward's only son. Born in 1832, which matches the information of the 1851 census. There was an Edward who died in infancy, before William was born, and three more Edwards after that who didn't survive.' She drew in a sharp intake of breath. 'And William died in 1854. In the Crimea.'

'*Theirs not to reason why,/Theirs but to do and die./Into the valley of Death/Rode the six hundred,*' Doris quoted softly.

'Tennyson,' Georgina said, recognising the poem instantly. 'I'm not sure if William was at the Charge of the Light Brigade or not, but that whole war was badly mismanaged. More people – on both sides – died from diseases like typhus, cholera and dysentery than from the actual fighting.'

'So it could have been disease rather than war that killed William. What happened to Anne?' Doris asked.

'I can't find a death record, even though we know she died

before the 1861 census,' Georgina said. 'I can't find a marriage record, either. Anne Lusher seems to have disappeared.' She winced, remembering the bones beneath the oak tree. 'I think we know why.'

'What about William's dad?' Doris asked.

'I've got his death record here,' Georgina said. 'He died four weeks after William. The cause of death is recorded as apoplexy – that's a stroke or a heart attack.'

'We did some of the history of the Crimean War for context with the Tennyson poem,' Doris said. 'It took about three weeks for news to get from the Crimean front to London.'

'So it's possible that Edward got the news about his son, had a heart attack or stroke as a result, and lingered for a week before dying,' Georgina said. 'That's very sad.'

'If William Berry was the William our Anne was in love with,' Doris said very quietly, 'she might not have wanted to survive him, either.'

'You think she might have killed herself? But then who buried her under the oak tree?' Georgina asked.

'I haven't a clue.'

'If she did kill herself... Suicide was really frowned upon, back then, but her death would still have been recorded,' Georgina said. 'Did she know that William had gone to war?'

'I'll add that to my list of things to ask,' Doris said. 'Once we've established that William Berry was *her* William. I don't want to make her feel even worse by blundering in.'

'Of course,' Georgina said. 'We'll keep looking.'

THIRTEEN

On Tuesday morning, Colin walked into Sammy Granger's office, ready to attend the post-mortem of Karen Berry's corpse. The pathologist took him to the examining room, where the body was laid out ready for analysis. The sharp smell of the examining room always made Colin feel slightly queasy, but he shoved it aside because attending the post-mortem would give him the chance to ask questions.

Plus he liked Sammy's brisk, no-nonsense attitude. In London, their usual duty pathologist had a tendency to waffle on about nothing, and Colin had hated the waste of time.

'I've already done the X-rays,' Sammy said. 'They show the kind of fractures I'd expect to see after a fall backwards from a height, where you landed on your back; it's the thoracolumbar area.'

'In layman's terms, that's where?' Colin prompted.

'The spine, between the waist and just below the neck – above that you have the cervical vertebrae, and below it you have the sacrum and coccyx. And there's a hairline crack on her skull where her head would've banged back against the floor. There are contusions to match, on both her back and the back of her head.' She showed him the X-rays and the photographs of the contusions on her laptop.

'Would the fractures have killed her?' he asked.

'If she'd made it to hospital, it's possible she could have survived,' Sammy said. 'It would depend on whether she developed a subdural haemorrhage, and whether that was treated in time.'

'Right.'

'Plus she banged her head on the way down.' She gestured to the wound on the side of Karen's head, made visible because Sammy had moved Karen's expensively highlighted fair hair out of the way.

'The SOCO team found a place on the wall where she might have hit her head,' Colin said. 'They're checking whether the blood matches with the sample taken from next to her body. Is it possible that someone could've struck her with something, to cause that wound?'

'Yes, but the chances of her hitting her head against the wall in exactly the same spot and at exactly the same angle as an earlier wound are low enough that I'd say this was more likely to be an accidental injury than a deliberate one.' She looked at him. 'Did you go into the ice house?'

'Only to the edge of the shaft. I didn't think that going down would be helpful to the investigation, and it might compromise the evidence. Though I've seen the photograph of her body in situ,' Colin said. 'I believe you went into the shaft?'

'To give me a better idea of the conditions where the body was found and help me estimate of the time of death,' Sammy confirmed. 'Which, yes, probably did damage some evidence.'

'But you needed the information and couldn't get it any other way,' Colin said. 'When do you think she died?'

'Given that she was found in a cool, damp place, I can't be accurate,' she warned.

'I know forensics can only give an estimate – and a lot

depends on the body composition, clothing and environment,' Colin said.

'I'm glad *someone* pays attention to what I say,' Sammy said with a grin. 'A body cools at nought-point-eight degrees centigrade per hour – or one-point-five degrees Fahrenheit, for you old-timers.'

'Oi, less of the old-timers,' Colin protested, laughing. 'I'm fifty-three. I grew up with centigrade, I'll have you know.'

Sammy laughed. 'Colin, you're the same age as my dad. I rest my case.'

Sammy was in her late twenties, and her comment suddenly made Colin feel old. How things could change in a couple of decades. His own life had gone from a place where he'd been happy down to a very dark place indeed; although he'd found a measure of peace since he'd met Georgina Drake, there were still bits of his past he couldn't face. Bits he still couldn't bring himself to share with Georgina.

He forced himself to sound light. 'All right. I give in. Time of death?'

'This particular body was slender, wearing very light clothing, and it had been in contact with a cool surface, in the shade,' Sammy said. 'The best estimate I can give you is that death happened between two and four on Sunday afternoon.'

He'd need to double-check when Posy had heard the door slam and thought Karen had left for London. Could there have been time for Karen to get to London and back to Hartington Hall? Or had she never left Norfolk in the first place?

Sammy went carefully through the post-mortem procedure, speaking her findings into a voice recorder and taking photographs as she went.

'I note the petechiae in the eyes,' she said, referring to the tiny, reddish-brown round spots on Karen's eyes. Colin knew they were caused by bleeding rather than being a rash. 'That would suggest strangulation, but there are no marks around the neck.' She made a deft incision. 'Plus the hyoid bone is intact.' That was the horseshoe-shaped bone in the neck that supported the tongue, larynx and trachea, Colin knew, and would be snapped if the victim was strangled.

'What else could cause the petechiae in the eyes?' Colin asked.

'Suffocation,' Sammy said. 'So I'll swab her nose to see if something was held over it and she breathed in any of the fibres.'

She deftly wielded the cotton swab, and held it under a daylight lamp. 'You're in luck. We have fibres.'

'From material held over her face?' Colin asked.

'The evidence points that way,' Sammy said. 'I'll check her fingernails in a second to see if there are any similar fibres underneath them. At the moment, you're looking for something beige and woolly.'

'Which could be anything from a scarf to a sweater to a blanket. Can you send me a close-up shot of the fibres, please?' Colin asked.

She nodded. 'I'll do it under the daylight lamp, so you get an accurate view of the colour. And I'll match the Pantone colour and send it to you – it'll be easier than trying to match things from a couple of tiny fibres.'

'Thank you.'

By the time Sammy had finished the post-mortem, they weren't much further forward. 'The point of impact was the victim's back,' Sammy said. 'Clearly she was standing with her back to the shaft when she fell.'

'Fell, or was pushed?' Colin asked.

'It could be a mixture of the two,' Sammy said. 'There are no signs of a struggle such as bruises from someone gripping her arms or any defence wounds on her hands, and her fingernails are clean; there are no fibres like the ones in her nose, and no scrapings of skin from an assailant or dirt from the floor where she was found.'

'Could she have jumped?' Colin asked.

'That's highly unlikely; she would have landed differently, and had different injuries,' Sammy said. 'I'd say the fall came as a surprise to her. Even if she knew how to avoid injury from a fall, she didn't have time to try and minimise the impact.'

'A fall of five metres onto a stone floor is enough to cause a lot of damage,' Colin said. 'What killed her: the head wound, the fall or the suffocation?'

'The head wound alone probably wouldn't have been enough to kill her instantly. Any subdural haemorrhage would've taken a while to kill her. If she hadn't been found for a few days, then hypothermia would've set in,' Sammy said. 'In my view, the fall wouldn't have killed her initially, but she would most likely have been unconscious after her head hit the wall on the way down.'

'Could someone have gone down to her after she fell and suffocated her to make sure she was dead?' Colin asked.

'It's a strong possibility,' Sammy said. 'If they'd suffocated her first and *then* pushed her into the shaft, they would've had to roll her body off the edge and she would've landed in a different position. I think the order's more likely to be the head wound, the impact from the fall and then suffocation.'

'When she was found, they had to go and get a rope to lower someone down to her,' Colin said. 'There wasn't a ladder in the tunnel, and the rungs in the side of the ice house had rusted away. So whoever suffocated her would've had to find something to lower themselves down, unless they brought a rope or whatever to the ice house in the first place and then took it away.' Bringing a rope would definitely indicate malice afore-thought, suggesting the murder was planned rather than done in the heat of the moment.

'Sadly, I can't help you with that one,' Sammy said. 'But it's unlikely she would've regained consciousness quickly. She doesn't appear to have resisted the suffocation. As I said, I can't see any evidence of self-defence.'

'OK. Thank you for all your help. I'll go back to base and update the team,' Colin said. 'When can I tell the family they can see the body?'

'Any time after tomorrow,' Sammy said. 'Just let me know when. I'll make sure she looks...'

Colin nodded, knowing what she meant. What they always had to tell the bereaved: that their loved one looked as though they were asleep.

FOURTEEN

Back at the station, Colin sat round the table with Mo, his DS, and Larissa, his DC, nursing coffees, as Colin briefed them on the post-mortem.

'Given the evidence that Karen was suffocated, I'm pretty sure we're looking at murder,' Colin said, looking around his team as the words sank in. 'So let's go through what we know. Karen Berry, Lady Ellingham, was last seen on Saturday by her stepdaughter Hattie, and on Sunday morning in the kitchen by her daughter Ellen. Later on Sunday morning, her stepdaughter Posy heard Karen having a row with Henry, Lord Ellingham. Henry said his wife stormed out after a row with him on Sunday morning and he assumed she went to London.' He shrugged. 'Apparently she usually went shopping in London after a row.'

'How did she get to London?' Larissa asked. 'Or did she get there at all?'

'Good questions,' Colin said. 'If she went to London, how would she get there?'

'Hartington isn't on a major bus route, and she doesn't sound like the type to use public transport anyway. If she left straight after the row and wanted to catch a train, she'd need to drive or get a taxi to the station in Norwich,' Larissa said.

'Her car is still at the house,' Colin said, 'so I think a taxi's more likely.'

'So we need to check CCTV at the station, and her phone records and bank account for payments to a taxi company or buying a train ticket?' Larissa asked, her pen ready to take a note.

'We've already applied for the phone records and bank account details,' Colin said. 'I'm surprised there doesn't seem to be any sign of her mobile phone or handbag. They weren't found near her body, nor around the ice house.'

'So maybe whoever pushed her over the edge – or suffocated her, or both,' Mo said, 'took the bag and her phone. Knowing the identity of her last few contacts by phone or text would be useful. It might give us an idea of who she met.'

'Without the phone itself, we have to wait for the records,' Colin said. 'They'll tell us if she called a taxi or a friend to get a lift to the station. Though she doesn't seem to have had any local friends.'

'What we know of her movements is pretty sketchy,' Larissa said.

'There's nothing that we can pin down between the argument on Sunday morning and her death,' Colin said. 'Which Sammy thinks is between two and four on Sunday afternoon.'

'It's two hours each way to London by train from Norwich, plus a good half hour between Hartington Hall and the train station, plus up to another half an hour waiting for the next train to depart,' Mo said. 'Possibly longer than that between Hartington Hall and London by car, depending on the traffic. Even if we say two and a half hours each way, she would've had to go to London, come straight back and be killed almost immediately. And if she was planning to go shopping in London, surely she'd want to spend a bit of time there, rather than come back as soon as she got there?'

'The timing's a problem,' Colin said. 'The evidence points to her probably not leaving Hartington in the first place. The next thing we know that happened to her after the row is that she was at the ice house. She fell off the edge into the shaft – or was pushed – and then somebody suffocated her.'

'It definitely happened in that order?' Larissa asked.

'Sammy says if she was suffocated before she was pushed over the edge, her injuries would have been different,' Colin said. 'Ditto if she'd jumped. There are a few people with a motive,' he continued. 'Posy and Hattie resented her. Their relationship with their father was strained anyway, and Karen made it worse. Apparently Lord Ellingham was planning to sell the house, which would've left them homeless – plus they see themselves as part of a long line of history.' He frowned. 'He told them in front of me that he was thinking of selling up, and from their reactions I don't think they knew that, so we'd better flag that as a possible rather than an actual motive.'

'What opportunity would they have to kill Karen Berry?' Mo asked.

'They lived on the estate and one or both of them had a key to the ice house. Posy definitely had a key, because she took Georgina to the ice house and discovered the door was unlocked,' Colin said. 'And Hattie had access, because she told me she had a key to the cabinet in her father's office that contained all the keys to the estate.'

'Why would Lady Ellingham agree to meet them, though, if she didn't get on with them?' Larissa asked. 'And why *there*?'

'Fair point. We also have the Pritchards – Karen accused Maggie, the former housekeeper, of theft. Maggie and her husband both resigned, and a few of the garden team resigned in support of the Pritchards,' Colin said. 'The Pritchards no longer live on the estate, but Brian Pritchard, as the former head gardener, would know where the ice house key is kept.'

'What about Karen's daughter, Ellen?' Mo asked.

'She wanted the ice house kept locked because of the bats,' Colin said. 'We need to confirm whether she had a key. What would her motive be?'

'Her mother hated the bats?' Larissa suggested. 'Several of the witness statements say that they'd argued about it. Though that's not enough of a reason to kill someone.'

'And then there's Lord Ellingham,' Mo said. 'He told us his wife hated it at Hartington. What if she'd threatened to leave him, and he continued the argument with her at the ice house?'

'What was the argument about?' Larissa asked.

'He was very vague about it,' Colin said. 'We need to ask him for more detail.'

'And why would they go to the ice house to finish the argument?' Larissa asked. 'Why wouldn't they just continue having a row in the house?'

It was exactly what Georgina had said.

'If we can find out why Karen Berry was at the ice house,' Colin said, 'we'd have a much better understanding of who might have killed her. At the moment, we're left with the fact that she either fell or was pushed off the edge of the ice house. Whoever was in the ice house with her then went down to smother her with something made from beige wool, then removed the ladder or rope or whatever they used to get to the floor of the ice house and pulled the door shut, so the building looked as if it was locked.'

'Which tells us nothing,' Mo said. 'And if whoever killed her had a key, why didn't they lock the door after themselves?'

'Good question. There is a theory,' Colin said tentatively, 'that maybe Karen met a dealer at the ice house.'

'What kind of dealer? You think she was taking drugs?' Larissa asked.

'No. I mean an antiques dealer. A fence, even,' Colin said. 'Though this is just a theory. There's no solid evidence, and it's based on hearsay.'

'In other words, your girlfriend filled you in on the gossip,' Larissa said, raising an eyebrow and smiling.

'She's not m—' Colin began.

'Yes, she is. And she's good for you. You're good for each other,' Mo said. 'Though, as you said yourself yesterday, she seems to be making a habit of finding dead bodies. Two in one day, yesterday.'

'The second body, strictly speaking, was a skeleton; and it was found by her dog,' Colin pointed out.

'It still counts, guv,' Larissa teased. 'So why would Lady Ellingham meet an antiques dealer?'

'According to Posy, she planned to sell the antique copper pans from the kitchen. And, again according to Posy, a very valuable book has gone missing from the library. Who would you go to if you wanted to sell old things from a stately home?'

'A dealer. Or a fence with good connections,' Mo said.

'I don't like coincidences,' Larissa said. 'Something's gone missing or it's about to go missing, and Posy discovers both instances. Could she be the one doing the stealing, but accuses her stepmother as a cover for her own actions?'

'We have to keep an open mind,' Colin said. 'But there's another similar issue; remember Karen accused the housekeeper of theft.'

'How long had the housekeeper worked at Hartington Hall?' Larissa asked.

'Decades. She was apparently there before Lord Ellingham's first marriage,' Colin said.

'If she was stealing things from the house, why did she only start taking things recently?' Mo asked. 'Or, if the thefts had been going on for years, why hadn't anyone noticed until now?'

'Maybe she wasn't the one stealing things,' Larissa said.

'And surely someone who'd worked at the Hall for years and knew where things were kept would be the most likely one to notice if something had been moved or gone missing?' She paused. 'Posy grew up in the house. Did she and the housekeeper get on well? In which case, the housekeeper might accuse someone she didn't like of being the thief, rather than someone she was fond of.'

'But why would Posy Berry take things from the house, when she was so protective of its heritage?' Colin asked. 'Why only recently? And why would she want the money?'

'Hattie said they lived off their trust funds,' Mo said. 'Supposing they were running out of money?'

'Or there could be someone in Posy's or Hattie's background,' Larissa said. 'Someone who wanted one of them to steal for them. Maybe a blackmailer, or someone who'd suckered them in with a sob story.'

'Or it could be Karen,' Colin said. 'You were with me at the Hall today, Mo. Posy and Hattie Berry said things were so tense in the house that they'd moved out. Posy, Hattie and the housekeeper were the ones who were most likely to notice things going missing from where they'd always been kept – and they'd all been pushed out of the house. The temps who covered for the housekeeper wouldn't know any different.' He looked at Larissa. 'You said Mrs Pritchard might have accused Karen of stealing in order to cover for Posy. But what if the housekeeper had told Karen she was going to tell Lord Ellingham about the missing stuff, and Karen accused her of theft in order to discredit her?'

'We need to talk to the Pritchards,' Larissa said.

'I agree,' Colin said. He called Posy and asked for Maggie Pritchard's number, then arranged to visit the Pritchards later that afternoon, as well as the family GP.

He was about to get on with paperwork when his phone rang.

'DI Bradshaw, do you have a minute to talk about the skeleton from Hartington Hall, please?' Rowena Langham, the Finds Liaison Officer, asked.

'Of course,' Colin said. 'What can you tell me?'

'We excavated the bones this morning. They definitely belonged to a female,' Rowena said. 'The shape of the skull and the pelvis told us that.' She paused. 'And I'm sorry to say that she was pregnant when she died. About four months, I'd say, judging from the size of the foetal bones.'

'Poor woman,' Colin said. 'Do you have any idea of her age?'

'I'd suggest she was in her late teens,' Rowena said. 'She still had growth plates in her leg and arm bones. The bones in the sacrum – the five vertebrae at the base of the spine – hadn't fused completely, nor had the collarbones, so she was definitely under twenty-five.'

Pregnant, in her late teens, and dead. Poor kid, Colin thought. His own daughter was in her mid-teens now. Please don't let anything like this ever happen to Cathy, he begged silently. Please.

'There's something else. Her death wasn't natural – well, you've probably already worked that out for yourself, from where she was buried,' Rowena said. 'The hyoid bone was snapped.'

'She was strangled?' Colin checked. 'Or could it have broken since she'd been buried – by a tree root or a rodent?'

'It's much more likely to be strangulation,' Rowena said. 'I can't date the burial precisely, without doing radio-carbon testing, but there were some remains of her clothing and their fastenings around her skeleton. From those, I'd say we're looking at the early 1850s – which is definitely more than a hundred years ago, so they count as bones of antiquity.'

'Thank you,' Colin said. 'Can I share this with my colleagues – and interested parties?' he added, thinking of Georgina.

'Yes. But I'd suggest it be kept low-key,' Rowena said. 'I need to speak to Lord Ellingham to arrange for burial of the remains.'

'Given that he's just lost his wife, and we're investigating the circumstances,' Colin said, 'I think you might be better off talking to his daughters, Henriette and Rosalind.'

'I'll do that,' she said. 'Thank you for your help.'

'And thank you for yours,' he said.

He typed a quick text to Georgina.

> Spoke to finds liaison officer today about the skeleton. Victorian, so definitely 'bones of antiquity'. Tell you more tonight C x

FIFTEEN

The Pritchards lived in a small flint-and-brick terraced cottage in Hartington. Like those of its neighbours, the front garden was bursting with summer flowers – climbing pale pink roses frothing round the front door, deep blue delphiniums and cream hollyhocks rising up at the back of the borders, sweet peas twirling round a tripod of garden canes, rose campion with their silver leaves and bright magenta flowers peeping through a froth of lavender, and scented herbs bordering the path. Colin thought of his tiny two-bedroomed first-floor flat and how uninviting it was in comparison. He didn't even have a window box.

He knocked on the front door; a short, round, bustling woman opened it. 'Detective Inspector Bradshaw?' she asked, looking ever so slightly suspicious.

He showed her his warrant card to confirm his identity. 'And this is my colleague, Detective Constable Larissa Foulkes.'

'Come in, come in.' Mrs Pritchard ushered them through to the kitchen: a bright room with yellow walls, blue-and-white gingham curtains, glass-fronted cabinets and what smelled like freshly baked scones sitting on a wire cooling rack on the countertop.

'My husband, Brian,' she said, introducing them to the man sitting at the scrubbed pine table with a mug of tea in front of him. 'Brian, this is Detective Inspector Bradshaw and Detective Constable Foulkes.'

'You have a lovely garden, Mr Pritchard,' Larissa said.

'It'll do,' Brian said, his expression dour. 'I'd rather be down the allotment, but the missus said you wanted to talk to us.' He tipped his head towards his wife.

'Hopefully we won't keep you very long, Mr Pritchard,' Colin said.

Once she'd made Colin and Larissa a cup of tea and placed a plate of scones, a dish of butter and a jar of home-made strawberry-and-rhubarb jam on the table, Maggie joined them at the table. 'Help yourselves to the scones. They're always at their best when they're warm.'

Colin thought about what the nurse had said to him about his blood sugar at his last check-up. Then he thought how offended Maggie Pritchard might be if he refused a scone. Or the luscious-looking jam. He wanted her on his side, so he had to take up her offer, didn't he? And, if you were going to eat something you knew you shouldn't, you might as well enjoy it properly...

He selected a scone, skipped the butter, added jam and took a bite. 'Oh, these are wonderful,' he said when he'd swallowed the mouthful. 'Lady Wyatt was right when she said you were a good cook.'

Maggie looked delighted. 'You know Lady Sybbie?'

'She's a friend,' Colin said, suddenly realising that it was true. In the three months that he'd been seeing Georgina, her friends had also become his. He'd even been invited to supper at Little Wenborough Manor and had enjoyed eating Cesca's fabulous food *al fresco* in Sybbie's beautiful garden.

'Lady Sybbie was a good friend to our Lady Millie,' Maggie said. 'And she does right by the girls.'

Maggie Pritchard had definitely nailed her colours to the mast, Colin thought; she was clearly Team Hattie and Posy rather than Team Karen.

'What did you want to talk to us about?' Maggie asked, seeming a little more friendly now.

'Firstly, I wanted to let you know that Lady Ellingham died over the weekend,' Colin said.

Her smile faded. 'It's all round the village already. That one won't be missed by anyone, except maybe her daughter,' Maggie said, her mouth twisting in a grimace of dislike.

'I don't know about that. She's made young Ellen cry before now. Always on about the way she looked – even *I* know you don't say that sort of thing to teenage girls. I reckon poor Ellen's better off without a mother who didn't really love her for who she was,' Brian added. And then he looked suddenly a bit aghast, as if he'd let something slip.

Colin was aware of Larissa writing notes by his side. Brian's comment was a reminder that he needed to follow up on what Hattie had already told him about the tension between Ellen and Karen. But he'd need to be really sensitive about how he investigated it, given that Karen had just died.

This was an equally sensitive matter. 'I'm sorry to ask, but could you tell us why you left Hartington Hall?' he asked.

'Didn't Posy tell you?' Maggie asked.

'Yes, but I'd like to hear the story from you,' Colin said gently.

'The official line is we retired,' Maggie said, her mouth tightening. 'For the sake of Lady Millie's memory and the girls, we went quietly.'

'What really happened?' Colin asked.

'*She* did,' Maggie said bluntly. 'That Karen. She's one of those who looks at you and works out how much what you're wearing costs, and then decides if you're worth talking to or ignoring. Why His Lordship married her, God only knows. It was obvious to everyone he'd marry quickly again after Lady Millie died – he's one of those who can't cope on his own – but why couldn't he have married someone *decent*? Someone who'd be friends with the girls, make a fuss of the dogs and be practical instead of wanting ridiculous things?'

It was very clear that Maggie hadn't seen eye to eye with Karen Berry. And she was yet another person who didn't think very much of Henry Berry.

'What I couldn't stand was the way she twisted everything and made out people had said or done things when they hadn't,' Maggie said, her brown eyes glittering with anger. 'The rows she caused, sidling up to His Lordship and claiming that the girls had said something to upset her, when they'd done nothing of the sort. He always took her part. Every single time. He never listened to what the girls or anyone else had to say.'

Colin was very interested in hearing what Maggie had to say about the thefts, so he waited. Would it tie in with Georgina's theory?

'His Lordship carpeted me in his study one day. He said he'd been talking to his wife, and he wanted to make it clear that she had the right to move anything she liked in her own house. Things didn't have to be kept rigidly as they were in Lady Millie's day.' She shook her head. 'It's so ridiculous. Of course I wasn't rigid. I'd worked there with Lady Millie for years and we'd found the most efficient way of doing things. Why change things just for change's sake?' There was a mutinous set to her jaw. Maggie Pritchard could be charming, Colin thought, but if you crossed her she'd be difficult. Not quite Mrs Danvers level but getting there. Enough to kill, perhaps? Or to be a willing accomplice?

'His Lordship said he wouldn't have me making her upset – she'd cried so much she had one of her migraines, and he reck-

oned it was all my fault.' Maggie shook her head. 'Blind as one
of Ellen's bats, he was, where *she* was concerned. Of course she
didn't have a migraine. They were crocodile tears. But he
wouldn't let me give my side of the story.'

'Which was?' Colin asked, to encourage her.

'I noticed things had been moved on the dressing table in
the Blue Room, and a little porcelain jar was missing. I didn't
think any of my team had taken it; none of them are light-
fingered. If any of them had broken something, they would've
come and told me – and brought me the pieces so it could be
fixed.' She shook her head for emphasis. 'But I couldn't find it
anywhere. And then I noticed the cabinet in the sitting room; a
little china figurine had gone and the rest of the stuff on the
shelves had been moved around to disguise its absence. But I'd
dusted that cabinet for years. I knew exactly what was in it. I
started keeping notes, then, and took photographs. She knew I
was onto her, and she wanted me out.'

'You think Lady Ellingham was taking things from the
house?' Colin asked.

'Like I said, none of my team would steal anything. I know
the girls took the pans from the Old Kitchen, but they warned
me about it first. If they took anything else to keep it safe from
that woman's sticky paws, I would've known about it.'

This definitely sounded like a power struggle between Lady
Ellingham and the housekeeper, Colin thought.

Maggie sighed. 'I knew I was going to have to try again with
His Lordship. I couldn't let her strip the house bare, could I? So
I asked him if we could have a private word. He dragged his feet
about it, the way he always does if he doesn't want to face something; he kept making excuses that he was too busy, and of
course he wasn't.' Her mouth thinned. 'He's always been too
weak to stand up and do his duty, even before he married Lady
Millie. He'll slink off to tinker with his cars instead. Anyway,
the next thing we know, His Lordship's banging on the door of

our house on the estate, saying he wants to search my house because *she* said we'd taken something of hers.' Maggie lifted her chin. 'I told him I hadn't taken anything and we'd got nothing to hide, so go right ahead and look wherever he liked. He went through my sitting room, then the kitchen – and right at the back of the spice drawer in the dresser was a pair of ruby earrings. I'd never seen them before in my life, but *she* said they were hers. I have no idea how they got into my dresser. I certainly didn't put them there.'

'How would Lady Ellingham have had access to your house?' Colin asked.

'I didn't give her my keys. Maybe there was a spare front door key in the estate office. It was a tied cottage, because Brian and I both worked for the Hall,' Maggie explained. 'But I know she was behind it all. Somehow she got into my house and she put those earrings in my dresser. The look of triumph in her eyes, behind His Lordship's back! Then she put on this big act about how she and His Lordship should be magnanimous, after all the years we'd worked at the Hall. If we agreed to retire there and then, they'd say no more about the earrings going missing then being found in my house.' Her lip curled. 'Hamming it up, she was, and His Lordship swallowed every single word.'

'Retire,' Brian put in, 'when it's another three years until we can claim our pensions. But I do odd jobs, and Maggie does a few hours in the village bakery. We manage to make ends meet.'

Maggie looked close to tears, though Colin couldn't quite work out if it was sorrow or anger driving them. 'There was nothing I could do or say. If I'd told His Lordship about the missing things after that – and they were all little, things you could slip in a pocket and take away without anyone noticing, like a silver snuffbox or a figurine or a miniature portrait – she would've pinned it all on me.'

'As a matter of routine, we checked to see if there had been any police inquiries at Hartington Hall in the last year. Nobody contacted us about anything going missing,' Colin said. 'If they had, we could have investigated. At the very least, we could have checked the earrings for fingerprints.'

'You wouldn't have found my fingerprints, but then she would've said I'd used gloves or something. The thing is, she accused me of stealing, and everyone would know it. Mud like that sticks,' Maggie said. 'I'm not a thief, but people would still talk, wouldn't they? So we didn't really have a choice.' She shrugged. 'We packed up and left. Luckily this place was for rent, and we could move in straight away.'

'I gather half the garden team resigned, too,' Colin said.

'Word got round, and they didn't want to work for someone who'd treat us like that,' Brian said. 'Plus they all knew if Her Ladyship took against any of them, they'd be out on their ear, too.' He sighed. 'It's hard, seeing the garden at the Hall looking – well, not at its best. I'd love to go back and sort it all out for young Posy, but I'm not going to work for someone who accused my wife of stealing something.' His mouth tightened. 'That's not my Maggie, and His Lordship should know that after all these years. I could strangle that woman.' He winced. 'Sorry. I know you shouldn't speak ill of the dead. But she was...' He grimaced, shaking his head.

'She wasn't a patch on Lady Millie. I hated the way His Lordship wiped my Millie out of the house, all for that woman,' Maggie said, her eyes narrowing. 'Broke the girls' hearts, it did. All the photos and her portrait put away. Shameful.'

'Do Rosalind and Henriette Berry know what happened?' Larissa asked.

'Yes. They came to see me, to apologise, and they said they knew I hadn't taken the earrings. But they can't do anything with their father.' Maggie rolled her eyes. 'His Lordship's always been a bit tetchy, but Lady Millie could always handle him and talk him round. Since she died, he's had that woman egging him on, starting fights between him and the girls.' She frowned. 'I think the girls only stay at the Hall now out of loyalty to their mum's memory.'

'Do you know anything about Lord Ellingham wanting to sell the house and move to London?' Colin asked casually.

'What?' Maggie looked shocked. 'No. His family's lived there for hundreds of years. I can't see him doing *that*. He might threaten it when he's in a mood, but actually doing something like that...' She shook her head. 'He's part of a long, long line of Berrys at Hartington Hall. You don't throw that sort of thing away on a whim.'

'Indeed,' Colin said. 'What can either of you tell me about the ice house?'

'It's two or three hundred years old,' Brian said. 'Years ago, before they had fridges, all the big houses had an ice house. They'd take the ice off lakes, ponds and ditches in winter and store it in the ice house. It'd stay frozen even through the summer – the walls are thick stone, and the sides are insulated by the ground. When they wanted ice in the kitchens, they'd send a lad out with a bucket to climb down and take a bit off the top. Once fridges came in, the ice houses weren't needed any more. Most of them were forgotten about or used as rubbish dumps – I was a young gardener here when they cleared ours out, in the 1970s. There was all sorts of stuff in there.'

'What about the bats in the ice house?' Colin asked.

'Young Ellen can tell you more about that,' Brian said. 'She's studying them as part of her course. She reckons there's a maternity roost in one of the trees that was blown down in the woods, a few years back, and they spend the winter in the ice house. We spent a while going through the best plants to attract insects for bats earlier this year, and I agreed to plant some for her.'

'How did people react to the bats?' Larissa asked.

'I don't mind 'em, and nor does the rest of the garden team. And I think having bat walks is a good way of getting people interested in the house and garden,' Brian said. 'I know Posy and Hattie were pleased that Ellen was taking an interest in the estate.'

'What about Lord Ellingham?' Colin asked.

'He's never been too interested in the land,' Brian said. 'The only things he cares about are his cars. He's got quite a collection in one of the old barns.' He rolled his eyes. 'Her Ladyship kicked up a fuss about them, but we told Ellen on the quiet that it'd be fine. It's a good idea to keep the ice house locked, because...' He shrugged. 'Well. What happened to her Ladyship, that could've happened to anyone who went in there and wasn't being careful enough about where they walked. Moss tends to grow in damp places, and it's slippery underfoot. The last thing Posy and Hattie need is one of the visitors falling in and hurting themselves or worse. Then nobody'd risk coming to visit the Hall, in case it happened to them.'

It sounded as if Brian thought Karen's fall was an accident. Or did he know something more?

'Can you think of a reason anyone would go to the ice house?' Colin asked.

Maggie shrugged. 'A visitor might be interested in the history, maybe. Or people who like quirky buildings, follies and the like. I think Posy's going to make an information board about it.'

'Or someone who wanted to study the bats,' Brian added. 'Though they'd have to get permission, first, to do that.'

'Jimmy said the ice house used to be a place for lovers to meet,' Colin said, dangling the bait. Would one of them say they'd seen Karen there with a lover?

'That was donkeys' years ago. I can't see any young ladies today being very impressed at being asked to meet someone in a damp, cold, dirty building,' Brian said. 'Even if you had a candle and a blanket. And there are the bats, too. Everyone knows about them. I reckon it'd put anyone off except young Ellen and her friends.' He frowned. 'Though, now I think about it, there was a bloke hanging around the place, a couple of months back. I assumed he was one of the visitors, but I saw him again on a day when the garden wasn't open. Not as fit as I was, though, so by the time I got over to him, he'd legged it.'

'Could you describe him for me?' Colin asked.

'Average height, wore a hoodie, needed a shave. In his forties, maybe?' Brian said. 'To be honest, I didn't take that much notice.'

Colin made notes. 'Thank you. Do you know who had keys to the ice house?'

'I did – but obviously I handed my keys in when we left,' Brian said. 'Posy and Hattie have a set of keys, and so does His Lordship. There's a spare or two in the estate office, but you'd have to ask His Lordship or Hattie for it. The keys are kept locked up, for insurance purposes.'

'Thank you both for your time,' Colin said. 'You've both been very helpful. And thank you for the tea and scones.'

'Thank you. They were delicious,' Larissa added.

'You're most welcome,' Maggie said.

'Just one thing before we leave,' Colin said. 'Do you have anything beige, made of wool?'

'Wool, yes; beige, no,' Maggie said. 'When I was the house-keeper, I always wore a white shirt and black skirt or trousers. Outside work, I like bright colours' – she indicated the fuchsia-pink T-shirt she was wearing – 'which is about the only thing I had in common with Her Ladyship. And it's pointless knitting my Brian a beige sweater or cardigan.'

'Why?' Colin asked.

Maggie laughed. 'Ah, you're not a gardener, are you, love? Any light-coloured sweater will always look grubby if you wear it in the garden, even after it's been washed. Earth gets ingrained so quickly into the wool, or there's moss, or pollen, or grass. I always knit or buy sludgy green sweaters for my Brian so they don't look so mucky. Why?'

'Just a line of enquiry,' Colin said, keeping things vague.

His meeting with the doctor was less helpful. Karen Berry had no medical conditions that might have caused her to fall, and her last consultation had been her annual medical review. The only medication she was on was the contraceptive pill, and she hadn't discussed pregnancy or IVF with her GP. The doctor confirmed that Henry Berry had high blood pressure, high cholesterol and arthritis, and was on tablets for all three conditions. But that left Colin no further forward.

SIXTEEN

Georgina had spent the morning sorting out the photographs of Hartington Hall, printing out a few of her favourites once she'd tweaked them on the computer. She called Sybbie at lunchtime. 'How are things?'

'Fairly grim. I think the burden of sorting out the funeral – when the coroner lets them have the body back – will fall on the girls.' Sybbie sighed. 'I can't really do too much more, here. I've made enough sandwiches and tea to feed an army, and nobody's touched more than a mouthful. Ellen's in her room and won't come out. I went up to see if I could coax her out, and I said she ought to talk to Hattie and Posy because they weren't much older than her when they lost their own mother, so they'd understand how she was feeling, but she told me to go away because she didn't want to speak to anyone.'

'It's hard losing a parent at any age,' Georgina said, 'but at that age it's even harder. She doesn't still think Posy or Hattie killed her mum, does she?'

'When she's had time to think about it and calm down a bit, she'll realise that of course they wouldn't,' Sybbie said.

'I was thinking of popping over with the photographs,'

Georgina said. 'I can give you a lift back to Little Wenborough, if you like.'

'That's kind, dear girl,' Sybbie said. 'Thank you.'

'Though I'm leaving Bert at home, this time. I don't want him to dig up anything else. See you in half an hour or so,' Georgina said.

'Can I come?' Doris asked, when Georgina put the phone down.

'Armed with a list of questions for Anne – or can you speak to her elsewhere?'

'I think only when I'm at the Hall,' Doris said.

'Then you're coming.'

Georgina had just settled Bert when her mobile phone pinged with an incoming text from Colin. 'Colin's just sent confirmation that the bones are Victorian. They count as bones of antiquity. So we're free to look into the case.'

'Good,' Doris said.

They listened to more of *Jane Eyre* in the car and switched it off as Georgina turned into the long, tree-lined drive. Georgina parked outside the stable block, where she'd parked before.

The three spaniels raced out to meet her, and she made a fuss of them. 'Sorry, boys. Bert stayed at home today.'

'Hello, Georgie. Aunt Syb said you were coming.' Posy greeted her with a hug.

'I know I could've just emailed you the photos,' Georgina said, 'but I thought you might like some hard copies as well.'

'That's so kind.' The younger woman had pale skin, despite spending so much time in the gardens, and the shadows under her eyes looked like bruises. Clearly she hadn't slept well, the previous night.

'How are things?' Georgina asked gently.

'Pretty bad. Papa isn't speaking to either of us, and neither's Ellen. She's not talking to Papa or Aunt Syb, either.' Posy sighed. 'I'd be the first one to admit I didn't like Karen, but I didn't wish her dead.'

Georgina forbore to remind Posy that she'd threatened to kill Karen, the previous day, for taking the Red Book; she was pretty sure that the outburst had been just words, driven by anger. Instead, she said, 'Posy, my daughter works for a probate genealogy company, and I suppose that's kind of made me interested in the story of a house and the people who live there. I'm researching my own house at the moment.'

'A house this big and this old would have lots of stories, over the years,' Posy said. 'Like our poor skeleton. DI Bradshaw rang me this morning; once the coroner confirms it, we can arrange for the remains to be buried. Though what do you put on a memorial stone, when you don't know the name of the person and don't have a clue where to start finding out?' She looked at Georgina. 'Unless you know how we can find out who they were?'

Just what Georgina had hoped for. 'If they're Victorian, we can look at the parish records to see if any death was recorded, and cross-check them with the census returns. I'm happy to do that for you.'

'That'd be wonderful,' Posy said.

'I know this might seem a bit of an odd question, but there's something that would help me. Do you have a family tree?'

'Yes, though Hattie knows more about the family history than I do. She was always the one for the library, when we were little, whereas I would be out in the garden with Granny Rosa,' Posy said. 'Come on in. Have you had lunch? Can I get you something?'

'I had a sandwich earlier, thanks,' Georgina said. 'Though, if you've got the kettle on, I'd love some coffee, please.'

'Done,' Posy said.

Sybbie greeted her with a hug. 'Dear girl. Good to see you.'

'Good to see you, too,' Georgina said.

Once she'd made coffee, Posy took Georgina and Sybbie over to the estate office to see Hattie. Georgina explained that she'd look up the census and parish records to see if she could find out who the body was, but didn't mention what she knew about Anne. 'Posy said you had a family tree, Hattie. That would help me enormously in finding the right census records,' Georgina said. 'And do you know if anyone kept correspondence in, say, the mid-1800s?'

'The family tree's easy,' Hattie said. 'I can sketch that for you now.' She grabbed a piece of paper and drew a quick outline.

'Posy and me – we were both born in the nineties. Papa and Mummy, who took over the hall in 2004,' she said, adding in Henry and Millie's names and dates. 'I assume you mean just the Berry side?'

'The ones who lived here, yes, please,' Georgina said.

'All right. Grandpa Henry and Granny Rosa – that takes us back to the late 1920s. They were the ones who took over after the Second World War and put the garden back to the original plans. Great-grandpa Henry, who was born in 1903, took over the hall between the wars.'

'All those Henrys,' Sybbie said with a groan. 'Shows no imagination, naming your child after yourself. Still, I suppose it could've been worse. Imagine if your great-grandfather was John Smith, son of John Smith, son of John Smith – how would you ever be sure you'd found the right one?'

'Bea has ways of checking,' Georgina said. 'But we interrupted you, Hattie. You were going to tell us about your great-great-grandpa – who I assume is also called Henry?'

'Absolutely,' Hattie said. 'He was born in 1878. His father, yet another Henry, was born in 1846. And our four-times-great-grandpa – I'm sorry, he's Henry as well – was born in 1818. He married Mary, who was the one who turned the Long Gallery into the library. Though, actually, he was never meant to inherit

Hartington, because he was the second son. His brother – Edward, born in 1807 – inherited the Hall, but Edward died in 1854, a couple of years after he inherited. And Edward's only son, William, was killed in the Crimean War. Family legend says that Edward died from a broken heart when he heard the news.'

More or less what Georgina and Doris had worked out, the previous evening; and Georgina knew the Victorians would have judged a heart attack or apoplexy to be the same as a broken heart.

'It was horribly sad, because William was also the second son,' Hattie said. 'The first son, Edward, died in infancy, along with another three Edwards after William, and the other four children were girls.'

'Child mortality was very high in that period,' Georgina said. 'My daughter says it's heart-breaking how many parents lost five or six children in infancy.'

'I think his mother insisted on calling him William in the hope that he'd live,' Hattie said. 'It's tragic to think he was the only one of their sons to survive childhood, only to be killed in war. Anyway, the house was entailed and Henry – as in our four-times-great-grandpa – inherited Hartington and the title. He made sure that Edward's widow, Sarah, and her daughters had use of the family homes here and in London; but he was the one who broke the entail so that if he or any of his children had only girls, the house would stay with them.'

'Do you still have the London house?' Georgina asked.

Hattie shook her head. 'It was a casualty of the Blitz,' she said. 'But we were very lucky, compared to a lot of people.'

'Do you have any documents about William?' Georgina asked. 'Just that I studied the Crimean War at A level, so if he sent any letters home, I'd love to see them.' It was true – just not the whole truth.

'I think there's some correspondence,' Hattie said. 'He was

meant to marry a London heiress, but obviously when he didn't come back from the war she married someone else.'

'I can show you the Muniments Room,' Posy said.

'Grandpa sorted it all out when we got the house back after the Hall was requisitioned. It's in date order, so it should be easy to find 1854,' Hattie said.

'And if you find anything relating to the garden, or anything interesting about the kitchen, please let me know,' Posy said. 'A Victorian recipe book would be wonderful, because we could maybe use recipes in the tea room and then publish it for the gift shop.'

'I'll let you know,' Georgina said with a smile. 'But I don't want to risk spilling my coffee over the documents, so how about I show you the photos from yesterday, first?'

SEVENTEEN

The Muniments Room turned out to be a rather dim room with a large table and chairs in the middle, a couple of map cabinets, some filing cabinets, and racked storage shelving filled with labelled boxes.

'I'll leave you to it,' Posy said. 'Give me a yell if you need anything. And, when you're done, if you wouldn't mind locking the room and bringing the keys back to me?'

'Of course,' Georgina said.

'So why are you really interested in William Berry?' Sybbie asked, when Posy had left. 'It's more than just because you studied the Crimean War for A level, isn't it?'

'It's some research I was doing yesterday, to see if I could find out the identity of the skeleton under the oak tree,' Georgina explained. 'William was listed in the 1851 census but not the 1861 census; and Lord Ellingham in 1851 was his father, Edward Berry – just as Hattie told us. In 1861, the census lists the head of the house as Lord Ellingham, Henry Berry. He was too old to be Edward's son, and I would've expected William to be Lord Ellingham after his father's death. I wondered what might have happened.'

'I see. And how does that connect to the skeleton?' Sybbie
asked.

'What would your first thought be if I said that the skeleton's female?' Georgina asked.

'Ah,' Sybbie said. 'And she was hidden under the oak
instead of being buried in the parish churchyard.' She wrinkled
her nose. 'Was she pregnant?'

'It's the theory I'm working on,' Georgina said. She
couldn't tell her friend everything she knew, but Sybbie was
bright enough to work things out. She'd be helpful. And she'd
assume that Georgina's knowledge came from Colin rather
than a pair of ghosts, so Georgie wouldn't need to lie outright
to her.

'And you think she was pregnant by William, and he went
to the war out of guilt at abandoning her?'

'Not necessarily,' Georgina said. 'Maybe he went out of
grief because he really did love her and she died.'

'What if she died in childbirth?' Sybbie suggested. 'Or some
complication of pregnancy?'

'That's assuming William was the father,' Georgina said.
'Hattie said he was meant to marry an heiress.'

'What if he fell for this other girl instead?' Sybbie asked.
'But if she wasn't the right class, or there was a scandal attached
to her family – well, nowadays, it wouldn't really matter.'

'But, back then, his father would've forbidden the marriage,'
Georgina agreed. 'William couldn't have married her without
parental consent until they were both twenty-one. But what if
he got a special licence, lied about her age and married her
secretly somewhere else?'

'Or if she was ill – a madwoman in the attic, like Bertha
Rochester,' Sybbie said thoughtfully. 'And not all deaths were
recorded back then, were they? Just as not all marriages were, or
births.' She paused. 'Or someone else could've been the father
of the child and she told William, who lost his temper, and then

was horrified when he realised he'd killed her – and he buried her before fleeing to war.'

'My gut feeling,' Georgina said, 'is that William loved her.' At least, Anne believed that he loved her. Then again, Colin had told her that to solve a case you had to keep the emotion out of it. Which was probably a nicer way of telling her to check her prejudices. 'Let's start by looking for a marriage licence.' She flicked into her phone's messages app. 'Bea sent me this example – actually, it's the marriage licence of Nelson's illegitimate daughter, Horatia, in 1822.'

Sybbie looked at it. 'Oh – it's partly printed! I wasn't expecting that.' She studied the image. 'So the handwritten bits will be the date, William's name and parish and if he's a bachelor or widower, her name and parish and if she's a spinster or widower, the church where they want to be married and his signature.'

'If you scroll up, there's another example just below it – it's after the Act of Parliament that repealed Hardwicke's Act,' Georgina said. 'At the time we're looking at, one of them had to be resident in the parish for fifteen days before they could marry.'

'Right,' Sybbie said. 'We know William died in 1854. So shall we work backwards?'

'Good idea,' Georgina said, and they took down the archive box for 1854. They carefully worked through the pieces, using Georgina's phone to photograph the papers they thought would be useful, and placing everything back in the box in the right order as they worked.

Two hours later, they'd found the letter from the Crimean front, confirming William's death, some letters addressed to Henry Berry giving their condolences on the tragic deaths of his brother and his nephew – and how sad that Edward's only son had died serving his country and poor Edward had had an apoplectic fit at the news – but no marriage licence. Maybe

Anne's William wasn't William Berry after all, Georgina thought, disappointed. Without a bit more input from Anne, via Doris, she didn't have a clue where to start.

The only information about Anne Lusher was in the household account books: she was a chambermaid, earning five pounds a quarter; her last payment was in July 1854. That narrowed the date of her death down to between July 1854 and William's death in October 1854.

But who had killed her and buried her body under the Great Oak?

If Anne had truly believed that William was going to get a licence to marry her, it didn't sound as if William would've been likely to murder her. Or had William known about the pregnancy and lied to Anne about the licence? Had he used it to lure her somewhere, killed her, then gone to war because he couldn't live with the guilt of what he'd done?

She'd need to get Doris to ask some questions.

Once they'd put the box back, they locked the Muniments Room and returned to the estate office. 'Thanks, Posy,' Georgina said, giving her the keys. 'Sorry, I didn't find anything about the garden or the kitchens. I found the condolences letters about William's and Edward's deaths though and photographed them – I hope you don't mind?'

'It's fine. We're only too happy to help,' Posy said.

'And, to be honest, it's good to have something to take our minds off what happened to Karen,' Hattie added.

Georgina remembered the question Colin had asked her last night. 'I'm so sorry if this is in poor taste, but how did Karen meet your father?'

'At his club in London,' Hattie said. 'He wasn't coping very well, here. I understand how he felt; I still walk into a room, expecting to see Mummy in her usual chair reading a book, or go into the garden, thinking I'll see her working on a plant with her secateurs, but instead there's this empty space where she ought to be.'

Georgina nodded. 'It was like that for me in London, when my husband died. I couldn't bear it there without him. That's why I moved to Norfolk.'

'About a month after the funeral, Papa went to London to stay with friends,' Hattie said. 'Karen was one of the staff at his club. I think he had a bit of a wobble, one evening, and she was kind to him.'

'It must be about the only time in her life when she was kind,' Posy muttered.

'The next thing we knew, he'd started seeing her. And then he told us they were getting married.' Hattie grimaced. 'Not that he needed our permission or anything – I don't mean it like *that*. And we knew he wasn't coping on his own, even with us to support him. I guess part of me was glad that he'd found someone else to lean on, because I was having a hard time myself getting used to Mummy not being around. So was Posy.'

'And, when we first met Karen, she was nice enough,' Posy said. 'We took her at face value. If she was good to him, then that was all right by us.'

'So they got married. Ellen had just finished her GCSEs, so I guess there could've been worse times for her to move – even though it must've been hard to move somewhere like Hartington when you're used to the buzz of London. Besides, going to sixth form somewhere different is often a good idea,' Hattie said. 'It starts preparing you to be independent when you go to uni.'

'But then things started to change,' Posy said.

'Karen always had a headache if they went out to see Papa's friends, so they'd have to come home halfway through the evening,' Hattie said. 'Or people would come here and she'd say she was too tired or too sick to come down to dinner. And, whenever they came back from visiting people, she never had anything nice to say. She'd criticise everything – what people wore, their make-up, the food, the décor. She had this horrible way of sneering, curling her lip and shaking her head at the same time.'

'People stopped inviting them out, and she stopped inviting people here,' Posy said. 'I wish she'd never met Papa. Or, if she was just setting him up for an expensive divorce, that she'd just done it quickly and let him find someone else. Someone who'd love him the way our mother did.'

'Do you really think she was planning to divorce Henry?' Sybbie asked. 'On what grounds?'

'Unreasonable behaviour, probably.' Hattie gave a huff of laughter. 'But if you manage Papa the way Mummy did, he's bearable enough.' She sighed. 'I'd like him to go and see the doctor. He needs some help to get him through this – whether it's antidepressants or a talking treatment or both. Right now, he's like Ellen. Refusing to come out of his room and, if you leave him food on a tray, he won't touch it.'

'That's him being a drama queen – well, *king*. He waited until we both went back to the cottage last night and then he made himself a sandwich,' Posy said, rolling her eyes. 'I know, because the kitchen was a complete mess in the morning, and Ellen always clears up after herself when she cooks. I don't know if she's even eating – I've taken her a couple of trays up, but she's left them untouched.'

'You're sure she's still here?' Georgina asked. 'She hasn't...?' She didn't want to ask the question; it was too horrible to contemplate.

'Done anything drastic?' Posy shook her head. 'Her car's here, and whenever I knock on her door, she tells me to go away.'

'Do you want me to try talking to her?' Georgina asked. 'It can sometimes be easier to talk to a stranger.'

'Would you?' Hattie looked grateful.

'I'll take you up. The house can be a bit of a warren,' Posy said.

Ellen's room was on the third floor, on the side of the house overlooking the lake. Georgina knocked on the door. 'Ellen? I'm Georgina, Sybbie's photographer friend. Sorry to disturb you. I was wondering if we could have a quick chat about the bats.'

'Not now,' Ellen said. She sounded hoarse, as if she'd been crying for hours.

'I know we don't know each other,' Georgina said quietly, 'but my husband died two years ago. So I know how bad it feels when you lose someone you love, and you're a couple of years younger than my children were when their dad died. Right now, I'm guessing you could do with a hug.'

'I'm fine,' Ellen said, but her voice was wobbly.

'Sometimes it helps to talk to a stranger. Someone who's not going to judge and will just listen.'

There was silence.

Georgina waited, giving the girl space.

A couple of minutes later, Ellen opened the door. She was dressed completely in black, as she'd been the day before, but this time she wasn't wearing make-up and her face was blotchy with tears. Wordlessly, Georgina wrapped her arms round the younger woman and let her cry.

When Ellen's shoulders had stopped shaking, Georgina sat her down on the armchair, sat on the arm of the chair herself and stroked Ellen's hair. 'I know right now you don't want to eat or drink anything. Everything's too hard. But I promise you, love, eating something will make you feel a bit better.'

'I *can't*,' Ellen said.

'I didn't know your mum, so I'm not going to spout nonsense about what your mum would or wouldn't have wanted you to do,' Georgina said. 'But I worried about my kids when their dad died. Neither of them lived with me, and I just needed to know that they were eating properly and they'd got someone close by to give them the hug I wanted to give them myself but couldn't because I was too far away.'

Ellen swallowed hard. 'I don't have anyone.'

'Yes, you do,' Georgina said gently. 'I only met Hattie and Posy yesterday – but my friend Sybbie, their godmother, loves them. Sybbie's a good judge of character, and that's enough for me.'

Ellen was silent, as if digesting her words.

'They weren't much older than you when they lost their mum, so they've gone through something similar. How they talked about you and the bats, yesterday, tells me they care about you.' Georgina took a chance. 'And they both know their dad's not good with emotional stuff. They'll be there for you, if you let them.'

'I...' Ellen dragged in a breath.

'Ten minutes. They're not going to judge you and they'll give you space,' Georgina promised. 'At least let Posy make you something to eat.'

Ellen said nothing, and Georgina didn't push her.

But eventually Ellen nodded. 'OK.'

'Well done,' Georgina said, and gave her a hug.

'That was kind,' Doris said as Georgina walked down the wide, sweeping staircase with Ellen. 'And I know this isn't the place or the time, but I have more to tell you about Anne. I was with you in the Muniments Room, so I know what you found out. I went looking for her – she was in the garden, near the lavender – and I asked her some questions.'

Georgina nodded, knowing that Doris would see the gesture and know she understood. Now definitely wasn't the time or place to have a conversation with a ghost.

In the kitchen, Posy put the kettle on; she made Ellen a cup of green tea and a hummus, falafel and rocket sandwich, garnished with baby plum tomatoes.

'We're not going to talk at you,' she said gently, 'because we lost our mum and we know how crap it feels to be in your shoes, and people just won't shut up. So we'll be quiet – but we're here if you want to talk, or want a hug, or if you want to rant and scream, OK?'

Ellen looked at her, and a tear ran down her cheek. 'I was horrible to you yesterday. I made out you...' She choked on the words.

'You were in shock and you're grieving. We know you didn't mean what you said,' Hattie said. 'Yes, I admit, Posy and I didn't get on so well with your mother, and that must've made life hard for you. I'm sorry for that.'

'Me too,' Posy said. 'We should've tried harder.'

'But we're here. And we can stay with you when the police talk to you, if you want our support,' Hattie said.

A shudder racked Ellen's body. 'And there's all the arrangements to make. The fu—' She clearly couldn't finish the word.

'We'll help. We won't take over, but we know what we needed to do for our mother, so we can help you. If you want us to do anything, then of course we will,' Posy said. She gave the younger woman a hug. 'The main thing right now is that you know you're not alone.'

Another tear spilled down Ellen's cheek. 'I don't deserve...'

'Yes, you do. It's fine,' Hattie said.

'We'll leave you now,' Sybbie said gently.

Georgina took a business card out of her bag. 'Here's my number, Ellen, when you want to talk about bats and photographs. Or if you want to talk to me about anything else.'

'Thank you,' Ellen said, putting it into the pocket of her jeans. 'And thank you for...' She welled up and shook her head, unable to speak.

Georgina gave her a hug. 'Any time. Take care.'

EIGHTEEN

'The bank details are here, guv,' Larissa said. 'And it's very interesting. As well as the accounts I'd expect to see, Karen Berry's got a bank account that only has cash paid into it. It was opened two years ago. The deposits are about once a month, but not on the same day of the month, and they're different amounts each time.'

'Are there any outgoing payments?' Colin asked.

'No. It's not an interest-bearing account, either, which is weird if it's a savings account. There's quite a bit in it.' Larissa tilted her screen so he could see it.

'The payments were made in various branches across London. Right. We need to talk to those branches and see if their records can narrow it down to the time the money was paid in,' Colin said. 'And we need the CCTV from the last three months, if it's available, so we can get an image of whoever paid the money in.'

'Provided they're not wearing a face mask,' Mo said. 'I know we're not under Covid restrictions anymore, but some people still wear face masks if they're out at the shops.'

People who had health concerns, Colin thought – but it was

also a useful excuse for people who didn't want their faces seen for any reason. 'Let's hope not,' he said. 'Anything on the phone records, yet?'

'Nothing that looks out of the usual,' Larissa said. 'Karen didn't make any calls on Sunday – definitely not to a taxi firm or a friend – so maybe she was planning to drive herself up to London.'

'Maybe,' Colin said. 'Can we do another check on the phone records for a couple of days either side of the dates for the last three times money was paid into that odd account? See if there's a pattern to the phone numbers – incoming and outgoing – and if any of them crop up around all three dates.'

'Will do,' Mo said. 'Though, if she's got a secret bank account, could she have had a secret phone as well? A pay-as-you-go she only uses to contact whoever puts the money in her account?'

'We'll need to do a search for that as well as a beige wool item. In the meantime, I'm going to have a chat with Maggie Pritchard and see if she still has her notes about the things that went missing,' Colin said. 'If Karen really was taking small things from the house and selling them, that might account for the cash deposits.'

Straight after the phone call, Maggie emailed Colin her notes and photographs.

'It seems as if something went missing from the house about once a month,' Colin said. 'It's beginning to look as if Maggie Pritchard was right to be suspicious. If Karen was taking these little pieces – and, from the amount of the deposits in that bank account, it's a strong possibility – who was she selling them to? And did that person meet her in London, or did they meet her at Hartington?'

'Maybe the ice house was their meeting point,' Larissa suggested.

'Maybe,' Colin agreed. 'Posy seemed to think Karen had

taken a book. Though that doesn't fit with the pattern of the other things taken, which are all small.'

'Or maybe it was worth a lot more, so it was worth the risk,' Mo said.

'Unfortunately, we don't have any idea what might have gone missing from the house since the Pritchards left,' Colin said, 'but I'll have a word with Rowena and see if she can give me a ballpark value for the last three things Maggie Pritchard says went missing. If there's a correlation between them and the deposits made in those months, that would be useful.'

He rang the Finds Liaison Officer.

'DI Bradshaw. I was just about to ring you,' Rowena said. 'The team have done a last sweep of the burial site under the Great Oak, and they found a ring and a chain. It looks as if our unknown woman wore the ring on a chain round her neck. The chain broke at some point, and over the years the ring must've slipped through the skeleton and sunk into the earth as the material of her clothes rotted and the roots moved.'

'Are there any identifying marks?' Colin asked. 'A date or initials engraved on it, or anything?'

'No. It looks like a typical mid-century wedding ring – it's gold, quite narrow, and engraved with leaves and flowers, which were fashionable at the time,' Rowena said. 'There's no hallmark but, then again, a lot of jewellery from the period wasn't hallmarked. I'll send you the photographs.'

'Thank you,' Colin said. 'I was going to ask if you could help with something related and maybe give me a ballpark valuation of a couple of items.' He was careful not to tell her of his suspicions.

'Send over the details, and I'll do what I can.' Rowena paused. 'Or maybe we can discuss it over dinner?'

Was she asking him on a professional basis, or a personal one?

Colin squirmed.

They hadn't even met in person; he was making a supposition that might not be there. Oh, to have Georgina's easy skills with people.

'Maybe,' he said, and then made a decision. 'Actually I was going to have dinner with my girlfriend, this evening. I was planning to tell her what you'd told me about the skeleton.' He'd intended to ring Georgina, but he was pretty sure he could talk her into dinner. 'She's a family friend of the Berrys, and she's looking into the historical side of the case. Would you like to join us? I'm sure she'd be interested in what you have to say, and she'll keep the rest of this confidential.'

'Oh – I, um, maybe another evening,' Rowena said hastily. 'Send me the details, and I'll try and get back to you in the next day or so.'

When he put the phone down, Colin was aware that both Mo and Larissa were looking at him.

'You've gone a bit red, guv,' Larissa said. 'Coming onto you, was she? The Finds Liaison, I mean?'

'I probably mistook what she said. I panicked. I think I might've behaved like an arse,' Colin said. 'I used Georgina as a kind of shield. That isn't very nice.'

Larissa patted his shoulder. 'You won't be the first to behave like an arse – or the last.' She raised her eyebrows. 'Or she might really have been coming onto you.'

'At least you've admitted now that Georgina's your girl-friend,' Mo said.

Colin closed his eyes for a moment. 'All right, you two. Settle down. I'll go and get the coffees in.'

'Just as the new boy should,' Larissa said with a grin, adding, 'guv.'

NINETEEN

In the front seat of Georgina's car, Sybbie closed her eyes. 'I'm glad to be going home.'

'I feel a bit rude, not even speaking to Lord Ellingham,' Georgina admitted.

'He was hopeless when Millie died, and he'll be just as hopeless now,' Sybbie said. 'I know I should feel sorry for him, but I think he feels sorry enough for himself.' She shook herself. 'And now I'm being unkind. I suppose I'm just cross about the way he's treated the girls, the past couple of years.'

'Do you think there's anything in Hattie's theory that maybe he has a medical condition?' Georgina asked. 'Could that have caused the change in his behaviour?'

'No. I know he has high blood pressure. Millie really struggled trying to get him to cut down on red meat and salt and do some proper exercise instead of just pottering round, tinkering with his cars. But I think we can put most of his behaviour towards the girls down to Karen dripping her poison into his ear,' Sybbie said dryly. 'If I die before Bernard and he tries any tricks like that with Giles and Cesca, I swear I'll come back and haunt him. Horribly.'

'She'd be the scariest ghost in the world,' Doris remarked from the back seat, and Georgina couldn't stifle a laugh.

'What?' Sybbie asked.

'Nothing. Just I can see where you get your reputation for being scary,' Georgina said.

'Me? I'm a pussycat,' Sybbie said. But to Georgina's relief her friend was smiling.

Back at Little Wenborough, Georgina dropped Sybbie off at the manor to be reunited with her husband, called into the shop briefly to pick up some salad and a tub of Cesca's home-made chilli pesto to stir into the gnocchi currently in her fridge at home, and headed back to Rookery Farm.

She sent her daughter a text to say she hadn't managed to find the marriage licence.

Bea messaged back.

> Did the family have a house in London, by any chance? If so, I can check the London Marriage Licence index for you. Send me the names, dates and any information you can. Love you xx

> They did – apparently it was a casualty of the Blitz.

Georgina typed in the information.

> Thank you, sweetheart. Love you, too xx

'It's not a complete dead-end, then,' Doris remarked.

'No. What did you find out about Anne?'

'She started at the Hall as a scullery maid, then worked her way up to laundry maid, parlourmaid and finally chambermaid – that's when she met William. They fell in love, and he wanted to marry her. They knew the family wouldn't approve, because she wasn't blue-blooded and he was supposed to be marrying this rich heiress,' Doris said. 'They tried to stay apart, but they couldn't. She knew they ought to be sensible, but...' She blew out a breath. 'Like me and Trev, I suppose. Sometimes you can't help yourself. You get carried away.'

'And she fell pregnant?' Georgina guessed.

'Yes,' Doris said. 'When she told him about the baby, he said he'd go to London and get a marriage licence. He was twenty-one then, so he didn't need his father's permission. She was still only eighteen, but she had no parents or guardians to give permission, so it didn't matter. He said if she asked for unpaid leave to visit a sick great-aunt in Norwich, he'd meet her there, take her to London and they'd get married.'

'I really hope he meant it,' Georgina said. 'It'll be so sad if it turns out that he was the one who killed her.'

'I don't think he did. The way she talks about him – it sounded as if he loved her, too,' Doris said.

Georgina's phone pinged.

> Got it. See screenshot below

> But remember that issuing a licence didn't necessarily mean it was used. Valid for up to three months, cost £2 12 s and 6d, and he would've got it from the office at the Doctors' Commons in St Bennet's Hill, St Paul's churchyard.

'That's a lot of money,' Doris said, clearly reading Bea's text over her shoulder.

'It'd work out at more than half a year's wages for our Anne. So he really did mean to marry her. And look, Doris! Berry, the Hon William of Portland Place, bachelor above twenty-one, and Anne Lusher of Hartington, Norfolk, spinster, daughter of John Lusher of Aylsham, Norfolk, deceased,' Georgina read aloud.

'Special licence, 15 August 1854. It's for All Soul's Church in Langham Place, which I assume must've been their nearest church.'

'The licence was issued, but – as Bea suggested – did they actually get married?' Doris asked.

'Let's find out.' Georgina texted Bea.

> Just what I'd been looking for. Thank you. Love you xx

Then she opened her laptop. 'Let's start with Anne, first.' She searched the Aylsham parish records for Lusher. 'Lusher, Anne, daughter of John and Anne, baptised 4 April 1836. We've found her,' she said. 'Let's see if she's buried in Aylsham.' She frowned. 'Anne Lusher, 4 April 1836, wife of John – it looks as if Anne either died in childbirth or shortly after, and she was buried on the same day her daughter was christened. How sad. And here's the burial of John Lusher, agricultural labourer, in May 1848. Our Anne would've between twelve. I assume she went into service around then?'

'Hartington Hall's not very far from Aylsham, so that's probably what happened,' Doris said. 'Let's see if the marriage really did happen in London.'

All Soul's Church parish records showed that William Berry and Anne Lusher were married by licence on 22 August 1854.

'I'm so glad that he didn't let her down,' Georgina said.

* * *

Colin stared at his mobile phone. He'd seen Georgina last night. Would seeing her two nights in a row be too much?

Then again, he was feeling out of sorts about the situation he'd misread with Rowena Langham, and a bit of gentle mockery from Georgina would help a lot with that.

He sighed, and video-called her. Funny how even seeing her on a screen made him feel instantly better. 'Hey. I promised to update you on what the Finds Liaison Officer said about the skeleton.'

'Female, and mid-1800s, you said?'

'Apparently there were buttons and fabric which helped her date it.'

'It ties in with what I've been researching,' she said. 'I went to Hartington today to drop off the photographs and give Sybbie a lift home. We spent a couple of hours in the archives, and Bea helped me find the marriage licence that wasn't in the family's records.'

He blinked. 'What marriage licence? And why were you looking for a marriage licence, anyway?'

'I think the body belongs to Anne Lusher. She was a chambermaid at Hartington Hall, and she's listed on the 1851 census but not the one after,' Georgina explained. 'The marriage licence in London is dated August 1854. It's for Anne Lusher and William Berry – who was the heir to the house and the title, except he was killed in the Crimean War. Edward – his father – died a month later, and that's when Posy and Hattie's four-times-great-grandfather Henry inherited the Hall.'

'That ties in with what the Finds Liaisons Officer's team found this afternoon,' he said. 'It's a wedding ring and a chain. I'll send you the photograph.'

'That'd be great,' Georgina said.

'She was pregnant, poor girl. About four months, Rowena – the Finds Liaison Officer – said.' His face felt hot, and he really hoped he wasn't blushing. He didn't even know what Rowena looked like. He didn't want Georgina to think he flirted with every woman he came into contact with. It might be early days between them, but she was becoming important to him.

'Sybbie and I thought she might be pregnant,' Georgina said, 'because that's one of the most common reasons for getting a marriage licence rather than banns. Sybbie wondered if maybe Anne died in childbirth or pregnancy. Though that isn't a reason to bury her under the oak tree.'

Colin sucked in a breath. That was the other bit he had to tell her. 'I'm sorry, Georgie. This isn't good news. Her hyoid bone was broken.'

'Which means?'

He winced. 'She was strangled.'

'Oh, no – the poor girl. But who would've killed her?'

'We'll probably never know,' he said. 'And I can't investigate it. Apart from the fact I'm working on a case now' – and he hadn't told Georgina that Karen's death was murder rather than an accidental death – 'it's too far back for us to find the evidence. You've done really well to find out who she probably was.'

'I'm going to keep looking, because maybe there's a letter or a diary or something that can tell us the truth,' Georgina said. 'Even if you can't arrest someone for murder, or get justice, at least it'll be closure.'

'True,' he said. 'Would they have known she was pregnant?'

'At four months, she could've hidden the pregnancy. But the servants who did laundry would've known when they didn't have to wash her menstruation rags – and they might have told someone. When she first realised, she was probably terrified of being dismissed without a reference.'

'Even though it takes two to make a pregnancy, and men of the day saw servants as fair game. If she was sacked, what would she do, with no money, nowhere to live and maybe a family who'd reject her because they thought she'd brought shame on them?' Colin asked.

'She'd have to go to the workhouse,' Georgina said. 'Except that's not what happened. William married her.'

'And we'll never know the rest,' Colin said. He sighed. 'It's feeling that way with this case, right now.'

'Talking of your case, I have information for you,' Georgina said. 'You asked how Karen met Henry. According to Hattie, it was at his club. He'd gone to stay in London after Millie's funeral – he couldn't bear it at the house – and she was one of the staff there. She was kind to him.'

Colin frowned. 'There's a bit of a discrepancy between that story and what everyone says about her.'

'You're the one who said I should keep an open mind and take the emotion out of it,' Georgina reminded him.

'Does that mean you have a theory?' Colin asked.

'It's not very nice,' Georgina warned. 'But maybe Karen realised Henry was lonely and quite well-off. Maybe she thought she could make a nice life with him.'

'She was a gold digger, in other words?' That would tie in with the missing pieces from the house and the secret bank account – yet more things he hadn't shared with Georgina.

'That's a horrible way of putting it, but maybe. And we don't know what goes on in other people's lives. Perhaps Karen's last relationship had been really awful and left her – well, damaged,' Georgina said. 'Maybe Henry made her happy.'

'Maybe,' Colin said. But Karen Berry had still ended up dead at the bottom of an isolated building, having been suffocated. 'I guess I'd better let you get on with your evening. Anything nice planned?'

'Bert and I will be going down to the river,' she said. 'Then I'm being very lazy and cooking shop-bought gnocchi and stirring some of Cesca's pesto into it. You?'

'Bit of work,' he said, wishing he was sitting in her garden with her instead of at his desk.

'If you have to stay late, try and get some fresh air to clear your head,' she said.

'Yeah. Enjoy your walk. Catch you later,' he said.

* * *

'You're not seeing our Mr Darcy tonight, then?' Doris asked.

'No. But that's fine.' Georgina paused. 'Are you OK? Because, now we know more about what happened to Anne, it must be a bit close to the bone for you.'

'It is, a bit,' Doris admitted. 'That, and the way Karen Berry died.'

Falling and hitting her head. Just as Doris had. 'I'm sorry,' Georgina said. 'I honestly never meant to drag you into any of this.'

'You didn't. I asked to come along,' Doris said. 'And then I met Anne. It's been good to talk to someone else who can hear me. And to feel useful again.'

'I haven't forgotten that I'm trying to track down Trevor, and find out what really happened to you,' Georgina said.

'I know,' Doris said. But her voice was slightly wobbly.

'What's happened, Doris?' Georgina asked.

'What Colin just said – about an unmarried pregnant woman's family thinking she'd brought shame on them.' Doris gulped. 'It's brought something back.'

'What?' Georgina asked, as gently as she could. She was sure there was no way Doris's family would have taken that sort of approach.

'That night – Trev didn't turn up to meet me.'

Georgina frowned. 'But I thought he was coming for dinner? You were making a special Valentine's meal for you both. And then you were...' She stopped, remembering what Doris had told her before.

'Doing the gin, hot bath and falling down the stairs routine, as recommended by the doctor,' Doris said grimly. 'We'd pooled our money and he was going to buy the gin.'

'If he didn't turn up, how did you get the gin?' Georgina asked.

'Someone else brought it round.' Doris took a deep breath. 'Irene.'

TWENTY

'Who's Irene?' Georgina asked.

'Irene Taylor. Trev's mum.'

Georgina felt sick. How could Trevor's mother possibly have supported the kind of medical advice that Doris had been given? Why had she brought the gin? Why hadn't she come to talk Doris out of even trying it and offer her support? But it wasn't tactful to ask. 'How did she know?'

'That's hazy,' Doris said. 'I'm guessing she saw Trev with the gin, then put two and two together. My family weren't big drinkers. Everyone knew what gin meant, in those days.'

'And she actually brought it round to you?'

'Yes.' Doris sighed. 'She obviously went on at him about it until he cracked and told her. I remember she came round, and she said I was a cheap little tart who should've been taught to keep my legs together.'

'What a *bitch*,' Georgina said, anger flooding through her. 'You're not a tart. Not at all. And what about Trev's part in it? It takes two to make a baby.'

'Back then, it was never the man's fault,' Doris said quietly. 'You know the saying. Boys will be boys.'

Those attitudes had continued long past the 1970s, too. 'I'm so sorry.'

'And that's when she said it. That I'd brought shame on her family.'

'That's so not true. Of course you hadn't.' Georgina bit her lip. 'Did she make you drink the gin?'

'She said she'd make sure I did what the doctor ordered,' Doris said. 'But that's as far as I can remember. The rest of it's still a blur.'

'Irene Taylor.' Georgina frowned. 'She might still be alive. I need to find her. I don't suppose you knew her maiden name?'

'No.'

'OK. Would Jack know?' Georgina asked.

'He was only a kid, back then. He'd know even less than I do,' Doris said. 'I always had to call her Mrs Taylor, even though my parents asked Trev to call them Albert and Lizzy and treated him as if he was part of our family. I think I only knew her first name because I heard one of Trev's cousins calling her "Aunt Irene".' She paused. 'Irene and... what was his name? Howard?'

'I'll get onto it now,' Georgina said.

'Not tonight,' Doris said. 'I really don't want to think about her any more tonight.'

'All right,' Georgina said. 'Tonight, we'll take Bert to the river, come back here, and watch something really silly and fun.'

'*Friends*,' Doris said. 'The one with the sofa. And the one where Monica gets a turkey stuck on her head.'

It was just the sort of thing Georgina would do with Bea – and, when she was younger, had done with her own mother. 'You're on,' she said.

* * *

On Wednesday morning, Colin and Larissa called in to the estate office at Hartington Hall with Felicity, the Family Liaison Officer, to see the Berrys and Ellen.

'You want to see all of us together?' Hattie asked. 'Has something happened?'

'I'll explain more when you're all here,' he said.

'I'll go and find Ellen and Papa,' Posy said.

'Come into the kitchen and I'll put the kettle on,' Hattie said.

The breakfast kitchen was large and had clearly been remodelled at some point in the last ten years, though the style was in keeping with the house; Colin wondered if Millie Berry had been the one to organise that. Hattie bustled about, filling the kettle and finding mugs and a teapot. He didn't really want a mug of tea, but he recognised that ritual often helped people cope when they were expecting to hear bad news.

By the time Hattie had sorted out the tea, Henry and Ellen had arrived in the kitchen with Posy and sat down at the table.

Sergeant Leonard had taken Ellen's statement on Monday; it was the first time Colin had talked to Ellen properly. 'Miss Newman, I'm Detective Inspector Colin Bradshaw, and this is Detective Constable Larissa Foulkes. You already know Felicity, your Family Liaison Officer. And we're all very sorry for your loss,' he said.

'Thank you.'

She looked tired, miserable and very young, he thought. And what he was about to tell them all was a huge bombshell. Accidental death was one thing to deal with; murder was quite another.

And the warmth of the July morning had built into muggy, oppressive heat. The sort of weather that made people's tempers scratchy and their reactions unpredictable.

'So how can we help you, Inspector?' Henry asked.

Colin exchanged a glance with Larissa. He'd ask some questions before the bombshell, he thought. 'I was just wondering if any of you had any idea why Lady Ellingham might have gone to the ice house.'

'No idea. She hated the place and the bats,' Henry said.

Posy and Hattie shook their heads.

Ellen looked a bit awkward, but Colin thought that was down to a combination of her age and the fact that she'd been known to argue with her mother over the bats.

'I'm afraid this is an insensitive question, but would any of you know where Lady Ellingham's phone might be?' he asked.

'Wasn't it with her, or in her handbag?' Henry asked.

'We haven't found a handbag, either,' Colin said. 'Could you describe her bag for me?'

Henry looked blank. 'I don't...' He shook his head. 'Sorry.'

'Her favourite one matched the shoes she was wearing,' Posy said. 'It was a Mulberry. Quite small.'

That didn't mean much to Colin, but he glanced at Larissa, who gave him the tiniest nod to indicate that she'd brief him later. Hopefully she'd manage to find an image on the internet.

'Thank you,' Colin said. Now for a tricky one. 'Do you know if Karen had more than one phone?'

'Why on earth would she have more than one phone?' Henry asked, giving him a disbelieving stare. 'This is all nonsense.'

'Hang on, Papa.' Hattie frowned. 'Karen always kept that handbag with her. She never let it out of her sight.' She looked at Colin. 'If her handbag wasn't with her... does that mean her death wasn't an accident? That someone killed her and stole her handbag?'

And possibly whatever she'd taken from the china cabinet or silver collection, which might've been hidden in said handbag, but he couldn't suggest that right now. Not when he'd come to break bad news, and definitely not without strong evidence to back up his suspicions. There might still be an innocent reason for the money in Karen Berry's secret bank account.

Hattie Berry had made the connection quickly. Too quickly? Did she know something about Karen's death?

Colin had briefed Felicity on the way, and now he gave her a small nod to let her know he was about to break the bad news. 'I'm sorry to have to tell you this, but I'm afraid the pathologist's findings suggest it wasn't an accidental death,' he said carefully.

Ellen let out a wail of distress and clapped her hands to her face. Posy scraped her chair back swiftly, walked round to the younger woman and wrapped her arms round her. 'Sweetie,' she said softly. 'Oh, sweetie. I can't say it's all right, because I know it's not. And I'm so sorry.'

'Are you saying somebody killed my wife?' Henry asked, his voice cracking. 'Then why the hell aren't you out there *looking* for him?'

Interesting that Henry immediately assumed the killer was a man, Colin thought. 'We're investigating,' he said. 'The Scene of Crimes team is sifting through the evidence, trying to work out what happened.'

'Someone killed Karen?' Hattie was pale with shock. 'But... Oh, my God. Who'd kill her? Why?'

The problem was, Colin thought, there were a lot of people with a motivation to want Karen Berry out of the way. Though it wouldn't be tactful or helpful to say that out loud. 'We're following a number of lines of enquiries. Though if we could have your permission to bring in a team to search the house, that would be helpful.'

'Why? What are you looking for?' Posy asked. 'How was she killed?'

'At the moment, and I know how bad this sounds, I can't say too much,' Colin said.

Posy dragged in a breath, her blue eyes widening in horror. 'Are you saying *we're* suspects?'

'At this stage, anyone on the estate or who might have been on the estate over the last couple of days needs to be ruled out of the investigation,' Colin said. 'I'm sorry to ask you this, especially while you're grieving. But the more you can tell me and the more information we have, the more likely we are to find out what happened and who killed Karen, so we can bring them to justice. I'm afraid I'll need you to go through your movements again.' He took deep breath. 'Do I have your permission to search the house, or would you prefer me to get a warrant?'

'I...' Henry's face crumpled, and he put his head in his hands, clearly overcome by grief. The lines on his face had deepened even in the few minutes Colin had been sitting here; he'd literally aged before Colin's eyes, but Colin knew that stress could do that to you.

Looking haunted, Hattie pushed her chair back and put her arms round her father. 'I know, Papa. I know. I'm here.' She looked at Colin. 'Yes, of course you can search the house. Anything you need, come to me. I have the keys, and...' She closed her eyes briefly. 'This is just...' She looked at Colin. 'Does this change anything about when we can arrange Karen's funeral?'

'I'm afraid so,' Colin said. 'And I know how difficult that is. That's why I wanted to tell you the news in person rather than over the phone.'

'That's considerate. Kind. Thank you,' Posy said.

Ellen hadn't said a single word. But what could you say to news like that? Colin wondered. 'The pathologist says you can go to see her any time you like, after tomorrow. When you see her, she'll just look as if she's asleep,' he said gently. 'I can take you there, or Felicity can if you'd rather. Just let us know when you want us to arrange it.'

'I don't want to see her,' Ellen said, wrapping her arms tightly round herself.

'There's no pressure, either way,' Colin said. 'You don't have to decide now.' God, he hated this bit of his job. Giving news that made a family fall apart. But as the senior officer, it was his duty to do it, and he'd never dump his responsibilities on his juniors. 'And thank you,' he added, 'for agreeing to let us search.'

Larissa called the forensics team while Colin took another statement from each of the Berrys and Ellen. It didn't add anything to what he already knew. What, he wondered, was he missing?

The team didn't find the pink Mulberry handbag or any phone belonging to Karen Berry, and the only beige wool things even close to the colour Sammy Granger had sent him were a cashmere sweater in Henry Berry's wardrobe, and a couple of old blankets in the dogs' bed. If the dogs' blankets had been used to suffocate Karen, there would have been dog hairs mixed with the wool fibres in her nose. He'd ask Sammy to check the fibres from the sweater, but it looked as if the killer had taken away whatever they'd used to suffocate Karen.

'Thank you for your help,' he said at the end of the search. 'I know it's been painful, and I apologise. We simply want to find out what happened and get justice for your family.'

'I know,' Posy said.

'I know you need time to grieve, but we need some information to help us piece together more about Lady Ellingham and who she might have interacted with over the last few months. Can I ask you for the contact details of her other relatives?'

'There aren't any,' Ellen said.

'No brothers, sisters, aunts or uncles, cousins?' Colin checked.

'Nobody,' Ellen said. 'Just me.'

'What about her friends? Former colleagues?' Larissa asked.

'Karen wasn't one for socialising. She was happy to be here,' Henry said.

And yet Henry had said yesterday that Karen was desperate

to go back to London. What was he trying to hide? Colin wondered.

It was clear he wouldn't get any more information right now. He needed to regroup and try a different tack. 'Thank you for your time. And, again, I'm sorry to be the bringer of bad news,' he said. 'Larissa and I will see ourselves out. Felicity will stay with you for the time being, to help out and answer any questions you might have.'

Ellen and Henry said nothing. Hattie's face was pinched. Only Posy gave him a small nod of acknowledgement.

'They're closing ranks,' Larissa said when they were most of the way down the tree-lined drive towards the narrow country lane.

'Agreed,' Colin said. 'It might be grief.'

'Or it might be they're not telling us what they know,' Larissa said.

'I think Posy's the most likely to tell us something,' Colin said thoughtfully. 'Or we can try the friends of the family that we do know, to see if they can suggest something.'

'Are you thinking of asking Sybbie?' Larissa suggested.

'I am,' Colin confirmed.

TWENTY-ONE

Georgina was sitting at the kitchen table with Bert's head on her knee, trying to find a marriage record for Irene and Howard Taylor on her laptop, when there was a rap on her kitchen door, and Sybbie walked in, her normally sunny expression grim.

Bert gave a small wuff and a wag of his tail in welcome; but, instead of making a fuss of the spaniel, Sybbie ignored him.

'I wasn't expecting to see you this afternoon. Is everything all right?' Georgina asked.

'No,' Sybbie said, and sat down heavily at the table. 'Am I interrupting?'

'It's fine. I'm interruptible,' Georgina reassured her, closing her laptop so she could concentrate on her friend. 'What's happened?'

'Did you know Karen's death wasn't an accident?'

She was fairly sure Colin suspected it, but as far as she knew he was still waiting for reports. 'Colin's not supposed to talk to anyone outside about his cases.'

'Not even in pillow talk?' Sybbie asked wryly.

'Not even in pillow talk,' Georgina said. 'I can talk to him, yes, but he can't confirm or deny anything. He did say that he was keeping an open mind until he'd had the pathologist's report back, but that's par for the course. Why? What have you heard?'

'Hattie just rang me. Colin told her the death wasn't accidental. He wouldn't say how Karen died, and he had a team searching the house. For the murder weapon, I presume. They took away one of Henry's old sweaters. And Karen's handbag's missing.'

Georgina knew about the missing handbag, but she could see how upset Sybbie was and decided not to make it worse by saying so. 'Surely someone didn't kill her just for a handbag?'

'Apparently it was a Mulberry,' Sybbie said. 'Limited edition.'

Georgina wrinkled her nose. 'Even if it was an expensive designer handbag, would people really kill for it?'

'People are killed for a lot less than that.' Sybbie's mouth tightened. 'Colin was asking about whether Karen might have had a second phone.'

Georgina felt her eyes widen. 'Why on earth would she have a second phone?'

'If Maggie Pritchard is right and Karen was taking little things from the house,' Sybbie said, 'then maybe she used a... what is it, burner phone, to ring the person she sold the things to? And *don't* tell me I've been watching too many of Bernard's TV dramas,' she added crossly.

'It's a theory,' Georgina said carefully.

'God, it's such a mess. The poor girls. Henry's going to be as much use as a chocolate teapot. Hattie said there was a policewoman there to help and answer questions, but most of the things that need to be done will fall on their shoulders.'

'Sybbie, forgive me for asking, but you don't th—' Georgina stopped abruptly.

'I do hope you weren't going to suggest that Posy or Hattie killed Karen,' Sybbie said, and the quietness of her voice was more terrifying than anything Georgina had heard before. 'I've known my goddaughters since the day they were born. There is no way – no *way*,' she emphasised, 'that either of them would've killed that woman. Lost their temper with her, yes. I can see that, very easily. But, under provocation, Posy always stomps off and does some hard pruning or weeding, and Hattie takes the dogs for a run. And they don't show their faces again until they can face people without screaming their heads off. Millie taught them that back when they were still stroppy teenagers.'

Georgina winced. 'I'm sorry, Sybbie. I wasn't intending to malign either of them. None of this makes any sense.'

'Well, I hope your boyfriend gets to the bottom of it. And quickly,' Sybbie said. She stood up abruptly.

'Sybbie, I don't want to fall out with y—' Georgina began.

'Which is why I'm leaving now,' Sybbie said.

Bert whined, and again Sybbie ignored him. 'I don't think we should speak again until we're both feeling more civilised,' she said.

Georgina stared after her friend as the kitchen door closed abruptly behind her; she heard the sound of wheels spinning on the gravel. She only hoped that Sybbie's way of dealing with things didn't involve driving too fast on the narrow country roads outside the village.

How could she fix this?

She called Sybbie's daughter-in-law.

'What can I do for you, Georgie?' Francesca asked.

'I'm really sorry to call you at work, Cesca, but I'm worried about Sybbie. We've just had a bit of a row,' Georgina said.

'You? But... you're not the sort to have fights with people,' Francesca said, sounding surprised. 'What happened?'

'Colin told the family that Karen's death wasn't an accident. I kind of started asking if she was absolutely sure that Hattie and Posy weren't, um, involved,' Georgina admitted. 'Which was a bit tactless of me.'

'Given that Millie was her best friend, she's a *leetle* bit protective towards them,' Francesca said. 'Give her a bit of time. She'll calm down. I'll drop some tiramisu over to her, after work, and try to jolly her out of it.'

'Thanks.' Georgina bit her lip. 'I'm sorry to be telling tales out of school. I just didn't want her to – well, be driving anywhere too fast, while she's angry.'

'No. Dearest ma-in-law is far too sensible for that. She'll go straight home, wield her secateurs in a way that warns everyone else to give her a wide berth, and then by the time her shoulders start aching she'll have worked herself out of her mood,' Francesca said. 'Are you all right, Georgie?'

'Yes. Just worried about Sybbie. And feeling guilty.'

'She'll be fine,' Francesca said. 'Actually, I know she feels a bit guilty about dragging you into another unexpected death.'

'What, like I did with you two and Jodie, a couple of months back?' Georgina asked.

'We're still the Musketeers,' Francesca said. 'When she puts the secateurs down, I'll get her to ring you.'

'Thanks,' Georgina said, meaning it.

Though she still felt guilty.

'If I could touch things,' Doris said, 'then right now I'd pour you a big glass of wine, stick a pizza in the oven, and while it was cooking I'd play some George Harrison and we could dance until you smiled again.'

'The thought's what counts,' Georgina said. 'Thank you.'

'Sybbie'll calm down, and it'll sort itself out,' Doris said. 'Pour yourself that wine and pretend I did it for you.'

'I'll stick to coffee,' Georgina said, 'but you're right. Keeping myself busy will stop me stewing over things.'

Georgina went back to researching Irene and Howard Taylor.

They'd married in 1950 in Little Wenborough's parish

church, and Trevor had been born in April 1953. Trevor had been their only child, and Howard had died in 2005, aged seventy-four.

If Irene had remarried, it hadn't been at Little Wenborough.

There was no record of Irene's burial, either.

Georgina widened her search to the whole of Norfolk. No remarriage, and no death.

Unless Irene had died and been buried the other side of the country from Norfolk, there was a possibility that she was still in Norfolk and still alive. At the age of ninety-four, Irene was likely to be living in sheltered accommodation. All Georgina had to do was find her.

All.

Billy in the butcher's ran the local historical society. He might know if Irene still had family locally – perhaps nieces and nephews – who could help Georgina get in touch.

And then, Georgina thought, she could find out exactly what had happened on Valentine's night, 1971.

TWENTY-TWO

'Ma's in the garden,' Giles said when he answered the door. 'But this might not be a good time to talk to her.'

'Why? What's happened?' Colin asked.

'I don't know, but she's pruning like a demon. Something's upset her,' Giles said. 'I'm steering clear until she's back to her normal self. If you want to go and find her, it's at your own risk.' He gave Colin a wry smile. 'Let me give you some dog biscuits. You can bribe Max and Jet to find her for you.'

Colin discovered Sybbie among her prized azaleas, scowling and pruning with precision yet at a speed that told him she was absolutely furious.

'I come in peace, Sybbie,' he said. 'With biscuits for Max and Jet.'

'Oh, *do* you, now?' she snapped, snipping a bit more.

'If you'd rather I asked you questions at the station, Lady Wyatt, that's fine by me.'

'Accusing *me* of bumping Karen off, now, are you?' she asked, her voice arctic.

Colin remembered that Francesca had once said her

mother-in-law could be scary. He'd dismissed it at the time. Wrongly, it seemed.

'No, I'm not,' he said. 'You know I can't discuss an investigation with you. But I have gaps that need filling, and those gaps should help to rule out your goddaughters from any investigation.'

Sybbie stopped pruning and narrowed her eyes at him. 'The girls were terribly upset. How can you possibly think they did it?'

'Routine questions,' Colin said. 'Like the ones I asked Georgina Drake yesterday, given that she found the body. And there are questions you might be able to help with. So are you going to do this as a friend of the Berrys, helping to exclude them, or would you prefer to talk formally at the station?'

Sybbie glowered at him again, then sighed and slipped her secateurs into her pocket. 'All right. I suppose you can have five minutes.'

'Thank you,' he said.

'What do you want to know?' she asked.

'Everything you know about Karen Berry,' he said. 'Bare facts.'

'She met Henry at his club in London, a few weeks after Millie died,' Sybbie said.

'Which club?'

'Alvanley's,' she said. 'It's one of these ridiculously old-fashioned places. Doesn't allow women – except to cook, serve drinks and do a bit of discreet admin. You know the sort. Utter arses.' She gave a brief and very acerbic impersonation of an upper-class politician waffling about nothing; Colin had to dig his fingernails into his palms to stop himself laughing. 'Apparently Henry had a bit of a wobble there one night, sobbing into his single malt or whatever, and she was kind to him. They got married in the register office at Chelsea, a couple of months later. Bit prettier than Westminster.'

Colin made a note. 'Did you go to the wedding?'

'Henry was hardly going to invite his late wife's best friend,' Sybbie said. 'It was a very small affair. Just Henry, Karen, Ellen and the girls. I think deep down he knew it was a bit on the hasty side.'

'Didn't any of her family attend?' Colin asked.

'I don't think she has any, or not that she admits to. No brothers, sisters or cousins. Hattie says she's always assumed Karen's parents are dead, because Ellen never mentions her grandparents – or her father. And you can hardly quiz someone on why their child never sees their father,' Sybbie said. 'I'm guessing it was an acrimonious split.'

'What about Karen's friends?' Colin asked. 'Didn't they go to the wedding?'

'Apparently not. It was very quiet.' Sybbie furrowed her brow as if trying to remember. 'Hattie said something about a man hanging round, but...' She spread her hands. 'I can't tell you any more.'

'Did any of her friends from London come to Hartington to see her?'

Sybbie frowned. 'Now you've made me think about it – no, I don't believe anyone did. Maybe Karen saw Hartington as a fresh start.'

Something definitely didn't feel right. Or maybe the new start hadn't been everything Karen had hoped for, and that was why she'd wanted to go back to London.

He needed to check out her former colleagues at the club. 'Where is Alvanley's?' he asked.

'One would assume that any reasonably competent detective would be able to work that out for himself,' Sybbie said crisply, 'given that so many gentlemen's clubs are based in St James's Street.'

She really was still angry. He sighed inwardly. 'Thank you for your help, Lady Wyatt. And I'm not casting aspersions on your goddaughters just for the sake of it. This is a murder investigation, and I need to be thorough.'

She sighed. 'I know, Detective Inspector Bradshaw. I just... The girls have had a hard enough time of it, lately. Though poor Ellen has it worse.'

'Last thing, and I'll leave you in peace. Do you know the date of the wedding?'

'It was in June 2019. I can't tell you the exact day.'

'That's good enough,' he said. She'd already told him which registry office. 'Thank you. I'll let you get on with your pruning. And I'm sorry that you and your goddaughters are going through this, Sybbie.'

Her shoulders sagged. 'Colin, I'm sorry for...' She shook her head. 'I just feel so helpless, you know? I can't do anything practical.'

'You just have,' Colin said.

'And I had a fight with Georgie, earlier. I've been snippy with her.'

He looked meaningfully at the pocket containing her secateurs. 'Figuratively, I hope. You're a bit fearsome with those things in your hand.'

'I suppose I am, dear boy.' She patted his arm. 'I'll ring her and apologise.'

'She'll understand. Put it down to a combination of worry and the weather,' he said. 'Call me if you think of anything else I might need to know.'

'I will,' she said.

* * *

Colin introduced himself on the phone to Michael Trafford, the secretary of Alvanley's Club. 'I wondered if I could talk to someone about a member of staff who worked at the club four and a half years ago, please?'

'I'm sure I can help,' Michael said.

'Karen Crawford,' Colin said, having checked the record of her wedding to Henry.

'I remember Karen. She ended up marrying one of our members, actually,' Michael said. 'What about her?'

'I was wondering what you could tell me about her,' Colin said.

'And you're from the police? Is she in trouble? She was always a quiet little thing. She did her job, got on with things and kept in the background,' Michael said.

'Not trouble,' Colin said. 'I'm sorry to tell you that she died over the weekend. As always, with an unexpected death, we're making routine enquiries.' It wasn't quite the truth, but he didn't want to broadcast the fact that this was a murder investigation. Not yet.'

'Oh, I say – I *am* sorry. What terrible luck for the poor girl.'

'What was her job?' Colin asked.

'She was part of the waiting staff,' Michael said.

'And how long did she work at Alvanley's?'

'Three years or so,' Michael said. 'The poor woman lost her husband, the year before she left us. He was quite a bit older than her, so I suppose it was only to be expected.' He gave a dry laugh. 'Heart attack, I think. It made the rest of us watch what we ate and drank for a few months afterwards – you always think but for the grace of God that could've been you – but it's so easy to slip back into the old bad habits, isn't it?'

Colin's antennae started twitching. Henry Berry was a good twenty years older than Karen. And now he was being told that her previous husband had also been a lot older. Was there a connection, or was he being oversuspicious?

'Did she have any particularly close friends among the staff?'

'Kept herself to herself, really. I think one of the bar staff might've been a bit sweet on her, but he didn't get a look-in,' Michael said.

'Thank you, Mr Trafford. You've been very helpful,' Colin said.

TWENTY-THREE

Georgina had just come back from taking Bert for his walk on Thursday morning when Sybbie rang her.

'I apologise,' Sybbie said. 'I was unfair to you, yesterday.'

'I was unfair, too, Sybbie, suggesting what I did,' Georgina said. 'It takes two to make an argument. I'm sorry.'

'Apology accepted,' Sybbie said. 'Are we still going to Pilates together tonight?'

'Yes,' Georgina said, and gave a wry laugh. 'Listen to us. We sound like a pair of daft old ladies.'

'You, dear girl, most definitely don't count as old,' Sybbie said. 'I'm not sure I do, for that matter.'

'Of course you don't,' Georgina said.

'I'm going with Posy, Henry and Ellen to the mortuary, today,' Sybbie said. 'Colin's meeting us there.'

'Do you want a lift over to Hartington?' Georgina offered on impulse. 'Just to give you some company on the way there and back, I mean. I don't expect to go to the mortuary with you. I'll take some more photographs for the website, if Hattie doesn't mind me wandering around with my camera.'

'That'd be kind. Thank you. Bring Bert – he can socialise with the other dogs,' Sybbie said.

'All right. When do you want me to pick you up?' Georgina asked.

'Would half past nine be all right?'

'Of course. I'll be there,' Georgina confirmed.

'Told you she'd come round,' Doris said when Georgina ended the call. 'To borrow a phrase from our favourite playwright, all's well that ends well.'

'Very funny,' Georgina said, but she was smiling. 'I assume you're coming to Hartington?'

'Yes. I want to try jogging Anne's memory about the wedding and William's family.'

'Are you sure?' Georgina asked. 'Given that what happened to her is so similar to...'

'What happened to me? Yes. That's why I want to do it,' Doris said. 'It's helping me remember things, too. And I need to know.'

Georgina settled Bert in the back of the car, then drove over to Little Wenborough Manor on the other side of the village.

Sybbie hugged her tightly. 'Dear girl. It's a sad business all round. And I'm glad you're not – well, sulking. After our fight.'

'I'm not a sulker,' Georgina said with a smile. 'You'll get sarcasm from me if I'm in a mood with you.'

'More like, you'll batter me with Shakespeare.' Sybbie smiled, but Georgina could sense a slight brittleness in her friend that wasn't usually there. Clearly the prospect of going to the mortuary was more upsetting than she was letting on.

When they reached Hartington, they discovered that Ellen wasn't at the house. 'The poor kid said she couldn't face going to see Karen's body,' Posy said. 'She's disappeared somewhere on the estate. Probably the woods, to check on her bats.'

'A garden can help bring you some peace when your heart's

troubled, whether it's a formal garden, a woodland garden or a lakeside one,' Sybbie said. 'Flowers are good.'

'*Here's flowers for you;/ Hot lavender, mints, savory, marjoram;/ The marigold, that goes to bed wi' the sun/ And with him rises, weeping: these are flowers/ Of middle summer*,' Georgina quoted.

'Knowing you, that's Shakespeare,' Sybbie said.

'It's one of Perdita's speeches from *The Winter's Tale*,' Georgina confirmed.

Sybbie sighed. 'Perdita. *Lost*,' she translated. 'I think young Ellen's a bit lost, right now.'

'I'm waiting for some calls to be returned,' Hattie said, 'so I'm not going to the mortuary, either.'

'I won't get under your feet, Hattie,' Georgina said. 'I've got a list of photos I'd like to shoot, if you don't mind?'

'That's fine by me,' Hattie said. 'Actually, we had a surprise package yesterday.' She bit her lip. 'I haven't got the originals – Felicity needed them for forensics to take a look at – but I was able to take photographs first. I meant to send them to you yesterday, but...'

'You've had an awful lot on your plate,' Georgina said.

Hattie nodded. 'It was about the inkstand that used to be in Papa's study – one of the things Maggie thinks went missing.' Hattie's expression tightened. 'Apparently whoever "bought" it' – she made quote marks with her fingers – 'found a letter in the inkstand. The address was ours, so they sent it back to us with an anonymous note, in case the letter had sentimental value.'

But why send it anonymously, if they'd bought the inkstand in good faith from a dealer? Georgina wondered. And, if they'd bought it knowing that it was stolen goods, why send the letter back at all?

'How did they find the letter?' Sybbie asked.

'Apparently, there was a secret drawer at the bottom, which they found accidentally. The letter was inside.'

'Maybe your father was the one who sold the inkstand,' Georgina suggested.

Hattie shook her head. 'Felicity already asked him. He didn't even realise it was missing. Felicity's getting the forensics team to see what they can find from the packaging. Anyway, I thought you'd like to see the letter.' She took her phone from her pocket and sent the photographs to Georgina.

'It looks as if William confided in his aunt and uncle,' Georgina said, when she'd finished reading the letter. 'And now we know the name of the woman he was meant to marry – Alice Featherstonehaugh.'

'Pronounced nothing like the way it's spelled,' Doris said dryly. 'Seeing that written down, I would've said Feather-stone-how, not Fanshaw.'

They weren't alone, or Georgina would've teased Doris that an Austen fan should know how surnames of the *ton* were pronounced. 'Edward obviously thought his sister was going to support him and her husband would "talk sense" into William, so he'd do what he was told and marry the heiress lined up for him. But she didn't,' Georgina said.

'I thought all the marriages among the *bon ton* were for dynastic reasons?' Hattie asked.

'Most of them were. But it looks as if the marriage between William's aunt and uncle was a love match, or at least it turned into one,' Georgina said. 'And I'm glad they were on his side. They knew he'd be unhappy with Alice.' She smiled. 'William's aunt actually reminded him that his father couldn't leave the house or title to anyone else, because it was entailed; and also, whatever he threatened, Edward couldn't disown William. And she offered to let William use their address for the marriage licence.'

William clearly loved Anne, if he was willing to make a stand against his father like that.

'Can we find the marriage licence?' Hattie asked.

'Already done. My daughter found it,' Georgina said. 'They got married in London. I know you said your family had another house in London at the time, but clearly William used his aunt's address.'

'Good. I know we haven't worked out why poor Anne was buried under the tree, but at least she and William were happy for a while,' Hattie said. 'If you want to spend a bit more time in the archives when you've taken your photos, you're very welcome.'

'That's a great idea,' Doris whispered. 'Anne says William kept a journal. That's when she first met him, when he was writing his journal and she went in to clean his room, not realising he was there. If you can find it, it might help.'

'Actually, I'd love to see the archives again. Now we've got this letter, it's fitted another piece into the puzzle,' Georgina said.

'I'll go and round Papa up,' Posy said, 'and we'll get going to Norwich.' She bit her lip. 'I have to admit, I'm dreading this.'

Sybbie squeezed her hand. 'I know, sweetheart. But Karen will just look as if she's sleeping. And I'll be there to support you – and your father,' she added.

Once Sybbie, Posy and Henry had left for the mortuary, Georgina took a few photographs and then left Bert playing with Hattie's spaniels while she looked in the archives.

'Sybbie and I looked through the box for the year William died. There wasn't a journal,' she mused.

'It took weeks to get news back from the Crimea,' Doris reminded her. 'And that would be just a letter. It would probably take even longer for his personal things to be returned to his family.'

'I'll try 1855,' Georgina said. 'Did Anne remember anything else?'

'Her wedding day,' Doris said. 'The sun was shining and the birds were singing their heads off. It was a very quiet ceremony, just herself in her best dress, William, William's aunt and uncle, and their two children with their nursemaid. She signed the wedding register with her own name, because William had taught her how to write. And they had the wedding breakfast at his family's house.'

'It sounds perfect,' Georgina said.

'They went to an inn in Newmarket for their honeymoon night, then took a coach travelling onward the next day to Norwich. They parted, then, and William stayed overnight in Norwich. He was going to meet his father to sort out some estate business, and he was going tell his father that they were married. She gave him their wedding certificate so he could prove to his father that the marriage was valid.'

'Of course it was valid. They had a licence.' But Georgina knew there hadn't been a happy ending. 'So she wasn't with him when he told his father?'

'No,' Doris said. 'She can't remember anything more. Just waking up and Hartington was different. Everything felt dark. I know what she means – it was like that for me, too, at Rookery Farm.'

'Let's see what we can find,' Georgina said.

She took the 1855 box from the shelf, set it on the table and carefully went through it.

The first thing of interest she found was from February 1855, a letter from William's captain, apologising that it had taken so long to return William's belongings but there had been an outbreak of sickness within his division. He enclosed William's watch, journal and personal effects.

And the very next thing, wrapped in brown paper, was a thin book, bound in black Morocco leather. Hardly daring to hope, Georgina held her breath as she opened the book. The paper was thin and delicate, and handwriting was neat and clear, in ink that had faded to brown.

The journal started in April 1854; clearly by this point

William was deeply in love with Anne. The entries told of how he taught her to read and write, how much she loved Wordsworth's poem about daffodils and they'd stolen a walk together behind the walled garden, finding their own daffodils to flutter and dance in the breeze.

William's description of the wedding day matched the one that Doris had given her from Anne.

And then came the entries that explained everything.

She read it with mounting horror. 'Oh, Doris. She must've trusted someone with their plans, and they betrayed her. Edward already knew about the wedding.'

'Was Edward the one who killed her?' Doris asked.

'I'm not sure. He confronted his father. Edward told William he already knew Anne was pregnant; he'd given her money and she'd gone. William said he'd find her and go after her – but, when he got back to Hartington, nobody had seen her and nobody knew where she was. One of the stableboys' – her voice hitched – 'said he'd overheard the grooms talking, the night before. They'd been drinking. And they said the old squire had given them the money and Anne Lusher wasn't going to be a problem anymore.' Georgina read on. 'William talked to the grooms, but they wouldn't tell him anything. And he had the final row with his father. Edward admitted he'd offered money to Anne but she didn't take it. That was the money he'd given the grooms. I think... maybe he paid them to do it,' Georgina said. 'And then bury her.'

Doris's voice was equally wobbly. 'Poor, poor Anne.'

Georgina wiped away the tears with the back of her hand. 'That's so sad. We can't even give her justice, because Edward died later the same year – well, he would've been dead by now anyway.'

'But her story's known now. She'll be able to rest,' Doris said.

Georgina carefully photographed the journal, marked

where it belonged in the box and took it to Hattie in the estate office.

'What have you found?' Hattie asked.

'William's journal. It fills in the rest of the story. But it's absolutely tragic,' Georgina said.

Hattie read through it, and her blue eyes welled up, too. 'That poor girl. My great-whatever-uncle was a monster. How could he have done that?'

'I'm not sure if he did it himself or just gave the orders,' Georgina said.

'Given the times he lived in, he probably gave the orders. He wouldn't sully his hands with a servant,' Hattie said, shaking her head. 'I'm not surprised William left. I think I would've done so, too, in his shoes.' She closed the journal with a sigh. 'I wish William and Anne had had the chance to grow old together. I know obviously that would've changed things for my branch of the family and we wouldn't have been living here, but...' She shook her head. 'That's so sad.'

'At least you know who she is now and you can put her to rest,' Georgina said.

'We'll ask if the vicar can bury her in William's plot, where she belongs,' Hattie said. 'I know his body isn't at Hartington – he's buried somewhere in the Crimea, with the men he fought alongside – but his memorial stone's here. She needs to be next to him, and her name recorded. Anne, beloved wife of William.'

'That'd be good,' Georgina said.

'I can hardly believe what's happened this week. Two bodies discovered here on one day. And both of them had been murdered.' Hattie bit her lip. 'I presume you know Karen's death wasn't an accident?'

'Sybbie told me. It's gone no further than me,' Georgina reassured her. 'Yes, I have a lot of friends who work in the media, but I don't gossip. You don't need to worry.'

'Thank you. I don't understand why she was at the ice

house in the first place, let alone who could've killed her.' Hattie's face was pinched. 'Aunt Syb said you're close to Colin, but you didn't say anything to the police about Posy's outburst, did you? I know she was angry about the Red Book, but she wouldn't have *killed* Karen. That's not who Posy is. She would've confronted Karen – threatened her with legal action or something if she didn't get the book back immediately.'

'I did tell Colin the Red Book was missing, in case it had some connection to Karen's death, but I know Posy didn't mean what she said, so I didn't tell him about that,' Georgina said. 'Actually, I've been thinking about it. You said Karen's split from Ellen's dad was acrimonious. If he thought there was still unfinished business between them, do you think he might have come here after her?'

Hattie's eyes widened. 'That never even occurred to me! I don't have a clue who he is, so I wouldn't have recognised him if he'd come here as one of the garden visitors or something. And why would he have waited four years to come here?'

Georgina grimaced. 'Maybe he couldn't come any earlier.'

'Because he was in prison or something, you mean?' Hattie frowned. 'There was a guy hanging about at the wedding, but none of us recognised him. Do you think that might've been her ex?' She shook her head. 'Ignore me. Obviously Karen's the only one who could've answered that.' She bit her lip. 'Oh, my God. If that *was* her ex, maybe he threatened Papa, and Karen was taking things from the house to pay him off so he'd leave Papa alone. And all this time Posy and I thought maybe she was selling things to make herself a – well, you know, a cushion, before leaving Papa. Maybe we got her wrong.' She wrapped her arms round herself. 'It would explain why Papa's been so difficult lately, if he's worried about Karen's ex.'

'You need to tell Colin anything you know about him,' Georgina said gently.

'That's just it,' Hattie said. 'I don't know anything about him, not even his name.'

'Colin can find out. Actually, I could probably find out, through the genealogy sites,' Georgina said.

'Would you?'

'Of course,' Georgina said. 'How's your dad doing?'

'Not great,' Hattie admitted. 'Though at the same time he doesn't seem to be quite... so all over the place as he was. He went to pieces when Mummy died, and Posy and I expected him to go to pieces again – which he has, sort of, but at the same time he's brighter. Easier to be with than he's been for months.'

'Did you manage to talk him into seeing the doctor?' Georgina asked.

'Not yet. And I can hardly ask Aunt Syb to nag him for me. He wouldn't listen to her.' She sighed. 'At least I can make sure he takes his meds. I think he's been forgetting them – he says all medication is rubbish and the doctor's a quack, but that's bluster to cover up the fact he hasn't been taking them properly. I bought one of those boxes that holds a daily dose for a week, so I can bring that day's meds in to him with a cup of tea and a digestive biscuit at ten every morning. At least I know now he's taking them and he's not going to get ill.' She wrinkled her nose. 'Sorry, that's hugely tactless of me. You said your children were about same age as Posy and me, and I'm not saying that just because you're over fifty you're hopeless. It's just... you kind of worry about your parents once they get to a certain age.'

Georgina smiled. 'I understand, love. I've been in the sandwich generation myself. My mum has dementia. She's in the early stages, so she lives in sheltered housing. I felt really guilty about leaving her in London, but she's happy where she is. Apart from the fact it's taken a layer of worry off my shoulders, because I don't analyse every moment I spend with her and wonder if I'm doing enough to look after her properly, it wouldn't have been fair to uproot her from a place where she's settled – away from her friends, her routines, and medics who've got to know her. My daughter drops in to see her every week, and I do regular Zoom calls and visits.' She smiled again. 'You've got a point about men being too stubborn to take their meds properly. I think my dad would've been a nightmare.'

'That actually makes me feel a bit better,' Hattie admitted.

TWENTY-FOUR

'I'm not going to ask how the viewing went,' Larissa said.

'I don't think it's anyone's favourite part of the job,' Colin said, 'but we need to support the bereaved.'

'I've got some news to cheer you up, though. The bank sent the CCTV through – a lot quicker than we hoped they would,' Mo said. 'And we have results.'

'Seriously? Already? I thought it'd be a dead end,' Colin admitted.

'The tech team say we owe them beer,' Larissa said. 'The thing is, people don't use ATMs as much as they used to. About forty per cent less than before lockdown, apparently. And more people are doing their bank transactions with apps – you can pay cheques into your account on your phone.'

'But you can't pay in cash,' Mo said. 'Which is why the bank could narrow it down for us on those three dates. The techs have stripped out the bits where there wasn't any activity. Here's the first one.'

'Three people of interest,' Colin said, when the short film had finished.

'This is the second set,' Larissa said.

Colin's eyes narrowed. 'The person with a peaked baseball cap – we can't see their face, as they've got a hand over their face to block the camera. Is that the same person as the baseball-cap wearer on the first set of people?'

'Wait until you see the third set, guv,' Mo said.

The baseball-cap wearer was clearly paying cash in when someone accidentally knocked into them, giving the camera a glimpse of the baseball-cap wearer's face, showing a couple of days' worth of stubble.

'Male, then. Can we be sure that person's the same in all three films?' Colin asked.

'The tech team did measurements. They're sure,' Larissa said.

'But it gets better. The bit where we actually see his face in the third film,' Mo said. 'The tech team enhanced it. They're running it through the database right now, to see if we get a retrospective facial recognition match.

'This,' Colin said, 'is about the best news we could get. I'm definitely buying them that beer.'

And it got better still, half an hour later, when the tech team rang Colin.

'We have a match,' Colin said, smiling, when he ended the call. 'And guess what? Gavin Hewitt has been sentenced for receiving stolen goods in the past.'

'He has form, then,' Mo said. 'I'd say, with the evidence from those deposits, we can arrest him on suspicion of receiving very recently stolen goods from a domestic burglary, selling them on and putting the money he got for them into Karen's account; if there are deposits in his account, too, we've got him.'

'Medium value items,' Larissa said, 'and we have three of them. There's a very high chance he's been involved in the previous transactions, too, even though we won't have the bank CCTV for them.'

'We'll be looking at a custodial sentence for that: maybe a couple of years,' Colin said. 'But, more importantly, we need to find out exactly where he was on Sunday and if he was the one who met Karen at the ice house. I'll have a word with London and see if they can bring him in for questioning. Then I'll talk to Hattie Berry. There must be some kind of inventory at the house, for insurance purposes if nothing else. If we can cross-check that with what's on display in the house, we might be able to find out what's missing.'

'We're a couple of steps closer, guv,' Larissa said with a smile.

'Do we have anything from the forensics team on that letter sent to Hartington Hall?' Colin asked.

'A couple of blurred prints, but nothing that matches with the database,' Mo said. 'It was posted in Brighton.'

'Which doesn't necessarily mean the inkstand was bought in Brighton – or that whoever bought it lives in Brighton, either.' Colin frowned. 'We need to find a link between Gavin, Karen and the inkstand.'

'Shall I ask the team at Brighton to come up with a list of likely dealers?' Larissa asked.

Colin nodded. 'That's a good place to start.'

* * *

Henry, Posy and Sybbie came back from the mortuary.

'Let me get you a cup of tea, Papa,' Hattie said.

Henry shook his head. 'I can't face anything. I just want to go into the barn.'

'Lord Ellingham, perhaps I could join you?' Georgina suggested. 'Your cars could be quite an attraction to visitors.

Maybe I could take some photographs of you with them, and you could tell me a bit about them.'

Henry looked surprised but nodded.

Georgina walked with him, not pushing him to talk, and he seemed to relax slightly.

'So the girls want my cars on their website?' he asked as he unlocked the door.

'Maybe a couple of shots of you with the bonnet up, peering at an engine,' Georgina said. She glanced at the cars; all of them were vintage sports cars, and all but one of them gleamed as if they'd been freshly polished. The one that wasn't shiny was set above a pit; clearly it was in the process of being restored.

'Did you restore all of them yourself?' Georgina asked.

'From a heap of rust, in some cases,' Henry said. 'I often wonder, if I'd had a son, if he might've been interested in my cars.' He looked disappointed. 'The girls aren't. At all.'

'I'm afraid I don't know a lot about cars,' Georgina said. 'I just drive something that's reliable. But I do enjoy going out in Sybbie's convertible.'

'The MGA,' Henry said. 'Lovely thing. You'd think it'd give us a point of contact, wouldn't you? But Sybbie's – well, Sybbie.'

'She loves her family, her dogs and her garden,' Georgina said quietly. 'And she's been a good friend to me.'

Henry's face tightened, as if he was about to lump Georgina in with the other women he didn't get on with.

Georgina decided not to give him the chance. 'After my husband died, I found it a bit hard to handle the world. It's why I moved from London to Norfolk. All the memories just haunted me. Sybbie helped me... connect with people again, I suppose.'

He looked contemplative, as if deciding how much of a connection her widowed state gave them. 'How long ago did your husband die?'

'Just over two years now,' Georgina said.

He nodded. 'But I'm guessing you know to the day, the same as I do. I miss Millie every single day.' He winced. 'Which sounds bad. Especially because Karen's just died.'

It did sound bad. But Georgina didn't comment.

Was this what would make Henry open up to her?

He flicked some imaginary dust off the bonnet of one of the cars. 'I know I rushed into marrying Karen. She was kind to me, and that was what I thought I wanted.' He looked away. 'But I should've considered how hard it would be for her here. How everyone would compare her to Millie – and everyone loved Millie so much. She was one of these people who made the world feel full of sunshine, even when it was raining.'

'Stephen was, too,' she said. 'And I still watch clips of him on the internet. There are a few of him reading Shakespeare's sonnets or one of the famous soliloquys.'

'Millie liked Shakespeare. She was thinking about making a Shakespeare garden. We don't have any connection with Stratford, of course, but she liked his flowers. That bit about the place where the wild thyme grows.'

I know a bank where the wild thyme blows... But she didn't correct him. This wasn't the time to be pedantic. '*A Midsummer Night's Dream,*' she said instead.

'I wouldn't know. Not very cultured. I leave that to the girls,' he said. He sighed. 'Karen didn't really like that sort of thing. She liked shopping, and the bustle of the city. It was too quiet for her here. If you haven't been brought up in the countryside, it takes a bit of getting used to.' He grimaced. 'I shouldn't have married her. It was selfish. Not just to her: I was just so miserable without Millie, I didn't stop to think how my girls would feel. There's a brick wall between us now and I don't know how to take it down.'

'You could try telling them what you've just told me,' Georgina said.

'They'll think I'm a silly old fool. Well, they already think that. Hattie even bought me one of those weekly pillbox things for my tablets, because she thinks I'm not capable of sorting them out for myself.'

'To be fair,' Georgina said, 'I would've done the same for Stephen. He got so wrapped up in his work that he'd forget. I would probably have put an alarm on his phone, too, to remind him.' She smiled at Henry. 'I bet you forget time when you're working on your cars.'

'I do,' he admitted. 'Maybe I did forget to take my tablets.' He shrugged. 'Don't like to think I'm getting old.'

'Taking the tablets will help you stay well – and young,' Georgina said. 'Posy and Hattie worry about you.'

'I know, and I feel guilty. It's half the reason I snap at them. Never been good at all that kind of stuff.' He flapped a dismissive hand.

Georgina smiled. 'Well, you can do something practical for them. Let me take your photo, and you tell me about your cars.'

Henry was enthusiastic on the subject of his beloved sports cars, and Georgina was surprised to find they'd been on the shoot for an hour.

'Sorry. I get carried away with my cars,' Henry said.

'Like me in my darkroom,' Georgina said.

'Funny, I didn't think you'd be like this. So easy to talk to,' Henry said.

'It goes with the job,' Georgina said. 'When you take a portrait of someone, the best shots happen when they're talking to you about what they really love. So I like to get people talking to me.'

Henry gave her a rueful smile. 'You're kind. And I probably don't deserve it. I made my wife unhappy, and I've made my daughters unhappy. I know I've got fences to mend, but I don't know where to start.'

'Talk to them,' Georgina advised. 'Tell them you want

things to be better between you and they'll meet you halfway. Ellen, too.'

'Ellen. Poor kid. We're all the family she has, now. Not much of a bargain. Karen said... Well, it doesn't matter anymore.'

Henry locked up the barn, and they headed back to the kitchen.

'I think I'll go for a lie-down,' Henry said.

Ellen had apparently come back from the woods just after Georgina had gone to the barn with Henry, but had gone straight to her room.

'We'll let you get on,' Sybbie said.

Hattie met Georgina's eyes and gave a small nod, as if to say that she'd fill Posy in on what had happened with Anne and William a bit later on.

Sybbie said goodbye to her goddaughters, and Georgina had just opened the back door of her car, ready to coax Bert into the back seat so she could clip his harness to the seat belt, when she became aware of a very strong scent of lavender. A second later, Bert gave a sudden bark and dashed off.

'Oh, Bert, now's really not the time for a fit of the zoomies,' Georgina said, and dashed after him.

Two seconds later, there was a crash behind her. She stopped dead and spun round, to see a stone ball lying in pieces on the gravel – in exactly the place where she'd just been standing to coax Bert into the car...

TWENTY-FIVE

'Oh, my God! Georgie, are you all right?' Sybbie shouted.

It felt as if her tongue was glued to the roof of her mouth, and she couldn't answer.

And then her knees buckled.

'Georgie. Oh, my God. I can't believe what nearly happened!' Hattie wrapped her arms round Georgina. 'Come on. Into the kitchen with you. Hot, sweet tea and a sit-down. Bert, *here*,' she ordered, and the spaniel pattered over, pushing his nose into Georgina's shaking hand.

'Everything feels blurry,' Georgina whispered.

'It's the shock,' Posy said. 'Let me make that tea. Did any of the gravel or a piece of stone fly up and hit you? Does anything hurt?'

'No, I...' Georgina rubbed a hand across her eyes. 'That was too close for comfort.'

None of them put it into words, but she knew they were all thinking it. That stone ball could've killed her.

'What – where did it come from?' she asked.

'The roof, I think,' Hattie said. 'I'll call the builder and get him to take a look up there, in case anything else is loose.'

'What's happened?' Henry asked, walking into the kitchen. 'Did I hear screaming?'

'One of the finials came off the roof and just about missed Georgie,' Posy said.

'Good Lord.' Henry stared at her, looking as shocked as she felt. 'Are you all right?'

'A bit shaken,' Georgina said. 'But I'll be fine.'

Ellen came down, too, clearly having heard the screams, and Hattie filled her in about what had happened.

'Sorry for scaring you all. I just panicked a bit,' Georgina said.

'But you could've been k—' Ellen bit the word back.

'Well, I wasn't,' Georgina said.

'Anne saw someone on the parapet,' Doris said, her voice sounding shaky. 'She told me to call Bert. If she hadn't...'

Saved by a ghost or two and a spaniel. Not that Georgina would be able to explain it to anyone, but she'd never felt so grateful in her entire life.

Posy insisted on making toasted cheese sandwiches for everyone, on the ground that they all needed comfort food.

When Georgina had finally stopped shaking, Sybbie put Bert in the back of the car and drove them home. 'My insurance will cover me to drive this. Don't worry, the last claim I had was a chipped windscreen and that was about ten years ago.'

Georgina couldn't summon up the energy to chat on the way home, and Sybbie simply spoke into the car's hands-free system to play classical music. 'Pachelbel's Canon. I don't care if it's overplayed – it's the best thing to drive to in the snow, dear girl – all nice and regular, no surprises, and you can just *breathe* to it.'

'It's not snowing, Sybbie. It's July.'

'I know, but I'm not playing Vivaldi's 'Summer'. It's a

stifling, horrible piece – precisely because he was asthmatic. This is lovely. Hum along, dear girl. That's it.'

'She's right,' Doris said. 'This is all calming and lovely. Hum.'

Georgina found herself humming through the piece, followed by Bach's Prelude Number One in C. By the time Sybbie pulled up outside Rookery Farm – where Bernard was waiting for them in his 4X4 – she was feeling calmer.

'Thank you for driving me home, Sybbie,' Georgina said.

Sybbie patted her shoulder. 'It was the very least I could do. Now, do you want Bernard and me to stay with you for a bit?'

'I'll be fine,' Georgina said. 'Though I don't think I can face Pilates class tonight.'

'No, you *need* to come,' Sybbie argued. 'If you stay here on your own, you'll have too much space to think. You need endorphins and then a big glass of wine in the Red Lion. It's Cesca's turn to drive, so no excuses – we'll pick you up at five forty-five and then collect Jodie.'

'All right, my dear?' Bernard asked. 'Sybbie told me what happened. Enough to shake up anyone.'

'I'm fine, thanks,' Georgina fibbed.

Though as soon as she'd let herself and Bert in through the kitchen door and Sybbie and Bernard had driven off, she sat at the table with her face in her hands and sobbed.

'Georgie,' Doris said. 'You're safe. It's all right.'

'You and Anne saved me. I'll never be able to thank you enough.' Georgina dragged in a breath. 'Can you thank her for me?'

'Of course,' Doris promised.

'If I'd died without the chance to tell Bea and Will and Mum that I love them,' Georgina said, the words feeling as if they'd been ripped from inside her. 'If I hadn't said goodbye to them... That's how it was for Stephen. He didn't get to say goodbye.'

'Neither did I, and it's pants,' Doris said. 'But you'd have found a way to tell them. Just as I got to tell Jack, through you.'

'Stephen hasn't found a way to tell me,' Georgina whispered.

'He will. When it's time,' Doris said. 'Right now, you're going to have a big sip of water, and then you're going to do those calming breathing exercises you lot learned at Pilates – and you *are* going to class tonight, by the way. It'll help you.' She waited until Georgina had filled a glass with water and taken a couple of sips. 'Breathe in for four.' She counted. 'Hold for four.' She counted again. 'Out for eight.'

Ten box breaths later, Georgina was feeling calmer.

'Better?' Doris asked.

'Yes,' Georgina admitted.

'Good.' Doris paused. 'I'm glad you're still here with me, than *here* with me. And I know that's not coming out right.'

'I know what you mean. And I'm glad, too,' Georgina said. 'I'm not ready to... not yet. There are things I still need to do. Things I want to be here for.'

'Will and Bea finding someone to share their lives with. Weddings. Grandchildren,' Doris said.

Georgina nodded. 'Things you wanted, too, and never got the chance to have.'

'Hey. I'm used to living vicariously. I've got my vicarious dog in Bert. I'll start working on the vicarious grandchildren, next.' Doris paused. 'Does that word come from vicar?'

'Probably.'

Doris coughed. 'I can't exactly check it on a phone myself.'

Georgina knew what her friend was doing: trying to take her mind off things. But she'd always found etymology interesting, so she went along with it. 'All right.' She looked it up. 'Vicar, from Latin *vicarius*, meaning substitute.'

'But spelled slightly differently,' Doris said, clearly looking over her shoulder.

TWENTY-SIX

Colin was more than disappointed to learn that Gavin Hewitt had a cast-iron alibi for Sunday. He'd taken a corner too fast on his way home from the pub at lunchtime, come off his bicycle and ended up in the Emergency Department with a dislocated knee; the hospital records and CCTV both confirmed it. He simply wouldn't have had time to get to Norfolk to meet Karen Berry at the ice house; even if he'd managed to get to Norfolk, with a dislocated knee he certainly wouldn't have been capable of getting to the floor of the shaft to suffocate her.

But the team in London was going to talk to him further about the bank deposits, where the money had come from and why he was paying money into someone else's account.

Colin rang Hattie to ask her about an inventory.

'Yes, we do have one,' she confirmed. 'That's a good idea, to check it against what's in the house.'

'Maggie Pritchard might be able to help you,' Colin suggested.

'That's a big ask, considering what Papa and Karen did,' Hattie said. 'She knows that Posy and I never believed any of that nonsense, but even so.'

'It'll vindicate her,' Colin said. 'And maybe if your dad apologised...'

Hattie gave a wry laugh. 'Papa doesn't do apologies. He might mumble something at her that's meant to give the gist of one, and she'll know that as well as I do. But I'll ask her.' She paused. 'Have you spoken to Georgina today?'

'No. Why?'

'She has a theory that maybe Karen's ex might be behind this – that he'd been threatening to do something to Papa, so she stole things for him to keep Papa safe.'

'Coercion, you mean? OK. What can you tell me about Karen's ex?'

'Next to nothing,' Hattie said, 'but Georgina's going to have a look on a genealogy site for me and see what she can find. Though not today.'

Because Thursday evening was Pilates class followed by a drink in the Red Lion with her friends, Colin remembered, though he didn't say so out loud.

'Because we had a bit of a scare at lunchtime,' Hattie continued. 'There was a loose finial on the parapet, and it fell down. It just missed her.'

'What?' A loose finial? A big chunk of stone falling down from the roof? Something like that could have *killed* her, or at the very least hurt her badly. Colin went cold with horror. 'Is she all right?'

'Yes. Luckily, when it broke, none of the fragments hit her, but she was a bit shaken up. Well, you would be, wouldn't you? Anyway, Aunt Syb drove her home.'

This had happened *hours* ago. And Georgina hadn't told him.

Neither had Sybbie.

He wasn't sure if it made him feel more hurt or angry that they'd kept it from him.

'Thanks for letting me know,' he said, as mildly as he could.

'We've got the builder who normally does things for us coming out late this afternoon, to make sure there's nothing else loose on the roof and it's safe,' Hattie said. 'He'll do the repairs later.' She sighed. 'Once we've argued through the usual red tape with the conservation people, which always takes for ever.'

'All right. I'll wait to hear from you about the inventory and what's missing. Though as soon as you can would be helpful,' Colin said.

Georgina wasn't answering her phone. Neither was Sybbie.

Given that Hattie had said Sybbie had driven Georgina back to Little Wenborough, he assumed they were together and sent them both a text telling them to call him if they needed him.

Georgina didn't call him, but Sybbie rang him back a little bit later to fill him in on the situation.

'And you're sure it was an accident, Sybbie?' he asked.

'Yes, of course. You know what old houses are like. Falling to bits, half the time,' she said crisply. 'Really, Colin. I do think your job makes you a tad oversuspicious.'

'Does it?' he asked, and waited.

There was a pause. 'Do you know something to make you think it might *not* be an accident?' Sybbie asked.

'I can't discuss a case,' he reminded her.

'But?'

'It's a coincidence,' he said, 'and I don't like coincidences. I haven't forgotten when Georgie was poisoned.'

'Neither have I, dear boy.' Sybbie huffed out a breath. 'She'll kill me for this, because you know how independent she is, but maybe you should drop in this evening to see her and give her a hug. Cesca's driving us to Pilates tonight. We're going to the Red Lion for the usual quick drink afterwards, but Jodie has to be back for Harry and she's the first drop, so we'll be back at Georgie's by, what, eight?'

'I'll be there,' he promised.

And he was waiting in his car three minutes before Cesca drove up the shingled driveway.

'Oh, good. It looks as if we're leaving you in safe hands *and* safe paws,' Sybbie drawled, with one of her trademark mischievous smiles. 'Call you tomorrow, dear girl.'

'Did you know about this, Cesca?' Georgina asked.

Cesca spread her hands. 'Well, that macaroni cheese I brought when I picked you up *was* a two-portion one,' she said.

'This is all an immense fuss over nothing,' Georgina grumbled, but climbed out of the car.

'Enjoy your dinner, guys,' Cesca said, waved to them, and turned the car round.

When they were out of sight, Colin wrapped his arms round Georgina. 'Why didn't you tell me what happened at Hartington?'

'Because I knew you'd fuss.'

He coughed. 'And the *last* time I fussed?'

'You were right about the poison. I'll give you that. But this was an accident. Hartington Hall's ancient, Colin. The roof's been up there for hundreds of years. Tiles and slates come a bit loose in bad weather, but you can't always see the problem – and eventually some little thing tips the balance and then they fall off.'

'It wasn't a tile, Georgie. It was a stone finial ball. And they don't fall off very easily,' he said, retrieving a bunch of stocks from his car and handing them to her. Her favourite ones, pink and purple.

'Thank you. These are so lovely.' She buried her face in the flowers, inhaling the sweet, spicy scent, then groaned. 'I think I'm going to change our name from the Musketeers to the Canaries – nothing to do with football, but because Sybbie and Cesca have certainly sung enough to you tonight. I bet Jodie was in on it, too.'

'No, actually, she wasn't.' He backtracked. 'Wait. You call yourselves the *Musketeers*?'

'It's our WhatsApp group name,' she said, unlocking the kitchen door and opening it for Bert's rapturous welcome before sliding the key into the lock on the inside of the kitchen door. 'Have you eaten?'

'Canteen sandwiches,' he said with a grimace.

'A late supper of macaroni cheese for two it is, then,' she said. 'Thankfully microwaveable.'

She bustled about putting the dish in the microwave and slicing tomatoes while he laid the table, taking the cutlery from the drawer and the crockery from the shelves and putting a bowl for the salad next to her. It was the kind of domesticity he'd forgotten how much he enjoyed. And how much at peace he felt here, in this kitchen, with this woman. With her, he could breathe.

When the microwave pinged, she poured them both a glass of elderflower cordial, topped up with sparkling water from the fridge, and they sat down at the kitchen table to eat. 'I really am all right, Colin. And your day can't exactly have been great, at the mortuary.'

'No, it wasn't,' Colin said.

'I talked to Henry, by the way. I used the excuse of shooting him with his cars.' She gave him a mischievous grin. 'As in *photographic* shoot.'

Colin narrowed his eyes at her. 'I know. I only made that mistake once. And you're trying to distract me.'

'Don't you want to know if Henry told me anything useful?'

'Yes,' he admitted, 'but I'm also cross with you for not telling me about that finial.'

'Because I knew you'd make a fuss. And you're not to tell Bea or Will,' she warned.

'As long as you promise *you'll* tell them,' he parried.

'All right,' she agreed.

'So what did Henry have to tell you?'

'He admitted marrying Karen was a mistake, because she never settled at Hartington. And he's admitted that he's rubbish at remembering to take his tablets. And that he's messed things up with his girls. I feel a bit sorry for him, actually.'

'Sybbie doesn't like him,' Colin said.

'Sybbie doesn't have patience with him,' Georgina corrected. 'And all that "his lordship" thing is an act. Henry knows he's not good at the stuff he ought to be good at, and that's why he can be obnoxious. Talk to him about his cars and he's a different man.'

'The photographer getting to the root of her subject?'

She nodded. 'Actually, I was thinking... I'd like to photograph you.'

And get him to spill all the stuff inside his head – the horror of the case that had nearly broken him? No way. 'Maybe,' he said instead. 'Anything else from Henry?'

'No. But I hope he's going to have a heart-to-heart with his daughters.' She smiled at him. 'Before all the, um, *excitement*, I'd had quite a successful day, if a bit upsetting.'

'Upsetting?' Colin asked.

'William and Anne. Hattie gave me the photographs of the letter that was found in the silver inkstand. I'm assuming the inkstand was stolen, as the letter was returned anonymously?'

'Yes. And the forensics team couldn't find anything useful from the packaging.' He sighed. 'I have a couple of lines of enquiry to follow up. Actually, have you ever seen this man?' He took his phone out of his pocket and showed her a picture of Gavin Hewitt.

'No,' she said. 'Have you asked the Berrys?'

'I'm planning to ask them tomorrow,' he said. 'Before I distracted you, you were telling me about your research.'

'I found William's journal.'

When she'd finished filling him in with what she'd learned,

he winced. 'So either Edward killed Anne himself when she wouldn't take his money and go away, or he paid the grooms to kill her – and then paid them a bit more to bury her. Did he really think William would cave in and marry the heiress, after that?' He blew out a breath. 'I'm not surprised William went off to fight a war instead. I would've done the same.'

She looked at him, then reached over to squeeze his hand. 'Colin, are you all right?'

He went very still. He knew she was perceptive; from spending so much time behind a lens and coaxing out little details, photographers tended to see things that other people didn't.

'It just touched a nerve,' he said, shrugging it off.

And then he made the fatal mistake of adding, 'Parental expectations.'

TWENTY-SEVEN

Georgina waited, saying nothing.

Colin knew this one. It was a standard technique he'd been taught years ago: leave a gap, and eventually the other person would speak to fill it. Even though he knew the drill and should've been able to keep his mouth shut, he could feel his resistance crumbling, feel the words rising up and spilling out. 'I was supposed to join my parents' chambers. They're criminal barristers – well, *were*, before they retired,' he said. 'Except I was seconded to a project in my final year at uni, and I found that I liked police work.'

She still said nothing.

He sighed. 'They were disappointed in me.' And it had always weighed heavily on him. The guilt that he'd let them down.

'It wasn't very fair of them to expect to run your life as well as their own,' she said, her tone mild. 'You have every right to make your own choices.'

'When it all went wrong in London,' he said, 'they saw it as vindication of what they'd always thought. If I'd done what they wanted and joined the family firm in the first place, I wouldn't have...' Could he say the words? Should he?

They came out anyway. '...had a breakdown.'

She didn't flinch or back away, just looked at him with those clear-seeing green eyes. 'If they'd stuck you in a pigeonhole that didn't suit you, it would've started to feel smaller and smaller every year. The chances are you would've hit a problem a lot sooner than you did.'

'That's what Tess said. My little sister,' he said. 'She also didn't join the family firm.'

'What does she do?'

'She's a psychologist,' he said. 'She works with criminal profiling. So we all worked in the same kind of area, I suppose. Just it wasn't what my parents had planned for me. Or for Tess.'

'When I first met you,' she said, 'I thought Stephen would've cast you as Claudius.'

'Hamlet's wicked uncle?' He stared at her, stung that she'd picked a character he loathed. 'But that's not—'

'—who you are. I know that now,' she said. 'But you turned up here, all handsome and arrogant.'

He ignored the semi-compliment. 'One of my girlfriends at university was an English student. She did her dissertation on *Hamlet*. She always used to say that Claudius is corrupt.'

'Claudius throws his weight around,' Georgina corrected, 'and that's what you were like when I first met you. I didn't think for one second that you were corrupt.' She reached over to squeeze his hand. 'You're honest and you want to make things right. You stand up for those who don't have a voice, instead of using yours to manipulate others.' She raised an eyebrow. 'If you *had* been more like Claudius, you would've made a good criminal barrister.'

He narrowed his eyes at her. 'Explain.'

'Skilled with language and with an eye on strategic moves,' she said. 'Your language is OK, but you're not Claudius. You're not trying to scoop every promotion going, or any promotion at the expense of other people.'

'What am I, then? Hamlet?' He narrowed his eyes at her.

'No. I haven't quite worked that out, yet. Maybe Benedick – who's one of my very favourite characters,' she mused.

'Benedick?' Colin scoffed. 'I know that play.' Mainly because he'd once really fancied Emma Thompson and he'd watched the film of *Much Ado* a few times over the years. 'He loves himself.'

'He stands up for Hero and he calls out his best friend on bad behaviour,' she said. 'The same way you stand up for people who don't have a voice anymore. Even if they're flawed and difficult, like Karen Berry, you make sure they're heard.'

He stared at her, taking in what she'd just said.

She really, really understood him. And that was huge.

'I think that might be one of the nicest things anyone has ever said to me,' he said, hearing the hoarseness in his voice but for once not minding the weakness it implied. He drew her hand up to his mouth, pressed a kiss against her palm and folded his fingers over it. 'Benedick. Though you're not as disdainful as Beatr—' He stopped. 'She's your favourite Shakespeare heroine, isn't she? That's why you called your daughter Beatrice.'

'Yes. And obviously Will was named after the Bard himself. But Stephen and I never expected Will or Bea to act,' she said gently, 'or to be a photographer or a journalist. We wanted them to follow their hearts and do what they loved, knowing that we'd support them. Bea was a born actor and wants to be the Beatrice of her generation, and Will's happy in his lab – though Stephen nicknamed him "Hubble".'

'After the telescope?' Colin asked.

'No,' she said. 'After the misquote everyone makes about Macbeth's witches. It's "double, double toil and trouble", not "hubble, bubble". A research chemist doesn't spend all his time mixing up weird potions, even though everyone thinks he does. Which is the point of the nickname.'

'I think,' he said, 'I would've liked Stephen.'

Georgina's smile warmed him all the way through. 'I think he would've liked you, too.'

'Good.' And, weirdly, it *mattered*. Because she was letting him close enough to admit how he felt about her. 'Though I worry about you, Georgie. First being poisoned, and now having a big chunk of masonry landing way too close to you for comfort.'

'It was an accident – well, the *masonry* was – and I'm fine,' she said.

'Are you?' he asked. 'Because you're a thinker, Georgie. And when you've had a near-miss, the might-have-beens can cast a long shadow.'

'You're right,' she said. 'I did have a bit of a meltdown after Sybbie brought me home. But I've cried it out of my system and Bert washed my face a few times. I'm fine.' She looked at him. 'Have you had near-misses?'

'It goes with the job,' he said lightly.

She folded her arms and gave him a speaking look.

'A couple of nicks, a couple of fractures, a few grazes.' He wasn't going to tell her the details. He remembered how much Marianne, his ex-wife, had worried when he'd been injured in the line of duty.

But it was the other might-have-beens that really haunted him.

The cases he hadn't been able to crack.

The young woman, almost the same age as Cathy, who'd died so horribly – and he hadn't saved her.

He pushed the thoughts away. This wasn't about him. This was about Georgina. 'Do Bea and Will know about Hartington?'

'Bea does, because she found William and Anne's marriage licence records for me,' Georgina said.

He narrowed his eyes at her. 'That isn't what I meant, and you know it.'

She sighed. 'No. And you're not to join the canaries and tell them. I meant what I said earlier, Colin. I don't want them worrying. I need you to promise you won't say anything.'

'And I meant what I said, too. You should tell them,' he said. 'If nothing else, to reassure them that you're OK. But all right. I'll keep it to myself.' He paused. 'Do you want me to stay tonight? I can sleep on the sofa.'

She smiled, stood up and kissed him before she cleared the plates from the table. 'No. I know full well you're planning to go back to work when you leave here, and you need to get some proper rest, not wrecking your back on my sofa.' She kissed him again. 'And I'm not ready to spend the night with you, yet.'

His skin went hot at the thought. 'Sorry. I wasn't being pushy. Well, I was. But I didn't mean *that*.' He sighed. 'We're taking this slowly. We agreed that way suits both of us. And I...'

'I know,' she said, and for a moment it felt as if she could see into his soul.

'Just promise me you'll let Bert sleep by your bed tonight.'

'He's already rescued me once today. If he hadn't barked and run in a different direction, I wouldn't have followed him. I was lucky.' Though there was a wobble in her voice, and he knew what was going through her head. He'd been there, too. A tiny amount of space could make a huge amount of difference. If she'd still been standing in that one spot instead of chasing after her dog, she could've been in hospital with a fractured skull. Or worse.

'Luckily for you, Bert seems to have a sixth sense,' he said dryly.

'There is that.' There was a strange expression on her face, but he couldn't quite work out what it was.

'Lock all your doors and windows tonight,' he said.

'Colin, it's July! It's going to be hot and disgustingly muggy tonight. I need my window open.'

'Then let Bert sleep in your room.'

'For pity's sake, nobody's ever going to get through the bedroom window.'

'It's a sash window. They're easy to op—'

'*Not* helping, Colin,' she said, raising her eyebrows at him. 'Anyway, Bert will bark if anyone turns up.'

'You don't wear your hearing aids when you're asleep. How will you hear him?'

'*They'll* hear him, and that'll deter them,' she said.

'I could work remotely. On your sofa. In one of your spare rooms.'

'No,' she said. 'I can cope on my own.'

'You're being stubborn.'

She sighed. 'Let me tell you a story. About five years ago, my hearing aids went wrong. It was some computery glitch or other, and they just packed up. I hadn't noticed how poor my hearing had become until I found myself without sound. I was meant to be going on a shoot that morning and, although I thought I could probably muddle through the job by lipreading or getting my clients to write things down, and then drop in to the audiology department to get my aids fixed later, I got to the front door and I realised just how much I couldn't hear. If a cyclist rode behind me on the path, even if they actually used their bell, I wouldn't hear it and they might crash into me. I couldn't hear anything at all behind me. Someone could barge past me and knock me into the road, or off an escalator. I couldn't even pop to the corner shop for a pint of milk, let alone handle going on the Tube. Feeling that vulnerable scared me – and I actually called Stephen to ask him to come to the hospital with me. Of course he dropped everything and did it, and he rearranged the shoot for me, too. But I lost my independence for that day. I felt *vulnerable*. And I hated every second of it.'

Now he understood. She needed to cope with this on her own. Giving in to the fear now would mean she'd feel that vulnerability again.

'I *minded*, Colin,' she said softly. 'It made me realise that one day I won't have my independence anymore. That I'll have to rely on other people to help me, and I'll feel like a nuisance. And that's not who I want to be.'

'I get that,' he said. 'But call me if you need to. Just so you know, you're on the list of people who can call me at stupid o'clock in the morning and I won't have a hissy fit.'

'Thank you,' she said.

But he knew she was going to be stubborn and not call him. 'And, so we're very clear on this, the offer's for *support*, not for smothering.'

This time, she kissed him. Long and slow and sweet. 'All right. I'll call you if I'm worried.'

It was enough to persuade him that she meant it. That she trusted him with herself. And it made him feel as if something was cracking around the edges of his heart.

'Thank you,' he said, and made a fuss of Bert to stop himself saying something soppy and embarrassing.

TWENTY-EIGHT

Later that evening, Georgina still couldn't sleep. She ended up sitting downstairs on the sofa with her laptop, Bert cuddled up beside her and a mug of hot milk and honey on the coffee table next to her.

'You need to rest,' Doris said.

'I know,' Georgina said.

'And blue light is bad for you. It blocks the body's production of melatonin and that messes with your sleep.'

Georgina chuckled. 'You read too many articles.'

'Over *your* shoulder, I might add. And blue light doesn't affect me in the same way it affects you,' Doris pointed out.

'Doris, it's pointless me lying upstairs, awake and fretting. I might as well do something useful,' Georgina said. She checked her email. 'Oh, good – Billy the butcher's come back to me.'

'The last thing he heard, Irene Taylor was still going strong and living in a nursing home in Norwich,' Doris said, reading the email over Georgina's shoulder. 'He thinks it's called Lake View.'

'I'll call them tomorrow and see if she's there, or if she's moved somewhere else,' Georgina said. 'Let's see what they say about opening hours and visiting times.' She found the website, checked the details and frowned. 'Even if I can visit, it looks as if this is a specialist dementia home.'

'You said yourself, your mum's pin-sharp when it comes to the old days and it's just the most recent months that she finds tricky,' Doris said. 'Maybe it's the same for Trev's mum.'

'I'll visit Irene Taylor and ask her what happened,' Georgina said, 'but I don't want you to get your hopes up that she'll remember. And I'm not entirely sure you should come with me when I go.'

'You can't leave me out. Not from *this*,' Doris said.

'If you were here physically,' Georgina said, 'I'd be saying the same thing. You've been hurt enough.'

Doris coughed. 'I'm dead, Georgie. She can hardly do anything else to me.'

'You still have feelings,' Georgina said gently. 'She was nasty enough to you at the time. I'm not giving her the chance to say anything else now.'

'Talk to Jack and Tracey about it,' Doris said. 'See what they think.'

Jack and Tracey Beauchamp, Doris's brother and sister-in-law, were the only other people who knew about Doris. They'd reacted badly when Georgina had first tried to tell them about the situation, but she'd finally convinced them that she was telling the truth – with a little help from Doris and the fireplace opposite where she was sitting right at that moment.

'All right. I'll talk to them tomorrow,' Georgina said. 'There's something else I want to look up. I promised Hattie I'd find out what I could about Karen's ex, and then at least we'll have a lead to give Colin when we ask if the ex might have anything to do with Karen's death.'

She flicked into the genealogy website and soon located Karen's wedding to Henry Berry in July 2019. Except Karen's surname wasn't what she expected to see. 'Karen Crawford, née

Newman. But Ellen's surname is Newman, not Crawford,' she said.

'Maybe Karen went back to her maiden name after the divorce, and changed Ellen's name, too,' Doris suggested.

'In that case, why was she still legally Karen Crawford when she married Henry? Why wasn't she Karen Newman?' Georgina asked.

'Don't ask me. Though don't they say the devil's in the details?'

'I'm going to trace this backwards,' Georgina said, and started making notes.

An hour later, she had a worrying list. Ellen Newman had been born in 2003 to Karen Newman; her father's name wasn't listed on the birth certificate.

Karen's first marriage had been to Robin Kennedy in 2012; he'd died two years later, aged sixty-four. The following year, she'd married Malcolm Crawford, who died in 2018, aged sixty-eight. And the year after that she'd married Henry Berry... who was currently sixty-five.

'Am I being unfairly judgemental?' asked Georgina, gesturing to her notepad.

'She married three older men in a row. Maybe she was looking for a father figure,' Doris said.

'But look at the pattern,' Georgina said. 'Her first marriage lasted two years before her husband died, and the second one lasted three years. She's been married to Henry for four years.'

'But Henry isn't the one who died,' Doris reminded her.

'I've got a nasty feeling about this,' Georgina said, and checked the death records.

Robin Kennedy had died from a stroke.

Malcolm Crawford had died from a heart attack. Georgina knew, from what had happened to Roland Garnett in her own barn a few months before, that a death could look like a heart attack but not actually be from natural causes.

'It could be a massive coincidence,' she said. 'But Henry takes medication... and Hattie thought her father might be developing another health condition. And she thinks he's been brighter since Karen died.' She took a deep breath. 'I thought maybe Karen was taking things from the house to pay off her ex because he was threatening Henry – but her ex is dead. So is the husband before that. What if she married men who are much older than her, men with a medical condition, and... speeded up the natural causes?'

'Did something to their medication, you mean? This is above my pay grade,' Doris said. 'I think you need to talk to Colin and get him to talk to a pathologist.'

But not at stupid o'clock in the morning, Georgina decided, whatever he'd said about not minding her calling him at any time. Tomorrow would be better.

TWENTY-NINE

The next morning, Georgina woke, feeling groggy, and was horrified to find it was half past eleven. How on earth had she slept in so late?

Well, that one was obvious – she'd been awake for most of the night before finally crawling back to bed.

She pulled on clothes over her pyjamas, sprayed herself with perfume, dragged a comb through her hair, brushed her teeth and put her hearing aids in. Mindful of what had happened to Doris, she negotiated her way carefully down the stairs, then rushed into the kitchen to let the dog out. 'Oh, Bert, why didn't you bark and wake me so I'd let you out for a wee?' she asked. 'And my poor guests in the barn are going to think I've deserted them!'

She followed Bert outside, ran down the garden path and headed for Rookery Barn, to find the kitchen door of the holiday cottage wide open, the washing machine going and Jodie cheerfully doing the cleaning. Jodie's seven-year-old son, Harry, was busy at the dining room table, building a car out of Lego.

'I'm so sorry. I should've been here to say goodbye to the

Parfitts,' Georgina said. The Parfitts were the first guests in the barn she hadn't said goodbye to before they left.

'Not a problem,' Jodie said. 'I was here to meet them before they left. I told them you'd been held up. You look as if you could do with a good strong coffee. Are you all right?'

'Yes. I just didn't sleep very well last night,' Georgina admitted.

'I'm not surprised, after the shock you had yesterday. If a lump of stone had barely missed my head, I wouldn't have been able to sleep, either. A lay-in will've done you some good.'

Dr Garnett, their less-than-congenial guest from a couple of months back, would've pedantically corrected Jodie's grammar to *lie-in*. Georgina, however, was concentrating on her friend's kindness and hugged her. 'I've not even had a shower yet – I just threw my clothes on over my PJs and squirted myself with perfume,' she confessed. 'Oh, God, I probably smell like Bert when he's rolled in something.'

'It's not as bad as *that*,' Jodie said with a grin. 'We've all done something like it at some point. At least you haven't got a hangover to make you feel worse! Go and have your shower. I'm sorting everything here. It's why I have a set of keys to the barn, remember?'

Georgina nodded.

'Georgie, can I play ball with Bert?' Harry asked, adding a swift, 'Please?'

'Of course you can,' Georgina said. 'Thanks, Jodie. I'll go and sort myself out – and was that a hint about coffee?'

'I wouldn't say no, if you're offering. Oh, and there's cake for you on the corner there.' She nodded towards a brown paper bag. 'Cesca says to ring her.'

* * *

'They're going through the inventory at Hartington Hall over the weekend,' Colin said into the phone. 'Can you get Gavin Hewitt back in, once we know what's definitely missing?'

'He'll be lawyered up by then, but it can't be helped,' his London counterpart said.

'You haven't managed to find out what links him to Karen Berry, apart from paying money into her account?'

'He says he's never heard of her.'

'Then why is he paying cash into her account? We've got him on CCTV, more than once,' Colin said. 'If he's fenced goods for her, then what's in it for him?'

'We'll keep pushing,' his London colleague said. 'As soon as you get images of what's been stolen, we can check among the usual crowd in case any of them have seen the stuff – or know who was looking for that sort of thing.'

'Do you think it was stolen to order?' Colin asked.

'Maybe.'

'I'll get the images over as soon as I can,' Colin promised.

Next, he wanted to check Gavin's photograph with the Berrys.

'I think he might be the guy who was hanging around at the wedding,' Posy said when he showed her the image. 'But I don't know who he is.' She looked worried. 'Is this Karen's ex?'

'It's a line of enquiry,' Colin said.

Hattie looked at the photograph, too. 'Yes, that's him. But I don't have a clue who he is, either.'

'Would your father know?' Colin asked. 'Or Ellen?'

'Ellen's not here. She's got a meeting with the bat people,' Hattie said. 'Papa's in the barn with his cars. I'll take you through.'

Lord Ellingham didn't look pleased to see Colin. 'What is it now?'

Colin bit back his impatience. According to Georgina,

Henry was much easier to handle if he was talking about cars. 'That's the most beautiful E-type,' he said instead.

'My pride and joy,' Henry said.

Shouldn't that be his daughters? But Colin went with it, and eventually he was able to show Henry the photograph.

'He looks like the man I saw hanging around the hotel after the wedding,' Henry confirmed. 'But I have no idea who he is. I've never seen him since, either.'

The last person Colin asked was Brian, who'd said in his statement that he'd seen someone hanging around the ice house. 'Yeah, that's the bloke,' Brian said. 'You don't think he's the one who...?'

Murdered Karen? 'I'm afraid I can't say anything, right now,' Colin told him. 'I don't suppose you remember the date, do you?'

Brian shook his head. 'Sorry. A few months back is all I can tell you.'

At least it was another link in the chain...

* * *

Georgina felt better after a proper shower. She headed back to the barn with two mugs of good coffee, and Jodie joined her for a quick coffee break with Cesca's cake.

She mouthed to Jodie, 'Can Harry have a chocolate biscuit?' At Jodie's nod, she said, 'Harry, I've got a chocolate biscuit for you.'

'What do you s—?' Jodie began, but Harry was already saying thank you.

'I'll share it with Bert,' he said.

'Best not, even if Bert looks sad, because chocolate will make him poorly,' Georgina said, producing a dog biscuit out of her pocket. 'But you can give him one of these, if you like.'

Harry couldn't persuade Bert to roll over, but Bert did sit nicely and lifted his paw to say please for the biscuit.

How lucky I am to live here, Georgina thought. To have good friends around me, my family, and such a lovely life.

She checked her phone and saw the message from Sybbie.

Did you good to sleep in.

In retaliation, she changed the name of their WhatsApp group to *Canaries*.

There was an immediate phone call of protest from Sybbie. 'What's that supposed to mean, dear girl?'

'You know perfectly well what it means,' Georgina said. 'I can't move without one of you telling the others what I'm doing – singing like a canary. Just like you talked to Colin and told him about that lump of stone nearly hitting me.'

'We do it,' Sybbie said, 'because we love you. Because we care.'

The phone beeped to say that Sybbie had changed the name of the WhatsApp group back to *Musketeers*.

Georgina huffed. 'I bet you've told Bea and Will as well, haven't you?' The very thing she'd made Colin promise not to do. She should've made Sybbie promise, too.

'All right, all right. Guilty as charged. But I also told them not to panic. And that I was siccing Colin onto you to look after you,' Sybbie said.

Georgina huffed. 'I'm perfectly capable of looking after myself, you know. *And* I have Bert.'

'I know.' Sybbie paused. 'Look, I'm going back to Hartington tomorrow. Maggie Pritchard's agreed to help start going through the inventory with Hattie, to see what's actually missing. I know it's a lot to ask, but you wouldn't be free, would you?'

Georgina thought of the moment that had stretched into

treacle yesterday. The smash of the stone on the gravel. The realisation that it could've been her head underneath that lump of stone. 'Just as long as we park well away from the house.'

'Bert can spend the day here, with Max and Jet.'

'All right. Are you taking the MGA?'

'I can do. We'll be two little old ladies in headscarves, roaring round the country roads in a vintage sports car with the top down,' Sybbie said, laughing. 'Well, one old lady and one middle-aged one. Wear a square headscarf, because it'll stay on better than a baseball cap. If you haven't got one, you can borrow one from me.'

'Would that be a Hermès one, like the Queen used to wear?' Georgina teased.

'Of course. We'll make a countrywoman of you yet. Green wellies, waxed jacket, headscarf. You've already got the dog, dear girl!'

Georgina knew that her friend was sending herself up, and grinned. 'All right. I'll bring Bert over in the morning. What time?'

'Nine. Then we can steal pastries from Cesca on the way out. I have it on good authority that she's baking cinnamon swirls tomorrow.'

'Done,' Georgina said. 'Catch you later.'

Assuming that Bea and Will were both busy at work, she sent them a text.

> Whatever Sybbie told you, I'm perfectly all right. Colin will do the nagging for you. Don't WORRY. Love you, Mum xx

Then she messaged Colin, knowing that he'd pick it up at some point.

Thank you for all the support last night. Have
done some research into Karen Berry's ex and I
could do with your views, when you get a
chance. G x

Next, she rang Jack, starting with the usual small talk of
asking how he was and how Tracey, the children and the grandchildren were.

'I'm guessing this isn't just a social call. What can I do for
you, Georgie?' Jack said.

'I've found Irene Taylor.'

'Trev's mum is still alive?' He sounded surprised. 'She must
be getting on for a hundred, by now.'

'Ninety-four. She's in a nursing home. One that specialises
in dementia patients.' Georgina paused. 'I was thinking about
visiting her. Just to see if she could tell me anything more about
what happened to Doris.'

'You just said she has dementia.' She could hear the frown
in his voice.

'People with dementia often remember the old days more
clearly than they do the last couple of weeks,' she said. 'It's like
that with my mum. Music always gives her a boost and seems to
open up her memories.'

'But what would Irene Taylor be able to tell you, Georgie?
You already know Doris died in an accident. A horrible, pointless accident because my sister followed that bloody doctor's
stupid advice.'

She couldn't tell him over the phone what Doris had told
her about Irene Taylor's involvement. Maybe she should've
arranged to go over and see him; that kind of news needed to be
broken face-to-face.

'She's at peace, now, Georgie,' Jack said.

No, she wasn't, Georgina knew. Doris was still missing
Trev. Still mourning the fact she didn't have a chance to say
goodbye.

'She knows we love her,' Jack said. 'I'd leave it.'

'Mmm-hmm,' Georgina said. Making a vague noise wasn't quite the same thing as telling a bold-faced lie, was it? 'Give my love to Tracey.'

'You weren't honest with him,' Doris said, sounding pained, when Georgina replaced the phone. 'You didn't tell him Irene brought the gin and said she'd make sure I followed the advice to the letter.'

'I upset him enough, the first time I told him what I knew about you. It's not fair to do it again,' Georgina pointed out.

'I suppose.' Doris sighed. 'All right. If you insist, go on your own. But it might be worth talking to Colin first. He might give you some tips on how to get the information out of her.'

'I'm hardly going to switch on an Anglepoise lamp and interrogate her, am I?'

'The look on your face right now,' Doris said, 'tells me you want to shake her.'

'I do. Until her bones and her teeth and everything else rattles,' Georgina admitted. 'But she's a ninety-four-year-old woman who's not very well, so I can't do that. Instead, I'll talk to her in a civilised manner. Ask her what happened.'

THIRTY

Colin messaged later that afternoon.

> I'm stuck on the case. Could do with a change
> of scene to get my head moving. How about
> we take Bert for a walk at Wells-next-the-Sea,
> then have fish and chips on the harbour?

> > Perfect. Come to me and we'll take my car. Text
> > me when you're on the way and I'll pack
> > Bert's bag.

> Bert's bag?

> > Water, bowl, snacks, spare lead and a towel

> Got it. See you soon. C x

An hour later, Colin arrived at Rookery Farm. 'How are you, really, Georgie?' he asked.

'Fine. Actually, I'm going back to Hartington with Sybbie tomorrow to help with the inventory.'

'Are you sure that's wise?'

'She's promised not to park anywhere near the house,' Georgina said with a smile. 'Anyway, I want to catch up with Hattie. As I told you earlier, I promised I'd look into Karen's ex for her, and I wanted to run a few things by you.'

'Strictly speaking, you're skating on the edges of interfering with the case,' he said.

'Really, I'm not. Hattie's just worried that Karen's ex might come after her dad.'

'Has she talked to her dad about it? Or Ellen?'

'It's difficult,' Georgina said. 'Henry and Ellen are both grieving, so if I can do some desk research to answer some questions and reassure Hattie… then that's a good thing. And it's not interfering with your investigation because I'm not talking to witnesses. I'm just looking things up on a genealogy website that anyone in the world can access.'

'Hmm,' he said. 'All right. Talk me through it.'

On the way to the beach, Georgina told Colin about the situation with Karen's marriages – including the fact that her two previous husbands had died; he'd known about one of the deaths, but the second definitely merited a proper investigation – and that Ellen's father was a secret.

'It could be that she had a really unhappy relationship with Ellen's dad and didn't want him to be involved with the baby,' he said. 'And maybe she married someone older because she thought he'd give them both some stability.'

'Robin Kennedy died,' Georgina reminded him.

'Not every death's a murder,' Colin said, his voice deliberately mild, even though he was actually wondering the same thing. But he'd rather not have Georgina investigating something that might put her in danger.

'I know – but there's a *pattern*, Colin. She's married to the first husband for two years, then buries him; she's married to the second one for three years, then buries him. She's been married to Henry for four years – and Hattie thinks her father might be ill. I know he takes tablets, because he told me that he wasn't very good at remembering to take them. And Hattie thinks he's been much more himself since Karen's death. What if Karen was doing something with Henry's meds, and she did the same to her previous husbands?'

'We have no evidence of her doing that to any of her husbands,' he said. 'Besides, the pattern's broken. Henry didn't die, this time; Karen did.'

'Not from natural causes. Hattie told me.'

'I'll give you that one, because you'll have heard from the family that the coroner won't release the body yet, and you know from experience what that means,' he said. 'But right now I'm out of leads. There are plenty of people with motivation and opportunity – and they have alibis.'

'You're the one who told me that you don't like coincidences,' Georgina said. 'Isn't it a coincidence that Karen marries three older men, two of them die and the third might be... unwell?'

'Where are you taking this?'

'I looked up the wills of her first two husbands,' she said. 'Robin Kennedy left her everything. Malcolm Crawford left her everything.' She waited a beat. 'Did Henry Berry change his will to leave everything to her?'

'That, I'm afraid, is between him and his solicitor,' Colin said. 'And possibly his executors, if he told them.'

'But supposing he kept his will the same as before they got married, so she'd have somewhere to live for life and some money, but the Hall and the estate would go to the girls? And supposing Karen wanted him to change it and leave the whole thing to her and he was dragging his feet about it?' she asked.

He frowned. 'I was under the impression Karen was trying

to get him to sell up and move to London, because she didn't like living in the country.'

'So why did she stay here for the last three or four years? Why didn't she get him to buy a place in London, so they could both live there instead of here?'

'You said yourself that very old houses cost a lot of money to maintain,' Colin pointed out. 'Maybe he couldn't afford a London base as well as owning Hartington Hall.'

'And maybe the reason things went missing from the house wasn't to protect Henry from her ex. Maybe the simplest reason is the most likely one, after all,' Georgina said. 'Karen was building a nest-egg, ready to leave him. Though, if she inherited everything from her previous husbands, what did she do with all that money?'

'If we knew the answer to that,' Colin said, 'it'd make a few other bits of the puzzle fall into place.'

They parked at the beach car park rather than in the town; it was almost full, but the cars were just starting to thin out as day trippers began to head for home after a day on the wide, flat sands.

They took Bert through the pine trees; the blackberries at the sides of the coast path had finished flowering and the first berries were appearing, some hard and green and some glistening red, promising juicy ripeness in a few weeks. Their footsteps were cushioned by fallen pine needles; the trunks of the trees seemed to stretch straight and endlessly to the skies. Right at that moment, Georgina felt a million miles away from all her worries.

'This is an amazing place,' Colin said.

'Apparently the forest was planted to stabilise the dunes and protect the fields on the reclaimed marshes,' she said. 'Sybbie said there used to be red squirrels here, but the last ones died thirty or so years back.'

'Maybe they'll get reintroduced as part of a rewilding

programme,' Colin said. 'I think there are a few places doing that now.'

But for now all they could hear was the chatter of birds.

'Do you know what kind of birds they are?' Colin asked.

'No,' Georgina admitted. 'We'd need Young Tom for that.' She grinned. 'But I *can* tell you they're definitely not rooks...'

They led Bert up the wooden stairs over the dunes to a gap between the beach huts; then Georgina took off his lead and put it in her backpack before slipping off her shoes and rolling up her jeans to just below her knees.

She and Colin walked along the sand, hand in hand. There were a few families with small children still eagerly building sandcastles, and a few dog walkers spread across the enormous sandy beach; pockets of teenagers were soaking up the sun on towels, playing music and chatting, beach cricket gear abandoned beside them.

Georgina whistled Bert back from playing on the sand with a little Westie, slipped her backpack off her shoulder and poured water from her reusable steel bottle into a small stainless-steel bowl. Bert lapped it up happily, then scampered off again, his plumy tail wagging behind him as he went in search of new friends.

'He loves it here,' Colin said.

'So do I,' she admitted, shaking out the last drips of water before repacking the bottle and bowl in her backpack.

The tide was out so they had to go a fair way to reach the sea itself; they held hands loosely as they strolled through the shallows. It was nice just to *be*, Georgina thought, with the water swishing gently onto the shore, seagulls floating on the air-currents above them, and the odd V-shaped skein of geese honking as they passed over the pine trees and headed for the salt marshes beyond.

Eventually they headed back towards the beach huts and

the car park, pausing to wipe their feet on the small microfibre towel from Georgina's backpack.

'Is that like Mary Poppins' carpet bag or something?' Colin asked. 'You manage to produce an amazing amount of stuff out of it.'

'Practically perfect, that's me,' she said with a grin.

'I'd agree we have enough evidence to say that,' he said, his grey eyes crinkling at the corners, and her heart felt as if it had done a backflip.

They drove back down to the harbour, parked and bought fish and chips. Georgina noticed that Colin separated out bits of fish for Bert before he ate anything himself, letting the hot flakes cool down for the dog at the side of the cardboard box. A man who was kind to animals was definitely one worth having around, she thought.

'I did a bit more investigating into the farmhouse, too, yesterday,' she said.

'That case you asked me about, with the coroner's report? The young girl who fell down the stairs?' he checked.

'Yes. I found her brother, a couple of months back, and he told me all kinds of interesting things about the farm.' She still couldn't tell him the true source of her information. 'The thing is... there's information about the case that didn't make it to the newspapers.'

'Such as?'

'She was pregnant at the time. You and I are too young to know what it was like in the early 1970s, but I'm guessing people's attitudes were a lot more straight-laced in rural places than they were in London.'

'She would've had a hard time,' he agreed. 'Are you saying you think she...?'

'Fell deliberately to kill herself? No, definitely not. I think she would've taken the standard medical advice of the day. Hot baths, gin, and fall down the stairs a couple of times.'

He winced. 'That's horrific. Poor girl. So it's a tragic accident.'

'But what if,' she said, 'someone... helped her?'

'How do you mean?'

'Jack – her brother – says their parents were lovely and they would've supported her. But her boyfriend's parents were a bit snooty. Especially the mum.'

'You think the boyfriend's mum helped her with the standard medical advice?'

She nodded. 'All of it.'

Colin's brow wrinkled. 'You're going back half a century, Georgie. Say Doris's boyfriend was the same age as her, and his mum was twenty when she had him – that'd make her pushing ninety, now. That's if she's still alive.'

Georgina tried to keep her voice casual. 'Supposing she *was* still alive though? And you could talk to her. What would you ask her?'

He looked at her. 'Are you telling me she still lives in Little Wenborough?'

'No.' When that dark-grey gaze met hers, she couldn't lie to him. 'She's in residential care.'

He winced. 'Georgie, you really can't go interrogating someone about something that happened fifty-odd years ago. Especially if the woman's in a care home.'

'I'm not intending to interrogate her. I just want to know what really happened.'

'If what she did led to the poor girl's death – deliberately, I mean, not an accident – she's hardly likely to confess it. And, even if she does admit to it, at that age she might not be well enough to stand trial,' Colin pointed out. 'What kind of residential care?'

Georgina sighed. 'A home specialising in dementia cases.'

'Then, even if she's guilty, it's definitely not going to court. She won't have capacity.' He shook his head. 'Georgie. I know you want to find the truth but I think you might have to leave this one.'

'Mmm,' she said. But, even if she didn't tackle Irene directly, the nursing home might be able to pass on her contact details to Trevor. And at least then she could help Doris say goodbye to the love of her life.

THIRTY-ONE

On Saturday, Georgina went to Little Wenborough Manor. Giles took charge of Bert while Sybbie dug out a spare headscarf and insisted on tying it 'properly' for Georgina.

'You look a million dollars,' Sybbie said when Georgina topped off the outfit with her favourite Ray-Bans. She laughed. 'We need a selfie. We can send it to the girls – and your kids.'

'Posed against the car,' Georgina said, and made sure that Sybbie's gorgeous 1961-built turquoise MGA was perfectly in the background as she took the snap.

'Just look at us,' Sybbie said, laughing. 'Who do we think we are?'

'A middle-aged Thelma and Louise,' Georgina drawled in a fake Arkansas accent, climbing into the car and fastening her seat belt.

'It's bad enough driving this gorgeous girl over a cattle grid. I'm certainly not going to drive her off a cliff,' Sybbie said, patting the steering wheel. 'Besides, neither of us is naïve enough to be Thelma, and we can't *both* be Louise.' She tutted. 'Upsetting film, really. That cop should've proved to them that they could trust him and he would've helped them sort everything out.' She shot Georgina a sideways look. 'Your Colin would've done it properly.'

'You're right. Colin's one of the good guys.' Georgina paused. 'I've been looking into Karen's past.' She gave Sybbie a quick rundown of what she'd learned about Karen's marriages.

'So either Ellen's father is a bad lot and Karen was trying to protect Henry by stealing from him and giving the goods to her ex to pay him off; or Karen is a serial marrier of old men and she stuffs them full of cholesterol and whatnot to bump them off, before cashing in on their estate. Neither's good,' Sybbie said. 'Was she going to do that to Henry, do you think? Or did she realise he has the constitution of an ox, so she was trying to feather her nest as much as she could before she gave in and left him?'

'Either. Both,' Georgina said. 'We don't have any evidence.'

'We can certainly get evidence of the stealing,' Sybbie said. 'That's what we're doing today.'

Sybbie was careful to park well away from the house when they got to Hartington, to Georgina's relief.

'No Bert today?' Hattie asked, her own spaniels pattering at her heels.

'Max and Jet are probably teaching him the delights of rolling in fox poo, the wretches,' Sybbie said.

'Our three could do that, too,' Hattie said with a grin.

'Trust me, Bert's already worked that one out for himself,' Georgina said. 'Let's just say that tomato ketchup is my new best friend.'

'Tsk. Bumped off the besties list for a bottle of red sauce. That puts my ego in check,' Sybbie teased. 'So who's on the inventory task force, Hattie?'

'You two, Maggie and me,' the younger woman said. 'Posy's up to her eyes in garden stuff.'

'Henry's not helping?' Sybbie asked.

'When there's a car to tinker with?' Hattie asked, rolling her eyes. 'And Ellen's off somewhere doing bat stuff. Which will probably be better for her than being cooped up inside with not enough to think about.' She ushered them through to the Hall's kitchen.

'Good to see you again, Lady Sybbie.' Sybbie was greeted by a short, round woman in her mid-sixties; her fair hair was streaked with silver, and her smile was warm.

'We haven't used that title for thirty-odd years, Maggie, and we're not going to start using it again now,' Sybbie said. 'Lovely to see you, too. Now, Maggie, let me introduce you to my friend Georgina Drake – Georgie, who's come to help us with the inventory,' Sybbie said. 'Georgie, this is Maggie Pritchard.'

Once they'd finished the introductions and arranged who was working in which rooms, they went through the contents of each room, checking them against the inventory.

'I can't face the library yet,' Hattie said when they broke for lunch. 'It will take for ever to go through the books. But I think books will be more difficult to sell than the stuff that we've found is missing. Miniatures, snuffboxes, silver and china – they're all very pocketable.' She sighed. 'I'll text everyone to say lunch is in the kitchen.' She grabbed her phone.

Posy turned up ten minutes later, but neither Henry nor Ellen replied to Hattie's texts, even though Hattie had told her father that Sybbie had brought the MGA in an attempt to entice him out of the garage.

'They'll just have to sort themselves out when they're hungry,' Hattie said. 'It's only simple stuff, anyway: bread and cheese and salad.' She looked hopefully at Sybbie.

'Yes, of course I snaffled something from Cesca. Cinnamon swirls,' Sybbie said. 'They're in the car – I'll just go and get them.'

Over lunch, Georgina updated Posy and Hattie on what she'd found out about Karen's past.

'So at best she was stealing to protect Papa but still taking things that weren't hers; and at worst... God, I wonder if that's why Papa was acting so strangely?' Hattie asked. 'If she wasn't nagging him to take his meds properly, or – oh, dear God – she was giving him things that made him ill...'

'Much as I disliked her – she wasn't a patch on dear Millie – it's not fair to make accusations when she can't defend herself,' Maggie said.

'That's incredibly generous of you, Maggie, given what she did to you and Brian,' Sybbie said.

'I don't feel generous, believe me,' Maggie said. 'I could cheerfully have poisoned the woman.'

Georgina and Sybbie exchanged a glance. That was a bit too close for comfort, given Georgina's brush with a poisoner in Sybbie's garden only a few months ago.

'Let's find the evidence and let that lovely detective sort it out,' Maggie finished.

'*Georgie's* lovely detective,' Sybbie said, digging Georgina in the ribs. 'Or are you still denying that he's yours?'

'He's a good man,' Georgina said.

'Yes,' Posy agreed. 'He was really kind to Papa at the mortuary.'

Georgina wasn't surprised. 'And he'll find out what happened.'

Hattie gave a start as Ellen walked into the kitchen. 'Ellen! I thought you were out.'

The younger woman shook her head. 'I had a bit of a headache. I'll go out now.'

'Let me make you a sandwich, love,' Maggie said.

'I'm not really hungry.' Ellen looked wary, and Georgina's heart sank. The poor girl must've overheard the housekeeper saying that she could've happily murdered Karen.

And maybe she'd overheard some of Georgina's own speculation about Karen interfering with her former husbands' medication. Georgina felt guilty, as if she'd been gossiping rather than trying to work out what was really going on. But how could she apologise without making everything even more awkward? At a loss, she said, 'At least have one of the cinnamon swirls. Sybbie got them fresh from Cesca's oven, and half of Little Wenborough queues up at the farm shop for these.'

The wariness was still in Ellen's expression. Clearly she *had* overheard most of what they'd said. But finally she nodded, as if she understood that the pastry symbolised the apology Georgina should've made. 'Thank you. I'll take it with me. I'm checking the maternity colony.'

'Brian sends his regards,' Maggie said, obviously also trying to make amends. 'He said he hopes those plants you put in together are attracting all the insects the bats like.'

Ellen gave her a wan smile. 'Tell him thanks. They are.'

'I'll make some green tea and put it in a travel mug for you,' Hattie said, pushing her chair back.

'It's OK. I've got my water bottle,' Ellen said, patting the bulge in a pocket of her cargo pants. 'See you later.'

'Let us know if you need anything,' Posy said.

'Yeah.' Ellen walked out of the kitchen without a backward glance.

They finished the inventory mid-afternoon, and Sybbie drove them back to Little Wenborough.

'It's such a perfect afternoon. I'm almost tempted to take a teensy detour to Holt,' Sybbie said.

The beautiful Georgian town was full of antique shops, which Georgina knew were like a magnet to her friend. 'Bernard would have my guts for garters if I let you loose in Holt with your credit card.'

'You could be my responsible adult,' Sybbie said.

Georgina laughed. 'Considering I like antiques as much as you do, Bernard's never going to put me on your Responsible Adult list.'

'Little Foo dogs,' Sybbie said longingly. 'I just *know* there's going to be one with my name on it...'

'No,' Georgina said.

'Spoilsport,' Sybbie teased. And then her tone changed. 'Oh, Christ. Georgie. The brakes have just gone spongy on me.'

'The brakes?' Georgina looked ahead. Noel Coward might have claimed that Norfolk was 'very flat', but it wasn't. There were gentle, hummocky hills – and sharp bends. Right in front of them was a hill, sloping downwards. With a sharp bend. And there was a massive, slow tractor pulling out of the junction...

THIRTY-TWO

'I'm going to have to do this old-school and hope to hell that the gears stand it,' Sybbie said. 'Hold on.' She changed swiftly down the gears to slow the car down; Georgina could hear the engine screaming.

'The handbrake's going on,' Sybbie warned, and pulled on it hard.

It wasn't enough. They were still hurtling towards the tractor.

Georgina braced herself, waiting for the head-on crash.

'I'm so sorry,' Sybbie said, and for a moment Georgina wasn't sure whether her friend was apologising to her or to the car. Then Sybbie wrenched the steering wheel to the left, making the car hit the verge.

There was a sickening crunch; Georgina jolted forward, and there was a sharp pain in her shoulder as the seat belt held her in place.

'*Not* the way I would've wanted to stop,' Sybbie said. She stroked the car's steering wheel. 'We'll fix you up again,' she whispered. She turned to Georgina. 'Are you all right?'

'I think so. Are you?' Georgina asked.

'I might hurt a bit tomorrow from the seat belt,' Sybbie said, rubbing her own shoulder, 'but not as much as my poor girl.' She fiddled with a switch. 'I'm glad Bernard made me have hazard lights fitted, the other year.'

'You didn't have hazard lights?' Georgina asked, shocked.

'They weren't fitted as standard on a 1961 MGA. And there are lots of things you don't have to do with a classic car that you do with a normal car,' Sybbie said. 'But he had a good point. It's safer.' She sighed. 'I'd better call the garage and see if they can tow her home. I hope you didn't have big plans with Colin, this evening.'

'No, I didn't,' Georgina said.

Bernard came to pick them up in his 4X4, following the mechanic from the garage in the tow truck.

The mechanic – a wiry man in his mid-thirties, with fox-red hair and a slightly scruffy beard, wearing a navy boiler suit – climbed out of the tow truck and patted the bonnet of the MGA. 'What happened here, Lady S?'

'The brakes went spongy and a tractor pulled out, Joe,' Sybbie said. 'Not the best of combinations.'

'I only serviced her for you in April and I know you're careful with her. How could the brakes have gone spongy?' Joe asked.

'I don't know, but I want her back to how she was,' Sybbie said mournfully.

Joe patted the car again. 'Beautiful girl that she is. We'll look after her, don't you worry. Though if you ever want to sell her...'

'No chance,' Sybbie said.

An hour or so later, Joe rang Sybbie's mobile. 'I know exactly why your brakes were spongy, Lady S. There's a puncture in the brake line.'

Sybbie frowned. 'What? How could that have happened?'

'I'd say it was deliberate. Done by someone who knew what they were doing.'

'Oh, my God,' Sybbie said.

'Were your brakes spongy on the way there?' Bernard asked.

'Of course not. I would've turned back and taken the VW instead,' Sybbie said. 'I'm not stupid.'

Bernard looked thoughtful. 'So they weren't spongy on the way there – but they failed on the way back. There's only one place this could've happened, and that's where you parked it.'

'But – who would've wanted to cut my brakes?' Sybbie asked. 'And who would know how to...' Her eyes widened and she cut off the rest of the question.

'Yes. Who at Hartington Hall would know how to cut the old-fashioned brake system of an MGA?' Bernard asked, his tone saying that he knew the answer perfectly well. 'I'm sorry, Syb. I know he was married to your best friend, but it has to be him.' He looked at Sybbie. 'Come to think of it, where was he when that bit of stone nearly squashed Georgie, the other day?'

'He'd just taken himself off to bed,' Sybbie said.

'And where was he today?' Bernard asked.

'Tinkering with his c—' she began, and stopped, a look of shock on her face. 'Oh.'

'Don't try to make excuses for him. I'm calling this in,' Bernard said.

Colin was there in thirty minutes. Grim-faced, he took their statements. 'And you're sure Henry Berry's the only one at Hartington who knows about vintage cars?' he asked.

'He's got quite a collection,' Bernard said, a muscle in his jaw tightening and his hands balling into fists. Unconsciously, he widened his stance, looking like a boxer about to land a punch to an opponent he loathed. 'Takes more care of them than he does of the estate. He leaves all that to his girls and wibbles on about *oh, I can't...*'

'Don't be cruel,' Sybbie said, elbowing him. 'He's had a hard time.'

'Henry Berry's a selfish sod and always has been. And, frankly, if Colin doesn't put him behind bars for this, then he'll have to arrest *me* for going over and breaking every bone in his body for putting you at risk,' Bernard shouted – the first time Georgina had ever heard him raise his voice.

'That,' Colin said, 'won't be necessary, Lord Wyatt.'

The use of his title had the effect of calming Bernard's temper. 'I'm sorry, Colin,' he said. 'But the idea of anything happening to Sybbie...' He gritted his teeth.

'I know,' Colin said softly. 'That was how I felt on Thursday. After the masonry incident.'

'There's something wrong at Hartington,' Bernard said. 'It needs sorting out.'

'I agree,' Colin said. 'That's my job.' He looked at Georgina. 'There is another way of looking at this. Sybbie and the car might've been collateral damage rather than the target.'

'How do you mean?' Georgina asked.

'That finial ball nearly hit you on Thursday; today, it was a car crash. Someone thinks you know something, and they're trying to stop you telling anyone else.'

Georgina shivered. Was he right? Was someone trying to stop her – trying to kill her? But why? She couldn't think what she might know that was so dangerous.

'You're staying here with us,' Sybbie said.

'No arguments,' Bernard added. 'Colin, we'll keep a close eye on her, but you're welcome to join us for supper tonight.'

'This is ridiculous,' Georgina said.

'I don't care. No more risks,' Colin said.

And Bert, who'd been sitting practically glued to Georgina's legs, woofed agreement.

THIRTY-THREE

Two hours later, Colin had Henry sitting in the interview suite, along with his solicitor.

'Guv, you shouldn't be doing this interview,' Mo said. 'You're involved.'

'I'm the senior officer on this case,' Colin said, his voice sharp. 'I can maintain detachment and do my job.'

'Guv,' Larissa said. 'Let us interview him. You can watch. Give us a list of questions, direct us, whatever works for you – but you *know* you can't interview him yourself. You can't go in and ask him why he tried to kill your girlfriend.'

Colin knew they were right, and he was glad his team had his back – but how could he sit here, doing nothing? 'I need to look into his eyes when he explains why he tried to kill Georgie.'

'You can. Just on a screen, not face-to-face,' Mo said.

Colin sat on a hard chair, watching the screen and listening intently. Mo and Larissa went through all the legal necessities for the tape: introducing themselves, making sure that all phones were switched off, stating Henry's name and that of his solicitor. They cautioned him that he was here for questioning under suspicion of an attempt to murder Lady Wyatt and

Georgina Drake, and made sure that he understood the caution. They were careful and methodical, and part of Colin was hugely proud of his team, while the other half was raging and wanted to shake the truth out of Henry Berry.

'Of course I didn't try to kill Sybbie. Why would I do that?' Henry asked, his voice full of scorn. 'That's utterly ridiculous.'

Larissa didn't answer him; instead she went with Colin's first line of approach. 'Tell us about your relationship with Lady Wyatt.'

'She's my wife's best friend – Millie, my first wife, I mean,' Henry clarified. 'They were at school together. She was one of our bridesmaids and she's godmother to both our girls. I've known her for decades.'

'How would you describe your relationship?' Larissa asked.

Henry shrugged. 'I don't really have a relationship with her.'

Larissa wasn't put off in the slightest. 'Are you friends? Do you rub each other up the wrong way?'

'I...' He sighed and drummed his fingers on the table. 'Sybbie's very strong-minded. I always felt she didn't think I was good enough for Millie.' All the bluster Colin had seen before suddenly went out of Henry. 'And she was right.'

'Tell me about it,' Larissa invited.

'I loved her. Millie, I mean, not Sybbie. From the moment I met her. And Christ knows what she saw in me. But there was something, and my parents loved her, and she loved Hartington – and I really thought it was going to work, you know?' Henry asked, his voice earnest.

Colin went cold. He'd been told that Mille had died from cancer. Was it a cover-up? Was Henry just about to confess that he'd killed Millie, next?

But then the words burst out of him. 'I often wish I'd been the second son instead of the only child. Then I wouldn't have had that damned house round my neck. It *eats* money. I could've just been a normal person, not having to live up to appearances and everyone else's expectations. I could've trained properly as a mechanic and tinkered with vintage cars all day.' He gave a mirthless laugh. 'Selfish bastard that I am, that's what I actually *do* all day. Except only on my own cars. I left the running of the estate to my mother and Millie – and the girls, as soon as they were old enough. But I've paid for it. Millie got cancer. Have you ever seen cancer eating away at someone you love, taking a little bit more of their lungs each day, giving them a little more pain?' His face was anguished. 'I would've done anything, given anything, to take it for her. But I couldn't. I couldn't give her a son, I couldn't stop her getting cancer, and I couldn't do anything to make her well again. All I could do was hold her hand at the end while her life slipped away.'

Tears were running down his cheeks now, unchecked.

Larissa silently poured him a glass of water.

'I didn't know what to do without her. Everywhere I walked in that blasted house had memories of her. Every inch of the garden.' Henry shook his head. 'Except she wasn't there. I couldn't stand it. I had to get away.'

This must've been what it was like for Georgina, Colin realised. And she'd loved Stephen with the same passion that Henry had unexpectedly shown just now. It shook him to the core. How would you ever have space left for anyone else, when a love like that had gone? Wouldn't it leave you an empty husk, unable to let anything else into that gap?

'So I went to London,' Henry said. 'Stayed with friends. They were Millie's friends more than mine, really – she was the one who kept everyone together – but they understood and let me stay. I went to my club one night and had some sort of break-down. Too much brandy, I don't know, but it all came out. And Karen was *kind*. She noticed what was happening and took me to a quiet corner out of everyone's way. She sat with me and listened.' He gave a wry huff. 'I took her out to lunch the next day, to thank her. And, I don't know, somehow she made me see that there could be life after Millie. That the sky could still be blue and the sun could still come out.'

Yeah. Colin knew that feeling. Georgie had been the one to show him that. But could he do the same for her? Was he enough?

He forced himself to concentrate on Henry's words.

'So I asked her to marry me. But she couldn't settle at Hartington. Everyone looked at her, remembered Millie and couldn't see past the fact that Millie wasn't here and I needed someone. They just saw Karen as second rate. Called her a gold digger, because she was a waitress and I had a title. It wasn't fair. I didn't care that she wasn't born an Hon or whatever. But it bothered *her*. We started to have rows, and she'd go to London and come back with piles of clothes. Money I should've spent on the estate, and the girls weren't happy about it.' He huffed. 'And it just got worse. She wanted another baby – but at my age? I couldn't do that. Not realistically. I'd be more like its grandfather. Technically, I could even be its *great*-grandfather.' He shook his head. 'She wanted me to sell the house and buy a flat in London. Mayfair, somewhere nice. And I thought about it. If it would make her happy, maybe I should. But then there were the girls. And there was Hartington. Whatever I did, I knew I'd disappoint someone.' He shrugged. 'Then again, I suppose I've been a disappointment, my whole life.'

The self-pity annoyed Colin immensely; but now he was beginning to see what made Henry Berry tick.

'Millie's dead. Karen's dead.' Henry closed his eyes. 'I just can't...'

'Let's have a break,' Larissa said, and recorded the time and date that she was stopping the interview.

While Mo sealed the CD, Larissa came out to see Colin. 'Are you all right, guv?'

'I'm fine. You did really well in there, letting him talk and get stuff off his chest,' he said.

'Mo's going to get him to read the written notes and sign them,' she said.

'Good.' He smiled at her. 'I owe you both dinner. Thank you for making me see sense.'

'You still want to shake it out of him, don't you?' she asked wryly.

'Yeah,' he admitted, 'but you're doing things the right way.'

After the break, Larissa spoke the time and date, introduced them all again for the tape, restated the reason for the interview and re-cautioned Henry.

'Lord Ellingham. Tell us about your relationship with Georgina Drake,' Larissa said, and Colin's fists clenched.

'Sybbie's friend, the photographer woman? I don't really know her,' Henry said. 'She seems nice. She's been helping with the girls' project to open the Hall to the public. They've taken to her.'

'Why did you try to kill her?'

'*Kill* her?' He looked shocked. 'But I've already told you, I hardly know her. I've only met her a couple of times. She took my photo and talked to me about my cars. Why on earth would I want to kill her?'

Larissa didn't answer. 'Why did you try to kill Lady Sybil Wyatt?'

'I've already told you that, too. I didn't try to kill Sybbie. We rub each other up the wrong way, but most of the time we tolerate each other. For the sake of Millie and the girls.' He winced. 'She's been good to them. Good to me, too, this week, I have to say. She came to the mortuary with us to see Karen.'

'Did Karen like her?' Larissa asked.

'No. I think because she knew seeing Sybbie reminded me of Millie, and I found that hard,' Henry said. 'So she didn't welcome Sybbie to the house.'

'Why did your girls move out of the Hall?'

'It stopped the rows,' he said tiredly. 'I should've been a better husband and a better father. Nipped it all in the bud instead of hiding behind my cars.'

'Are you a qualified mechanic, Lord Ellingham?' Larissa asked.

'I've never taken formal exams,' he said, 'but I've spent the best part of fifty years working with vintage cars, restoring them. I know my way around an engine and how to fix problems, if that's what you're asking.'

'So you'd know how the brake systems work for a sixty-year-old sports car,' Larissa said.

Henry nodded.

'For the tape, Lord Ellingham, I need the words, please,' she said quietly.

'Yes,' he said.

'If you know how the system works, then it follows that you'd also know how to make a brake system *not* work?'

Henry sat up straighter. 'Hang on. What are you suggesting?'

'Do you recognise this car?' Larissa showed him a picture of Sybbie's crumpled car.

'Yes. It's Sybbie's MGA. Dear God, what happened to it?' Henry asked.

'The brakes failed on it this afternoon.'

'What? Is she all right?'

Larissa didn't answer. 'Did you cut her brakes?'

'No! I'd never do anything like that!' Henry protested.

'Where were you today?'

'In the barn, tinkering with my cars. I'm restoring a Lotus Elan,' Henry said. 'A 1973 model. Red.'

'Did anyone see you there?'

'No. I was on my own in the barn, just me and the radio.'

'So you have no alibi,' Larissa said.

'Are you really saying you think I tried to kill Sybbie?' Henry asked. 'But that's ridiculous!'

'We're not sure who the intended victim was: Lady Wyatt or Georgina Drake,' Larissa said.

Henry raked a hand through his head, all fight gone out of him again. 'I didn't try to kill either of them. And I would never damage a car as beautiful as Sybbie's. I would've liked to add the MGA to my collection, but I could never persuade her to sell it to me. And *that* doesn't mean I'm the kind of man who sulks and smashes something up if he can't have it.' He shook his head in apparent resignation. 'Sybbie's right about me. I'm weak. I just give up.'

But worms could turn. Colin had seen it happen before.

Had Henry Berry killed Karen, as the only way out of the impasse between her demands and those of his daughters? And then, thinking that Sybbie and Georgina were close to uncovering the truth about what he'd done, had he tried to kill them?

THIRTY-FOUR

'Can I at least go home and get some fresh clothes?' Georgina asked.

'No, dear girl, you'll have to slum it and borrow mine,' Sybbie said.

'Sybbie, you're taller and thinner than me. I can roll the legs of things up, but there's nothing I can do about things actually fitting round my middle,' Georgina protested.

'Then we'll get Jodie to pick stuff up for you. I'm not letting you out of my sight. It's more than my life's worth.'

'*Cabin'd, cribb'd, confin'd,*' Georgina grumbled.

'Don't try to Shakespeare your way out of it. Colin would either murder me or have me locked up if anything happens to you.' Sybbie gave her a sunny smile. 'You're staying put, and that's that.'

'Am I at least allowed to make a phone call?'

'You probably ought to tell the kids, actually,' Sybbie said.

Georgina shook her head. 'They'll panic and try to bubble-wrap me. Let's wait to hear from Colin first.'

'Is that who you're going to call? Colin?'

'No. It's... to do with Rookery Farm. The girl who died there, fifty or so years ago,' Georgina said.

Sybbie frowned. 'I thought you'd already looked into it and it was a tragic accident?'

'Maybe. Maybe not.' Georgina didn't want to go into details right now.

'All right. I'll give you space, as long as you promise not to disappear,' Sybbie said. 'Bert, don't let her do a runner. Or there will be no sausages for you, ever again.'

The spaniel woofed and put his head on Georgina's knee.

When Sybbie had withdrawn, Georgina rang the nursing home where Irene Taylor was living.

'Hello,' she said, when the receptionist answered. 'My name's Georgina Drake, and I recently moved to Little Wenborough, where Mrs Irene Taylor, one of your residents, used to live. I got your number from your website. A friend of the family suggested she might be able to help me with a research project.' It was the truth. Just slightly tweaked.

'I'm afraid that's unlikely,' the receptionist said. 'I can't talk to you about Mrs Taylor, because of patient confidentiality, but I'm sure you realise from our website what kind of care needs our residents have.'

'Dementia. Yes. My mother has dementia,' Georgina said, 'and looking at old photos makes her really happy. And music. The home where she lives has a singer come in once a week to go through some of the old songs, and it really brightens up everyone's mood.'

'That's true,' the receptionist said. 'We have a singer here every week.'

'And visitors always give residents a boost,' Georgina said, ready to work her way round to the subject of Trevor.

'She doesn't get many visitors,' the receptionist admitted. 'I think her son lives abroad. He always sends her flowers every two weeks, but I guess when you live that far away you can only visit a handful of times a year.'

'Why don't I pop in some time next week?' Georgina said. 'If she's not up to seeing me – well, never mind. But maybe it will give her a bit of a lift.'

'All right,' the receptionist said.

It was a start. And, when she was there in person, she could ask the home to pass her details on to Trevor.

'I can't talk about what's happening,' Colin said later that evening in Sybbie's garden. 'But I can tell you we're holding Henry overnight, so you're safe for now.'

'I can't quite see Henry as a murderer,' Bernard said. 'He wouldn't have the guts. He'd rather hide away with his cars.'

'If he's the one who cut my brakes so I crashed my poor car, I'll kill him myself,' Sybbie said.

'Get behind me in the queue,' Colin said, 'and no smart comment about "ladies first".'

'Even though she's an actual lady with a capital L?' Georgina teased.

'*Not* funny,' Colin said.

'We're all right, Colin,' Sybbie said. 'Women like Georgie and me, we don't break. We simply dust ourselves down and get on with things.'

Colin looked at Georgina and thought of what Henry had said about his love for Millie, and again he wondered if Georgina's life could stretch to fit him, or whether it'd be kinder to them both if he walked away from her now.

She took his hand briefly and squeezed it. 'Stop brooding.'

'Brooding,' Sybbie said. 'That's it. It's been driving me mad since I first met you.' She snapped her fingers. 'I've just thought who you remind me of, Colin.' She grinned. 'Mr Darcy. The Firth version.'

Doris wasn't here, because she hadn't gone with them to do the inventory at Hartington, but Georgina could imagine her reaction if she was: a laugh, followed by a gleeful, 'Told you so.'

Colin groaned. 'Oh, for pity's sake, Sybbie.'

'She's got a point,' Georgina said with a smile.

Colin groaned again. 'I got a lot of grief at the station when that series was on the telly. Notes on my desk with a picture of Darcy glued to them, saying I was needed to sort out a public affray... and the location would *always* be a pond or a lake. And when I moved to CID my old squad gave me one of those frilly shirts as a leaving present.' He closed his eyes and shook his head. 'It all started up again when *Love Actually* came out. Pictures of typewriters left on my desk and fake Portuguese accents when anyone talked to me. And you don't want to know about *Mamma Mia!*'

Sybbie and Georgina immediately laughed and launched into the chorus of 'Take a Chance On Me'.

'Rookie error, Colin,' Bernard said pityingly. 'I'm going to open a bottle of red.'

'And you can chop the salad while I grill some chicken,' Sybbie said. 'Colin, you'll stay for dinner with us, won't you?'

'Thank you. That'd be great,' Colin said.

When Sybbie and Bernard had left them on the terrace, Colin took Georgina's hand. 'First that stone finial, and now this. I'm beginning to think I need to get you a ton of bubble wrap and a suit of armour to keep you safe.'

'I'm fine,' Georgina said. 'But Bernard's got a point. I don't think Henry's the murdering type.'

'So who do you think is?' Colin asked.

'I think Karen was,' Georgina said. 'I know you said that a heart attack doesn't necessarily mean murder, but what if she really did do something with her last two husbands' medication? Hattie thought her father might be developing some sort of illness: what if Karen had been messing with his medication, too? He'd be the third rich, much older husband...'

'If Karen really was killing her husbands, and Henry was the next planned victim, who stood to lose most from his death?' Colin asked.

'Posy and Hattie,' Georgina said promptly. 'Because they'd already lost their mum, and losing their dad as well would be so hard. But they're not killers. I know you told me to take the emotion out of it, because of course I wouldn't want to suspect a close friend's goddaughters, but you've met them. You *know* they're decent people. Besides, my theory about Karen is only a theory. There isn't any real evidence that she was planning to kill Henry.'

'Let me rephrase that,' Colin said. 'If people *thought* Karen was trying to kill Henry, who would want to stop her?'

'Posy and Hattie,' Georgina said again. 'But I think they'd be more likely to talk to the police than take matters into their own hands.'

'Unless they thought Karen could hide her tracks well enough to make it look as if they were making a fuss over nothing, and nobody would believe them,' Colin said. 'Who else?'

'I guess anyone who might lose their job if Karen inherited the Hall and sold it?' Georgina asked.

'Discounting the Pritchards: they'd already lost their jobs and their homes,' Colin said. 'Although revenge might still be a motive for them, and I don't think Maggie's the sort you want to cross, I'm not sure she's a killer. Remember, she was compiling evidence about the things going missing from the Hall. I think Maggie Pritchard's the sort who'd want Karen to see exactly who'd stopped her carrying out her plans and tell her to her face that she did it for Millie's memory.'

'Agreed,' Georgina said. 'So if we discount Henry's daughters and the staff at Hartington, that leaves Ellen. But why would she kill her mum?'

'Maybe she thought her mother would sell the Hall and that would be the end of the bats?' Colin suggested.

'Whatever happened to the house and the estate, the bats are protected by law,' Georgina reminded him.

'Ellen seems to care as much about the house and the estate as Hattie and Posy do,' Colin said. 'I think we need to talk to her again. Though that can wait until tomorrow.'

THIRTY-FIVE

The next morning, Colin picked Georgina up from Sybbie's, leaving Bert behind to play with Max and Jet, and drove to Hartington Hall. They were halfway there when a call came in from Larissa.

Colin glanced at Georgina before answering the call on hands-free. 'Anything you hear—'

'—is confidential,' she finished. 'Got it.'

'Guv, how close are you to Hartington?' Larissa asked.

'Halfway there. I'm with Georgina, and you're on speaker,' Colin said.

'Right. Felicity – the FLO at Hartington – just called. Ellen Newman's gone missing.'

'I'll be there in twenty minutes,' Colin said. 'Can you send Felicity's number to me?'

'Will do,' Larissa said, and Colin's phone pinged with a text shortly after she ended the call.

'Can you ring Felicity for me, please?' he asked Georgina. 'It'll still come through on my hands-free when she answers.'

'And anything I hear is still confidential,' she added. 'Sure.'

Felicity answered immediately.

'It's Colin Bradshaw, Felicity,' he said. 'I'm on my way over. I understand Ellen's gone missing?'

'Yes. We've already checked the ice house,' she said, 'because that would be the obvious place for her to go. But she's not there and none of the garden team have seen her in the woods. She's left a note.'

'What does it say?' he asked.

'That she's sorry for everything. Posy's scared that Ellen's done something stupid,' Felicity added.

'Is Ellen's car still at the Hall? Or is anyone else's vehicle missing?'

'I'll check and let you know,' Felicity said. 'In the meantime, Hattie's using the estate office as a central point. She's getting the search teams to check in with her every fifteen minutes, and she's marking the areas they've searched on a copy of the estate map.'

'That's sensible. OK. We'll be there soon,' Colin said. 'Call me if anything comes up.'

Felicity rang back, ten minutes later. 'There are no missing cars, including Ellen's. I got the spare key for Ellen's car from Hattie and there was an overnight bag in the boot, which Hattie said belonged to Karen. I've left it where it is – I didn't touch it, and I used gloves to open the tailgate – and I'm getting Forensics onto it.'

'Good work,' Colin said. When he ended the call, he blew out a breath. 'Either Ellen borrowed the bag from Karen and was planning to go away somewhere, or that bag's full of Karen's stuff. We'll find out when Forensics get there.'

'Are you thinking Ellen might have been the one who killed her mum?' Georgina asked.

'If the contents belong to Karen, that's looking like a stronger possibility,' Colin said. 'Why didn't Ellen tell us about that bag?'

When they reached Hartington Hall, he parked on the

gravel – deliberately out of reach of any potential falling tiles or masonry – and Georgina led him to the estate office.

'Thank you for coming so quickly,' Hattie said. She gave them a rundown of who was on each team and where they were looking.

'That's good planning,' Colin said. He sniffed. 'Is it me, or is there a really strong scent of lavender in here?'

Lavender. Bert had saved her, Georgina thought, the last time she'd smelled lavender. Anne and Doris had helped the dog. But Doris wasn't here, this time, and Georgina had no point of contact with Anne without Doris. Except maybe through this one scent that everyone seemed to smell when Anne was around.

Was this perhaps Anne telling her that she knew where Ellen was and could lead the dogs there?

Keeping her fingers crossed that she was doing the right thing, Georgina asked, 'Might the dogs be able to find Ellen?'

'We've never even done gun-dog training with them, let alone tracking,' Hattie said. 'They're pets. Daft as brushes, the three of them.'

'So's my Bert, but it's worth a try,' Georgina said.

'Let me go to Ellen's room and get her pillow or something so they can find her scent,' Hattie said. She came back with a pillow, which the three spaniels sniffed.

'Find her, boys. Let's get her home safely,' she said. 'Find her.'

To Georgina's intense relief, the dogs padded about; then they seemed to pick up the scent and rushed out of the estate office.

Given that strong scent of lavender, it had to be Anne they were following, Georgina thought. Anne would lead them to Ellen.

She chased after the dogs, Colin right behind her.

'Where are they going?' he asked as the dogs streaked up the stairs.

'Hopefully not just to her room,' Georgina said.

The dogs took the next two flights of stairs, and pattered along the corridor. At the very end, they stood by a door, whining. 'What's behind that door?' Colin asked.

'At this level of the house, I'd assume it's the attic,' Georgina said. 'I'm sure someone said something about Ellen looking at a bat roost in the attic.'

'Let's hope she's there,' Colin said grimly. 'And that we're in time.'

He twisted the round brass door handle, trying to push aside the memories of the last time he'd gone into an attic. The darkness. The metallic aroma of blood, so harsh that you could almost taste it. The girl, lying there, her wrists scored with a blade and blood seeping out. The pallor of her skin. The fact she didn't move when he called her name. The coldness of her forehead, her skin almost waxy as he checked her temperature...

He took a deep breath. This wasn't the same thing at all. He remembered what the counsellor had said about grounding himself. Something you could touch: the round metal handle in his hand. Something you could see: the door itself, unpainted and panelled, dark with a patina of age. Something you could hear: the dogs' paws clattering on the uneven oak floorboards. Something you could smell: a coppery scent he recognised.

Blood.

There wasn't time for this. Not now. Not if Ellen was up here.

Given that he could smell blood, what had she done?

He shoved the door open. 'Ellen? Are you up here?' He couldn't see a light switch, so he grabbed his phone and switched on the torch. The room was cavernous, piled high with boxes and ancient trunks under the enormous rafters, unwanted furniture mixed in with ancient toys.

Where was Ellen?

One of the dogs squeezed past him, ran to the end of the room and barked.

Colin followed.

What he saw drove all the breath from his body. He wasn't sure if he hesitated for milliseconds or minutes, because time seemed to flow like treacle. But then his training snapped in. 'Call an ambulance,' he yelled back to Georgina, and knelt down to check Ellen's pulse.

'On it now,' Georgina said. 'What can I tell them?'

'She's cut her wrists. She's unconscious, but she's breathing and has a pulse. We need to bind those wounds and elevate her arms while we wait for the ambulance,' he added. He stripped off his T-shirt and ripped it into strips before using them to bind the wounds.

'The ambulance is on its way,' Georgina said. 'What can I do to help?'

'Let's get her out of here. Somewhere more comfortable and more accessible,' Colin said. He hadn't been able to save Carly, but he was determined to save Ellen. 'Can you hold my phone, so I can see where I'm going?'

'Of course,' Georgina said.

He picked Ellen up as gently as he could and carried her out of the attic, followed by Georgina and the dogs.

'Good boys. You found her,' Georgina said, making a fuss of the dogs.

Back in the estate office, Colin lay Ellen on the sofa and put cushions under her legs; lifting her legs higher than her heart would increase the blood flow to her heart and brain. Then he used bandages to secure the dressings he'd made from his T-shirt, so the pressure was enough to stem the bleeding. He turned her head gently to the side, making sure her airway stayed open, then covered her with a blanket.

'Talk to me, Ellen,' he said. 'Everything is going to be all right. Help's on its way.'

'Ellen, the bats need you to be OK,' Hattie said, joining him. '*We* need you to be OK. Whatever's happened, we can sort it out together. Posy and I will help you.'

But there was no response.

All they could do was wait for the ambulance.

THIRTY-SIX

Two days later, Colin sat at the side of Ellen's bed, Larissa on the other side. 'Are you sure you're up to this, Ellen?' he asked.

The young woman's skin was pale and there were dark smudges underneath her eyes, but she nodded. 'I want to talk. That's why I asked to see you. You have to release Henry. He hasn't done anything wrong. He's all right, Henry, even though he sometimes sounds like a bit of an arse.' She took a deep breath. 'I know I'm going to be locked up for what I did. But I never meant to hurt anyone, really I didn't...'

'We know. Just tell us what happened in your own words, love,' Larissa said.

'Larissa's going to write everything down, and ask you to read it through and sign it to say she's got it right,' Colin said. 'But we'll do a proper interview with you when you're a little bit better.'

Ellen looked at him. 'I don't know where to start.'

'Anywhere you like,' Colin said. 'We've got all the time you need. There's no rush. We're listening.'

She swallowed hard. 'Mum never wanted me. She always said I ruined her life.' Her breath hitched. 'My dad... I don't know who he was, but I do know he was married to someone else. And he wouldn't leave her for Mum, even when she got pregnant. She said it was my fault. She had boyfriends after him, but none of them stayed because they didn't want me. I was a nuisance.'

If Karen hadn't wanted the baby, why the hell hadn't she given her daughter up for adoption, so Ellen could've had a family who wanted her? Colin wondered.

'And eventually she met Robin. I must've been eight or nine. He was really old, but he was all right. He didn't seem to mind me. And he married Mum so she had a nice house, the sort of clothes she liked. I thought everything was going to be OK,' Ellen said, 'but then he died. He had a stroke. Mum had a fight with his family over the will, and they won, and we ended up in this pokey rented flat with mould on the ceiling.' She looked miserable. 'Then she met Malcolm. He was really old, too, but he wasn't nice like Robin was. I didn't like him, so I used to stay in my room as much as I could.' She bit her lip. 'Mum got angry with me for messing up the wallpaper because I pulled my bed across the door and it scraped against the paper and ripped it.'

Larissa glanced at Colin, and he knew they were thinking the same thing. The same horrible, horrible thing.

'Why did you pull your bed across the door, Ellen?' Larissa asked gently.

'Because of Creepy Malcolm. The way he looked at me,' she said. 'He touched me, a couple of times. Not as – not as bad as it could've been, but I didn't want him near me. He said it was just a joke, touching my tits, and I should take it. That's – that's when I started cutting myself. To make me feel clean.' She shuddered. 'He made me feel dirty, the way he looked at me.'

Colin had heard this kind of story before. If Malcolm hadn't been dead, Colin thought, then he would most certainly have been in court for this. And Colin would've made sure Ellen got the justice that Carly h—

No.

Not now.

'He didn't have the right to touch you,' Colin said, forcing his voice to sound a lot calmer than he felt. 'You did nothing wrong.'

'But I think Mum did. Something wrong. Not because he touched me, I mean,' Ellen clarified. 'When Malcolm stopped buying her things... He took medication. For his heart. I think Mum might have... I don't know, fiddled with the dose, or something. And he died.'

Colin blinked. 'You think your mother killed Malcolm?'

Ellen nodded. 'And then I thought about Robin. How he died and left everything to her, just like Malcolm did. And I wondered – but then I thought I was being stupid.'

Georgina had suspected that, too.

'And then she met Henry.' Ellen sighed. '*Another* old man. Posher than Malcolm and Robin. And they got married so quickly. She said he was lonely and so was she. And I wasn't to ruin things like I had with Robin and Malcom. I was sixteen, and I knew I only had to put up with it for two more years before I could get away from her, so I went along with it. All I had to do was wait it out. Even if I didn't go to uni, as soon as I was eighteen, I could leave and never have to live with her again.' She gave a rueful smile. 'Except Henry's family was *nice*. I didn't expect to like them, but I do. And I love Hartington. I love the woods, and the bats. And Hattie and Posy stuck up for me. It was like having big sisters, for the first time in my life. An actual family who cared about me. And they had pets. I mean, I never even had a goldfish or a hamster when I was growing up, but at Hartington there's a pile of dogs to cuddle up to. And it was a *proper* home, not like the damp flats in London or the houses with the old men where I didn't belong. Hartington was a place where I could settle.'

Poor kid, Colin thought. The poor, lonely kid.

'Mum wanted Henry to sell the house. I mean, he can't – his family's lived there for hundreds of years. But she wanted him to buy a place in London. She hated the country. She hated the dirt and the insects. She hated the dogs; she said they were filthy and they smelled and they dribble water all over the floor all the time.'

'Spaniels never swallow—' Colin began.

'—the last mouthful,' Ellen finished, and gave him the first genuine smile he'd seen from her. It changed her utterly from sulky near-teenager to the bright, sweet young woman she clearly hadn't had the chance to be. 'That's what Posy says. And Maggie Pritchard.' She closed her eyes. 'Oh, God, the Pritchards. I have to say sorry to them. For what Mum did.'

'The earrings?' Colin asked.

Ellen nodded. 'Henry was dragging his feet over selling the house. Mum must've realised he'd never do it. Henry's not one for making decisions. He says things sort themselves out if you leave them alone for long enough. So Mum started taking things. Just like before.'

'Before?'

'In London. She used to clean other people's houses. And, every so often, when the landlord threatened to evict us because she was behind with the rent, suddenly it was all paid up.' She bit her lip. 'Mum said she won the money on a lottery card, and I was young enough to believe her. But then I overheard her talking to Gavin.'

'Gavin?'

'Someone she was at school with,' Ellen said. 'I think he might have been her boyfriend, years ago. And I think he was a bit dodgy.'

'Do you know his last name?' Colin asked carefully.

'I'm not sure. Does it matter?'

He took his phone from his pocket and showed her Gavin's photo. 'Do you know this man?'

'Yeah, that's Gavin,' she said.

'Thank you,' Colin said.

'Why do you have his photo?' she asked.

'Later,' Colin said.

'You were telling us about London,' Larissa reminded her.

'Mum was taking things from the houses. Nothing big, nothing like a painting or anything, just a little thing here and there at random. She'd give them to Gavin, then he'd flog them for her and give her the money.'

Bingo. They'd got him, Colin thought. His London colleagues would be pleased.

'And she was taking stuff at Hartington, I was sure of it. I could see the signs. Maggie noticed things had been moved and were missing, and I overheard her telling Hattie about it. Maggie didn't like Mum – she'd been at the Hall for years and she really loved Hattie and Posy's mum. Towards my mum, she always acted a bit like Mrs Danvers, though she was always all right with me. Probably because I was interested in the plants and I used to talk to her husband, Brian, about my bats. But I knew Mum wanted Maggie out. Maybe she'd twigged that Maggie knew about the stealing, or maybe she just wanted to prove she had the power to get Henry to do whatever she wanted. So she did that thing with the earrings.' She bit her lip. 'I should've told the police, but I knew it'd be my word against Mum's, and who are you going to believe? The ugly weirdo who cuts herself and likes bats, or Lady Ellingham?'

'You're not ugly and you're not a weirdo,' Larissa said firmly. 'You can get help with the cutting. And the world needs people to stick up for bats and the environment.'

Ellen's eyes filled with tears. 'And Henry was changing, too. He could be a bit of an arse, but that was just to cover up the fact he knew he was hopeless at anything except his cars. But he barely talked to me anymore. If I went into the garage where he was restoring the Lotus, he didn't chat to me about the bats or show me what he was doing with the car. Not like the way he used to.' She bit her lip. 'And it scared me that maybe Mum was doing to him what I thought she'd done to Robin and Creepy Malcolm. So I tackled her about it. I got her to meet me at the ice house so nobody would be likely to overhear us – and I told her it had to stop, the stealing and whatever she was doing to Henry, or I'd tell Posy and Hattie about it and we'd go to the police. She screamed at me. I thought she was going to hit me. I ducked when she took a swing at me and she lost her balance – all because of those stupid, *stupid* shoes she always wore. She slipped and fell off the edge. I heard her scream, then nothing.'

'What happened then?' Colin asked.

'I'd been at the ice house with the bat surveyor, a few days before. We'd used a rope to get to the bottom – there are iron rungs in the wall, but half of them have rusted and broken away, and I wouldn't trust them with anyone's weight. I hadn't put the rope back, so I used it to get down to Mum. I put the light on my phone. And she – there was all this *blood*. She was hardly breathing. And the way she was lying... If she'd got brain damage from banging her head, or broken her back and was going to be in a wheelchair for the rest of her life, she would never have coped. I don't know what I was thinking,' Ellen said, 'but I'd been wearing one of Henry's old cardigans – I like it, because it's big and baggy and hides me. I just took it off and held it over her face until she stopped breathing.'

'What did you do then?' Larissa asked.

'I don't know,' Ellen said. 'I don't remember climbing up the rope again or shutting the ice house door. I think I threw the cardigan away. I might've thrown the rope away, too. I threw Mum's phone and her pink handbag in the lake – I just put a stone in the bag so it'd be heavy enough to sink. Then I remember throwing up until my stomach hurt and I thought I'd pass out.' She swallowed hard. 'I knew Mum had had a fight with Henry that morning; she'd packed an overnight bag and told me she wanted me to drive her to the station. I'd already put her bag in my car, and I just left it there. I thought everyone would assume she'd gone to London in a strop.' She closed her eyes. 'And then Georgina came to take the photographs and found her.'

'The finial that nearly hit Georgina – do you know what happened there?' Colin asked.

'It was loose. I found that out when I'd been checking the roof for signs of bats. I meant to tell Hattie, so she could get the builders to take a look at it, but I forgot. That day, I just went on the balcony and pushed it off. I didn't mean to *hurt* Georgina,' Ellen said. 'She was kind. I just wanted to scare her, so she'd stop digging up the past and find out about what Mum did.'

'What do you know about Lady Wyatt's car?' Larissa asked.

Ellen closed her eyes. 'I'd watched Henry do the brakes on one of his cars. I knew where to put a hole. Not big enough to make her crash – just enough to give her a warning. I heard them all talking about Mum and they were getting a bit too close to what she'd done with the medication. With Robin and Creepy Malcolm, I mean, and whatever she was doing to poor Henry. I only meant to scare her and Georgina a bit and make them back off. I'm sorry. I never meant to hurt anyone. I just wanted it all to stop, and for everything to be all right again.' She looked Colin in the eyes. 'I'm going to go to prison, aren't I?'

'I'm not a judge,' he said. 'I can't predict what kind of sentence you'll get. But you do need help, Ellen, and we'll get that for you, I promise.'

'I'm sorry,' Ellen said. 'I'm so, so sorry...'

THIRTY-SEVEN

A week later, Colin sat on the terrace at Little Wenborough Manor. Giles and Will were tending the barbecue, with Bert, Jet and Max at their feet, waiting hopefully for a bit of grilled chicken to come their way. Cesca had sorted out a table full of side dishes and was busy topping up everyone's glasses, aided by Bea. Jodie was sitting with Harry on her lap, reading him a story. And Bernard, he noticed, was holding Sybbie's hand very tightly.

'So your theory was right, Georgie. Karen was marrying old men, bumping them off and pocketing their estates,' Sybbie said. 'Not to mention stealing things that Hartington will never get back. And the Red Book's still missing.'

'Maybe I should be searching your library, Sybbie,' Colin teased.

'Hah.' Sybbie gave him a grin. 'I wish.'

'All the dealers have it on their lists, now. When it finally surfaces, they'll say something to whoever brings it in about needing to check some details, and they'll call the Met's Art and Antiques unit and get it back to Hartington,' Colin said.

'What's going to happen to Ellen?' Georgina asked.

'She'll have to face charges,' Colin said. 'Karen's fall was an accident – and I believe her about that. But it's what Ellen did afterwards. Smothering her, instead of calling for help.'

'She'd had a hell of a life, from what Posy said. Can't she claim diminished responsibility?' Bernard asked.

'Possibly,' Colin said. 'I can't comment.'

'The Berrys are standing by her,' Sybbie said. 'Posy and Hattie realise she was trying to keep Henry safe. It seems that Henry hadn't been taking his medication properly for a while. We're not sure whether Karen "tweaked" his meds by not giving him enough of the stuff he needed, or adding things that made him ill, but he's grumbled his way through a thorough overhaul by the doctor. And Ellen's bat bricks are still going ahead.'

'Ellen really didn't mean to hurt Sybbie or me,' Georgina added. 'She just didn't want us to dig too deeply.'

'Hmm,' Colin said. 'Well, yet again you've helped me crack a case. And you solved what happened to Anne Lusher.'

'With help,' Georgina said. From Doris and Anne, though she couldn't acknowledge that publicly.

'Maybe I should get you on my team as a cold case consultant,' Colin mused.

Just then, Bea's phone rang.

'I know, I know – the rule is no tech at dinner,' she said. 'Normally, I'd put my phone on silent, but I'm waiting for—' She shrieked as she glanced at the screen. 'Oh, my God! Sorry, I really, *really* need to take this.'

'Break a leg,' Georgina said, clearly having a good idea what her daughter was waiting to hear about.

Bea rushed off to a quieter spot in the garden. She returned a couple of minutes later, with the broadest grin Colin had ever seen. 'That was my agent,' she said. 'Peter Newton just rang her. You're all looking at the new Lady Macbeth for his next production at the Regency Theatre in London. I got the job!'

'Fantastic! Well done, darling,' Georgina said, hugging her warmly. 'And we're all coming to the first night.'

'Including me,' Will said, coming to hug his sister. 'Dad would've been thrilled.'

Bea's eyes sparkled with unshed tears.

'He'll know,' Georgina said.

'He'll definitely know,' Doris said quietly in Georgina's ear.

Did that mean Stephen had made contact with Doris? Did Doris have a message from him? Georgina's pulse leaped. But she couldn't have that conversation with the ghost who lived with her – not right here and not right now. Nobody else here knew about Doris, and the explanations would take too long. Plus they needed to celebrate Bea's success; Sybbie had already despatched Bernard to bring champagne.

'We'll talk later,' Doris said, as if understanding Georgina's dilemma. 'Just know that he's glad to see you look so happy.'

Colin took her hand and squeezed it. 'OK?'

Yes. No. Both at once. And she couldn't talk about it. 'Just mulling over your not-so-serious job offer,' she said lightly.

'It might be a serious offer. I don't know, yet. Though, the next photography job you take, will you promise me *not* to find a dead body?' he asked.

'I'll try,' Georgina said with a smile.

Though she hadn't finished digging, yet. She still needed to find out the truth from Irene Taylor, if she could. Starting with a visit to the nursing home, arranged for Wednesday morning...

A LETTER FROM THE AUTHOR

Huge thanks for reading *The Body in the Ice House*. I hope you were hooked on Georgina, Doris and Colin's journey. If you want to join other readers in hearing all about my new releases and bonus content, you can sign up for my newsletter!

www.stormpublishing.co/kate-hardy

If you enjoyed this book and could spare a few moments to leave a review that would be hugely appreciated. Even a short review can make all the difference in encouraging a reader to discover my books for the first time. Thank you so much!

This series was hugely influenced by three things. Firstly, I grew up in a haunted house in a small market town in Norfolk, so I've always been drawn to slightly spooky stories. (I did research it when I wrote a book on researching house history, but I couldn't find any documentary evidence for the tale of the jealous miller who murdered his wife. However, I also don't have explanations for various spooky things that happened at the house.) Secondly, I read Daphne du Maurier's short story 'The Blue Lenses' while I was a student, and... I can't explain this properly without giving spoilers, so I'll say it's to do with how you see people. Thirdly, I'm deaf; after I had my first hearing aid fitted, once I'd got over the thrill of hearing birdsong for the first time in years, my author brain started ticking. The du Maurier story gave me a 'what if' moment: what if you heard something through your hearing aids that wasn't what you were supposed to hear? (The obvious one would be someone's thoughts, but that's where my childhood home came in.) It took a few years for the idea to come to the top of my head and refuse to go away, but *what if you could hear what my heroine Georgina ends up hearing?*

And so Georgina Drake ends up living in a haunted house in a small market town in Norfolk...

The Body in the Ice House comes from my interest in social history: in this case, the ice houses built in the 1700s and 1800s in the grounds of stately homes. My romance writer side has always wanted to use an ice house for an assignation; my crime writer side had other ideas! The cold case in this book again comes from my interest in social history; my first-year subsidiary subject at university was Victorian Studies, so I wanted to set it in that period. What happens if you fall in love with the 'wrong' person?

Little Wenborough isn't a real place, but the name is a mash-up of the town where I grew up and the river where I walk my dogs in the morning. But Norfolk is an amazing place to live. Huge skies (incredible sunrises and sunsets), wide beaches (aka my best place to think, and the Editpawial Assistants are always up for a trip there), and more ancient churches than anywhere else in the country (watch this space!).

Thanks again for being part of this amazing journey with me and I hope you'll stay in touch – I have so many more stories and ideas to entertain you with!

All best,

Kate Hardy

KEEP IN TOUCH WITH THE AUTHOR

www.katehardy.com

facebook.com/katehardyromanceauthor
x.com/katehardyauthor
instagram.com/katehardyauthor

ACKNOWLEDGEMENTS

I'd like to thank Oliver Rhodes and Kathryn Taussig for taking a chance on my slightly unusual take on a crime novel; Emily Gowers for being an absolute dream of an editor – incisive, thoughtful and great fun; and Shirley Khan and Maddy Newquist for picking up the bits I missed! I've loved every second of working on this book with you.

Gerard Brooks has been a particular star with location research, coming with me to visit ice houses and taking it in very good part when I was on tiptoe at Felbrigg Hall with one hand through the bars at the doorway of the ice house, taking a photograph of the bottom of the shaft and asking whether he thought pushing him off the edge would be enough to murder him, or if I'd have to go down and finish the job... (He did say, rather loudly, 'I hope anyone who just overheard that realises you're a writer and you're not *really* planning to kill me!')

Special thanks to my family and friends who cheer-led the first Georgina Drake book, made useful suggestions about ice houses/cake/ghosts and are always there through the highs and lows of publishing: in particular Nicki Brooks, Jackie Chubb, Siobhàn Coward, Sheila Crighton, Liz Fielding, Sandra Forder, Philippa Gell, Rosie Hendry, Rachel Hore, Jenni Keer, Lizzie Lamb, Clare Marchant, Jo Rendell-Dodd, Fiona Robertson, Rachael Stewart, Michelle Styles, Heidi-Jo Swain, Katy Watson, Ian Wilfred, Susan Wilson, Jan Wooller and Caroline Woolnough. (And apologies if I've missed anyone!)

Extra-special thanks to Gerard, Chris and Chloë Brooks,

who've always been my greatest supporters; to Chrissy and Rich Camp, for always believing in me and being the best uncle and aunt ever; and to Archie and Dexter, my beloved Editpawial Assistants, for keeping my feet warm, reminding me when it's time for walkies and lunch, and putting up with me photographing them to keep my social media ticking over while I'm on deadline.

And, last but very much not least, thank *you*, dear reader, for choosing my book. I hope you enjoy reading it as much as I enjoyed writing it.

Printed in Great Britain
by Amazon

47331764R00152